D0397684

Facials Can Be Fatal

A BAD HAIR DAY MYSTERY

FACIALS CAN BE FATAL

NANCY J. COHEN

FIVE STAR

A part of Gale, Cengage Learning

GALE
CENGAGE Learning·

Farmington Hills, Mich • San Francisco • New York • Waterville, Maine
Meriden, Conn • Mason, Ohio • Chicago

GALE
CENGAGE Learning·

Copyright © 2017 by Nancy J. Cohen
Five Star™ Publishing, a part of Cengage Learning, Inc.

ALL RIGHTS RESERVED.
This novel is a work of fiction. Names, characters, places, and incidents are either the product of the author's imagination, or, if real, used fictitiously.

No part of this work covered by the copyright herein may be reproduced or distributed in any form or by any means, except as permitted by U.S. copyright law, without the prior written permission of the copyright owner.

The publisher bears no responsibility for the quality of information provided through author or third-party Web sites and does not have any control over, nor assume any responsibility for, information contained in these sites. Providing these sites should not be construed as an endorsement or approval by the publisher of these organizations or of the positions they may take on various issues.

LIBRARY OF CONGRESS CATALOGING-IN-PUBLICATION DATA

Names: Cohen, Nancy J., 1948– author.
Title: Facials can be fatal / Nancy J. Cohen.
Description: First edition. | Waterville, Maine : Five Star Publishing, [2017] | Series: A bad hair day mystery
Identifiers: LCCN 2016037336 (print) | LCCN 2016049125 (ebook) | ISBN 9781432832827 (hardcover) | ISBN 1432832824 (hardcover) | ISBN 9781432834760 (ebook) | ISBN 1432834762 (ebook) | ISBN 9781432832681 (ebook) | ISBN 1432832689 (ebook)
Subjects: LCSH: Shore, Marla (Fictitious character)—Fiction. | Women detectives—Florida—Fiction. | Murder—Investigation—Fiction. | Beauty operators—Fiction. | BISAC: FICTION / Mystery & Detective / Women Sleuths. | FICTION / Mystery & Detective / General. | GSAFD: Mystery fiction.
Classification: LCC PS3553.O4258 F33 2017 (print) | LCC PS3553.O4258 (ebook) | DDC 813/.54—dc23
LC record available at https://lccn.loc.gov/2016037336

First Edition. First Printing: February 2017
Find us on Facebook– https://www.facebook.com/FiveStarCengage
Visit our website– http://www.gale.cengage.com/fivestar/
Contact Five Star™ Publishing at FiveStar@cengage.com.

Printed in the United States of America
1 2 3 4 5 6 7 21 20 19 18 17

ACKNOWLEDGMENTS

My gratitude goes to aesthetician Carmella Hershcovich for sharing her expertise and for answering my numerous questions about facial procedures. She's an exemplary professional who treats her customers with care.

Also thanks to Roxanne Hedlund, my hairstylist, for graciously filling in the blanks for me when I ask, "What would you do if. . . . ?" or "What's the procedure for . . . ?" Roxanne styles my hair for upcoming meetings, conferences, and speaking engagements while offering her insights into the beauty biz.

And I would be remiss if I didn't mention Stacey Miller and Jessi Basilone, nail technicians, who listen to my plotting ideas with a smile while polishing my nails to perfection.

A word of thanks, too, for the staff at Design 4000 who've created a bright and cheerful environment, including Leslie and Nadine at the front desk. Their telephone reminders keep me on track.

CAST OF CHARACTERS

Andrew Fine —Public Relations Director for Friends of Old Florida (FOFL), a historic building preservation society

Anita Shorstein —Marla's widowed mother

Ashley Hunt —The headliner model at Yolanda's fashion show

Biggs Kahuna —Manager of the hotel where FOFL's holiday ball takes place

Brianna Vail —Dalton's teenage daughter; nickname is "Brie"

Carla Jean Hatfield —A sales rep for Luxor Products

Dalton Vail —Marla's husband and Brianna's father; homicide detective in Palm Haven

Dr. Ian Needles —A board member for FOFL, he's a plastic surgeon who is also a scuba diver

Gabriel Stone —A funeral home director in Parkland

Henutt Soe Dum —Yolanda Whipp's husband who may have a connection to the Asian mob

Howard Cohn —Treasurer for FOFL and a banker who has a fascination for shipwrecks

Jason Faulks —A photographer who takes pictures at the holiday ball

John & Kate Vail —Dalton's parents, both retired

Joyce Underwood —Makeup artist at the fashion show

Katherine Minnetti —A detective on the Palm Haven police force and Dalton's partner

Lora Larue —A board member for FOFL who produces the annual ball and acts as liaison to other historic building preservation groups across the country

Marla Vail —Owner of Cut 'N Dye Salon in Palm Haven, Florida; married to Dalton Vail

Nadia Welsh —A friend of Val's and a customer at Marla's day spa

Nicole Johnson —Hairstylist at Cut 'N Dye Salon

Rick Rodriguez —A real estate magnate who covets historic sites for redevelopment

Robyn Piper —Marla's neighbor and the receptionist at her salon

Rosana Hernandez —An aesthetician who gives Val Weston a facial

Sam Flint —A journalist in Key West

Sean Knight —Val's brother-in-law who was married to Cathy, Val's deceased sister

Solomon Gold —President of FOFL, he administers the day-to-day business at their office

Sue Ellen Wyatt —Secretary for FOFL, she handles ticket sales for the group's gala fundraiser

Tally & Ken Riggs —Tally is Marla's best friend. Ken is her husband; their baby is Luke

Traci Warner —Receptionist at day spa

Valerie Weston —Val is a major donor for FOFL

Yolanda Whipp —An upscale boutique owner and fashion designer who puts on a show at FOFL's annual fundraiser dinner

CHAPTER ONE

Marla was busy sorting foils at her salon station when screams pierced the morning air. She glanced up, her nerves on edge. And here the day had started so peacefully.

Nicole, one chair over, paused in the midst of cutting a client's hair. "What is that God-awful noise?" the other stylist asked.

Marla dropped the foils on her roundabout. "I don't know, but it sounds as though it's coming from our day spa next door. Maybe someone found a palmetto bug."

But as she hurried outside and across the pavement to the adjacent spa facility—a recent expansion under her ownership along with the Cut 'N Dye hair salon—she doubted those blood-curdling shrieks could be due to an insect. They sounded too shrill and terrified.

A black bird squawked and dipped over the parking lot. Along with November and the season's first cold front, the birds had returned from up north to South Florida. That wasn't a vulture portending some disaster, was it?

Inside the day spa, patrons in the waiting area stood with their cell phones lifted, taking videos for social media. Her mouth compressed, Marla sped past them toward the rear, where staff members in smocks gathered. They all stared in one direction.

Traci, the receptionist, spied Marla and called out to someone beyond her range of vision. Just as abruptly as they had started,

9

the screams stopped.

Marla reached the group huddled in front of one of their facial and waxing rooms. "What's going on?"

An aesthetician, her complexion white as her lab coat, wiped her teary eyes. "I am sorry," she said with an accent, her voice wavering. "Val was fine when I put the cream mask on her face. I only left for ten minutes to let her relax. When I returned, she didn't move and I thought she must be asleep. I did not realize at first she was not breathing."

"I've already called 911," Traci said in a quiet undertone. "The cops and medics should be here any minute."

"Your customer isn't breathing?" Marla pushed past the crowd to enter the room and administer CPR, but the sight inside made her stop midtrack.

A woman lay supine half off the table, her hands encased in cloth mitts and her mouth wide open. Her face, coated with a greenish substance, aimed a glassy stare at the ceiling. New Age music played in the background, the soothing melody an incongruence to the scene. Air-conditioning blasted cool air into the room with a citrus scent. A discarded towel lay on the floor.

"Oh. My. God." It might be too late for CPR if the woman had lain like this for longer than ten minutes. Could she have suffered a seizure? Her bluish lips could indicate anything.

Marla forced herself to at least palpate for a pulse at the lady's neck. She tamped down the bile in her throat at the clammy feel of her skin. The hardened face mask gave the lady an almost alien appearance. Was that consistency normal for a facial?

Not feeling a beat at the carotid, Marla backed away. The best thing she could do would be to secure the room until the cops arrived.

She swallowed uneasily, anticipating her husband's reaction.

Would Dalton, a homicide detective with the Palm Haven police force, arrive on the scene when he heard the address from the dispatcher? From previous experience, she knew that unattended deaths were investigated. That would apply in this case since the aesthetician had left the client alone.

Returning to the corridor, she drew the sobbing woman aside. "What's your name?" she said, her brain foggy under the circumstances. Consuelo? Magdalena? It hovered on her tongue.

"Rosana Hernandez. Do you think she had a heart attack, *senora*? Val might have been trying to get up and call for help." Her gaze misty with tears, Rosana bent her head.

"Yes, you could be right. Had you done a medical survey on her?"

Rosana, a couple of inches shorter than Marla's five feet six, nodded. "*Si.* Val had been with me for years. She followed me when I came here from my last salon in east Fort Lauderdale. She did not have any history of heart problems or other sicknesses."

"So you've known her for quite some time." Marla glanced inside the room and grimaced. "What are those things on her hands?"

Rosana drew a deep breath. "I was giving the lady a paraffin treatment. She had a manicure scheduled next. I don't know how this could have happened."

Stomping footsteps drew their attention. The other staff members parted like the Red Sea under Moses' command. A pair of uniformed rescue workers headed their way carrying a load of equipment. Following at their heels were two patrol officers and a tall, broad-shouldered fellow whose piercing gaze made Marla's heart flutter.

She exchanged glances with Dalton but avoided embracing him in front of the staff, even when she wanted nothing more than to sink into his arms.

"I'm glad you're here," she told the EMTs. "The patient is in that room. I don't think you'll be able to do much for her."

A quick examination on their part confirmed her assessment. Dalton and one of the uniformed cops entered the room while the other officer began questioning onlookers.

"What happened?" Dalton asked Marla, tucking his cell phone away as he rejoined her. He must have made a call from inside the room.

"Rosana was giving her customer a facial. She put on the woman's face mask and left the room for a few minutes. When she returned, the lady wasn't breathing."

"Can I speak with Rosana somewhere private?"

"Sure. How come you're here? Did you recognize the address from the dispatcher?"

"That's right. Good guess." The corners of his mouth lifted. This was far from the first time he'd been summoned to her place of business.

"We can use one of the empty massage rooms," Rosana suggested in a weak tone.

Marla introduced the aesthetician to her husband. She patted the woman's shoulder. "It'll be all right. Dalton will ask you some questions, and then you can take the rest of the day off. Traci will notify your clients."

Dalton pulled out a notebook and pen and followed Rosana into another treatment room. Marla joined them, intending to offer moral support to her staff member. To her gratitude, Dalton didn't object. But then, he'd come to value her contributions. He had even identified her as his unofficial sidekick to an Arizona sheriff during their recent honeymoon.

"Okay, can you please tell me exactly what happened?" he asked Rosana.

Her lower lip trembled. "I was giving Val a facial. She has

12

been my customer for years, and we never had a problem before."

"Her full name is . . . ?"

"Valerie Weston. She lives east on the Intracoastal. Anyway, when I took the job here, Val followed me to this salon even though it was distant for her."

"So you've given her facials before. And she's never had a bad reaction?"

"No, sir." Rosana gave a visible shudder. "Everything was fine. I put the facial mask on, set the timer for ten minutes, and left the room so she could relax. I went to get a cup of coffee. When I returned, I found her . . . like that." Her voice choked on a sob, and she covered her face with her hands.

"Rosana, why don't you make a copy of your client's medical survey for Detective Vail?" Marla suggested.

"*Si*, I get it now." The white-coated woman shuffled from the room like a condemned prisoner on her way to execution.

Marla's heart went out to her. She knew how horrible Rosana felt. She'd been in the same position of losing a client when crabby Mrs. Kravitz died in the midst of getting a perm. The image of her head lolling against the shampoo sink remained with Marla even now. How many years ago had that awful incident occurred? She'd met Dalton, the detective assigned to the case, as a result. Back then, he'd suspected her of poisoning the woman's coffee creamer.

"Won't you be reassigned?" she asked him, leaning against the treatment table. "I mean, I own this place. You have a conflict of interest here." *Same as when our neighbor was found dead in his house next door after we'd argued with him.*

"We're short-staffed this time of year. A couple of the guys requested vacation time before the holiday crush. Come here."

He held out his arms, and she rushed into them. She leaned

her head against his solid chest, her anxiety easing under his embrace.

"I'm glad you came, even if your partner takes over later. I suppose you'll order an autopsy?"

"It's normal procedure. Does the woman have any close relatives nearby?"

"I have no idea. I'd never met her myself."

"What can you tell me about Rosana? Is she an immigrant? Does she have citizenship papers?"

Marla stepped away, perturbed by his return-to-business tone. "Yes, she's from Venezuela and married an American. Rosana is very good at what she does. Her customers highly recommend her."

"What was her relationship to Valerie Weston?"

Marla spread her hands. "As Rosana said, Val was her customer, and they'd known each other for years."

Rosana approached and handed a paper to Dalton. "Here is Val's client survey."

"Thank you." He scanned the contents. "It says here Ms. Weston had a latex allergy."

"That is correct, Detective. I was always careful not to use latex products in her presence and to wash my hands before touching her."

"May I take a look?" Marla snatched the paper from his fingers.

The Confidential Consultation Card, as the survey was labeled, consisted of three sections. Marla scanned Val's responses on the general health record. Topics ranged from dietary habits to female problems, sun exposure, implants, disease listings, skin-related ailments, and medications.

She nodded at that last one. Meds could affect hair as well as skin reactions. Most people didn't think to tell their hairdressers when they started on a new drug, but certain medications could cause a stronger response to chemicals such as bleach.

According to this report, Val Weston appeared to be in good health. The next two sections regarding skin care and the beautician's analysis didn't raise any red flags.

"Was she married?" Dalton asked the beautician. "Do you know who her next of kin might be?"

"She was single. No children. I know she had a sister who died recently from breast cancer."

Dalton asked a few more questions before dismissing Rosana.

Marla walked her out. "Go home and get some rest. This wasn't your fault. Val might have had an unknown medical problem to cause her death."

Rosana sniffled. "*Gracias, senora.* It is horrible."

"I know, but the police will find out what happened."

Once the staff member had left, Marla sought her husband again. He'd been conferring with one of the other officers and broke off at her approach.

She drew him aside. "What's your theory about Val's death?" The woman's image kept replaying in her head. The glassy eyes and weird greenish tint of the facial mask became increasingly grotesque in her imagination. Her stomach lurched.

Stow it, Marla. You have to remain strong.

Dalton's gaze grew warm as he regarded her. "Could be anything. Brain hemorrhage? Aortic aneurysm? Heart arrhythmia? Who knows?" His cell phone buzzed, and he squinted at an incoming text message. "The M.E. is here. Marla, you can go back to work. I'll catch you later."

"Shouldn't I stick around to support the staff?"

"It's not necessary. I'll help the uniforms interview witnesses, and then we'll close down the day spa until we complete our investigation. I know you want to keep chaos to a minimum, so I'll tell the body removal guys to use the rear entrance."

"Thanks. That'll help." *But not by much.* "I know this might sound harsh, but I don't need the negative publicity right now. I'm in the running for that educator position with Luxor Products, and this won't look good."

"You're right. It does sound harsh in view of a woman's death. That's unlike you, Marla." The fine lines around his mouth tightened.

She knew her husband wasn't thrilled about her accepting another job, especially one that would mean more travel. They were celebrating their one-year anniversary in a couple of weeks, and she had enough to do between work and her new family. While it was a second marriage for both her and Dalton, they'd become a tight unit in a short amount of time. Marla still felt odd as Brianna's stepmother, but the role had grown on her. The teenager needed a woman's guidance.

Still, gaining the new position meant a lot to her. She had contacted the hair product company—whom she'd worked for at a beauty trade show—to let them know she'd like to do the models' hair on any advertisements they shot in the area. They'd called back saying they had an opening for an educator and asked if she would be interested. Her affirmative response had prompted the admission that they were considering one other candidate as well. Would this incident jeopardize her chances?

At any rate, Dalton was correct. She shouldn't be thinking about herself right now. As the day spa's owner, she was ultimately responsible for Val's death. And poor Rosana. This would hang over her head. Marla should see to it that the rest of the staff didn't hold it against her.

She went from person to person, speaking to each staff member in turn and reassuring them the place wouldn't stay closed for long. Her own state of nerves wasn't as steady as she appeared. Her stomach felt increasingly queasy, and she had a strong urge to sit down before her knees folded.

Nonetheless, she took time to apologize to any clients still waiting to be interviewed. "If you're here for your hair or nails, we'll fit you in next door. Just see Robyn at the front desk. Otherwise, Traci can reschedule you for next week."

"That poor woman," one of the ladies said with a sorrowful expression. "To die in the middle of getting a facial, which is supposed to be a relaxing treatment."

"I hate them myself," retorted a young blonde. "All that steam in your face, and then they squeeze open your zits. It hurts. I don't find anything pleasurable about it."

"Rosana cares about her customers," Marla said, defending her employee. "She must be doing something right, since her appointments are almost always filled."

"She messed up this time," said Miss Sourpuss.

Marla stared the woman down. "No one can predict the sudden onset of a life-threatening medical emergency. Rosana had done a thorough assessment on her. The lady didn't have any known heart conditions."

"Maybe she had a reaction to one of the products," the other customer offered with a frown. She was a middle-aged lady with tinted auburn hair, and she wore skinny pants that belonged on a thinner woman.

"Rosana would have used the same lotions on her before," Marla replied in a patient tone. "Val had been a long-term customer."

"Val, as in Valerie? That wasn't Valerie Weston, was it?" Redhead gaped at her.

"Yes, it was, although the police detective will urge you to keep this information quiet. They have yet to notify next of kin." Marla pressed her lips together. Gossip would be bad enough, but they didn't need rumors flying along with videos.

"I have tickets to her fancy ball next month. I hope they don't cancel."

Marla had a sudden sneaking suspicion that made the hairs on her nape rise. "What ball do you mean?"

"The annual holiday fundraiser for Friends of Old Florida. It's a historic building preservation society. They do the best party, especially with Yolanda Whipp showcasing her latest fashion designs. I can't wait to see what she's come up with this year."

Marla's heart sank. The dead woman had been *the* Valerie Weston? Oh, no. Putting two and two together, she slapped a hand to her mouth. Val's demise in her day spa would have more repercussions than she'd thought. What would this mean for the fashion show?

She'd been hired, along with her stylists, to do the hair of the models backstage at the highly anticipated event that took place during FOFL's annual gala. Why hadn't she realized the connection earlier?

Because I'd been upset. Val's death threw me for a loop. And it hadn't been Val who'd hired her team. Marla's contact had been someone else from the group.

Dear Lord, this was much worse than she'd anticipated.

Stunned by her new knowledge, she addressed Traci once she was free. The receptionist's usual calm had given way to a frazzled exterior as she tapped at the computer keys to change people's appointments. This was Wednesday. Marla hoped they'd be allowed to reopen by next week.

"Tell me, did Ms. Weston show any signs of trouble when she checked in earlier?"

Traci shook her head, her shoulder-length layers framing a face that looked pale in contrast to her sangria lipstick. "She seemed fine. I liked her. Val always had a pleasant smile and something upbeat to say."

"Do you know if she had any relatives nearby?"

"Just a sister who died recently. She called FOFL her family.

That's Friends of Old Florida, an organization where she devoted her time. Somebody from there made her appointment for today."

"Oh, really? Can you give me their number?"

Traci squinted at the computer as she retrieved the data. "Here it is." She wrote it down on a scrap of paper, while Marla wondered if it could be the same person who'd hired her staff for the fashion show.

"Do you remember the person's name who called? So you're saying it wasn't Val?"

"That's correct. Sorry, I don't remember much else."

"Male or female?"

Traci's shoulders lifted and lowered. "Could have been anyone. I field a lot of calls every day."

"Okay, please let me know if anything else comes to mind."

"There is one more thing. Patty didn't come in to work today. I've called her cell a few times, but it goes straight to voice mail."

They had hair stations here for backup when the salon got too full. Patty, the shampoo assistant, helped with cleanup and other assorted tasks. She should have come in today.

"That's odd. Didn't we just hire her?"

"She's only been here two weeks. She applied when our last girl had an accident on her bike, remember?"

"And you don't have any other contact number?"

"Nope."

"That's not good. She should call in if she can't make it to work." Marla shoved the scrap of paper into her skirt pocket. "After you settle things here, why don't you take the rest of today off? Tomorrow, you can work with us at the salon. Robyn could use the extra help. And thanks for your quick action. You did good calling 911 right away."

Not wanting to keep her own customers waiting any longer,

Marla hurried next door. She'd have liked to tell Dalton her latest revelations, but he was busy. And if he stayed on the case, it would mean a late night for him.

She drew in a shaky breath as she entered her salon. The bright lights, familiar sounds, and chemical scents calmed her. No matter what her problems, she needed to keep her cool and get through her appointments for the day. Customers relied upon her.

Plastering a smile on her face, she approached Robyn and gave her the rundown in a low voice so others wouldn't overhear. To her credit, Robyn gave her a reassuring grin.

"We'll do fine, Marla. Your eleven o'clock is waiting. I told her you'd been delayed, but she didn't mind."

"Now I'm off schedule. Thanks, Robyn. I'll tell you more later." She'd been lucky to hire the marketing expert after Robyn had been laid off from her corporate job. They'd become good friends aside from work.

Nicole intercepted her in the backroom where she went to mix her customer's highlights solution. Shelves of bottles and boxes faced her as she selected the proper products and then brought them over to the sink. After double-checking her client's profile card, she grabbed a bowl and began measuring components.

"So what happened? Who was screaming? I saw all the flashing lights outside." Nicole pursed her lips and leaned against a counter. The dark-skinned stylist looked svelte in a maxi-dress with a matching sweater wrap.

"You'll never believe it. Rosana, the aesthetician, was giving her customer a facial. She applied the mask and left the room for a few minutes. When she returned, the lady was dead."

"What? How?"

Marla paused to think things through. "Dalton said it could have been anything from a heart attack to a brain aneurysm.

The only problem that showed up on Val's medical survey was a latex allergy, but Rosana knew this. Val had been her client for years, when she'd worked in east Fort Lauderdale."

Nicole folded her arms across her chest. "So I gather the spa will be closed for a few days?"

"Yes, but I hope we'll be able to reopen by next week. I told Traci to send all their hair and nail people over here today. Are you between clients now?"

"I'm waiting on a touch-up." The stylist glanced at her watch. "Ten more minutes."

"Traci will help Robyn tomorrow at the front desk," Marla said. "We're bound to be busier if she shifts some of the spa appointments to the salon."

"Careful, hon, you don't want to add that 30 volume bleach."

"Oops, I guess I'm more rattled than I thought." She retrieved the correct item and added it to her bowl. Her hand shook as she mixed the chemicals with a brush.

"You need to calm down."

"I can't. We have to handle the overflow. But that's not the worst of it. The woman who died was Valerie Weston from Friends of Old Florida."

"So? What does that mean?"

"FOFL is the group that hired us to do the hair at their fashion show in a few weeks. I don't want to lose that gig." She didn't mention her educator opportunity, not wishing to spring this news on her staff until it was a done deal. It would mean more hours away from the salon.

"But was this client someone you recognized? Is she the person who spoke to you about doing the show?"

"No, it was somebody else." Marla put down her brush and spared a glance her way. "Lora Larue contacted me. She's one of the board members."

"So you don't know how this Valerie was connected to the group?"

"Not really. I hope they don't blame us and cancel our contract."

"You're jumping to conclusions. How can it be our fault? That woman might have dropped dead anywhere if she'd had a true medical emergency."

"Rosana left her unattended for a brief interval. Otherwise, she might have called for help sooner." Visions of a lawsuit entered her mind. Oh, God. Marla clutched her stomach.

"Hey, come here. Give me a hug." Nicole strode forward to embrace her and pat her on the back. "We'll be okay. Things will get back to normal."

Marla sprang away, grasping the bowl and brush before the moisture behind her eyes turned into a waterfall. "I know. And I appreciate your support, as always."

She didn't express her misgivings about the negative publicity affecting her personal goals. But she wasn't to be let off the hook so easily. Her customer, displeased at having to wait for her appointment, demanded Marla relate the whole story. She gave an abbreviated version, aware of listening ears around the salon. Her rendition left out any mention of the dead woman's medical history.

"Have you heard of this organization?" Marla asked, hoping to gain some information. She knew pitifully little about the group for whom her staff had been hired. Her fingers moved automatically to section off a strand of hair, place the foil under it, brush on the solution, and fold the foil over.

"Sorry, I haven't. How's that husband of yours, dear? Won't next month be one year you'll be married?"

"That's right," she said. "Our anniversary is December eighth."

"Any little ones in the barn yet?"

"Excuse me?"

"Are you planning on having children?"

"Dalton already has a teenage daughter. She's taking driving lessons. That's enough anxiety for us, thank you."

The woman's dark eyes met hers in the mirror. "You're young yet. You can still get pregnant. I'm sure you'd make a great mother."

All right, we need to change the subject. "Let's discuss you instead. Weren't you about to go on vacation when I saw you last?"

Marla skillfully steered the conversation away from her personal life. What concern was it to others if she and Dalton meant to expand their family? With her past history, she didn't want children of her own. She had enough to do without the added responsibilities and constant worry. Besides, she looked forward to traveling, something she hadn't had much time to pursue on her busy career path.

While she worked, part of her mind kept track of the cop cars coming and going outside, along with the scudding clouds overhead that heralded another cold front. It wasn't until later in the afternoon that most of the police vans had left.

The body must be long gone by now, she thought, signaling for her next client to get shampooed. She was still behind schedule, but she'd catch up. And keeping busy prevented her from thinking too hard about what was happening next door. How long would it take before the autopsy results came in? She'd feel more vindicated if the woman had died from natural causes that couldn't have been prevented or treated. Would Rosana quit her job there? Or if not, would she still want to work in that room?

"Hey, Marla." Robyn approached her station, a friendly smile on her face. "There's a sales rep here to see you from Luxor

Products. Shall I send her over while your customer is getting washed?"

"Luxor Products? Oh, no!" She gulped. "I mean, yes, please send her on back. I have a few minutes free."

Dear Lord. Luxor was the company where she hoped to work as an educator. Was this person truly a sales rep or someone come to evaluate her? If the latter, she was doomed.

CHAPTER TWO

Marla's jaw dropped as she spied a familiar blonde heading in her direction. She hadn't seen Liesl Wurner, another stylist, since their jobs at the Supreme Show in Fort Lauderdale.

"Hello, luv." The tall, willowy woman embraced her. "It's good to see you again."

"Likewise, Liesl. What are you doing in town?" They split apart and regarded each other with critical appraisals.

"I had an exit interview with the area supervisor. I'm finally moving to London. I got the position at a high-class salon in the theatre district that I've always wanted."

"Good for you." Marla beamed at her, genuinely happy that Liesl's dream would come true. "I suppose you've heard I've been asked to apply for an educator position with Luxor."

"Bang on. That's part of the reason why I'm here. I hope you get the position, but you have competition."

"So I've heard."

"I'd really like to see you succeed, although it seems like you've already struck gold." She swept her arm to encompass the salon bustling with customers. "But a word of caution. You'll be scrutinized carefully. After that disaster at the show, the company is very careful about whom they select to represent them."

"They asked me if I'd be interested in the job."

"That doesn't mean you'll get it. Don't do anything to jeopardize your chances."

"It's too late for that warning." Marla sank into her empty salon chair and rubbed a hand over her face.

"What is it?" Liesl asked, her eyes reflecting her concern.

"We've just had a death next door at the day spa. I own the place."

"Good heavens. What happened?"

Marla groaned inwardly. She didn't care to repeat herself innumerable times, but it was inevitable. In a brief summary, she gave Liesl a rundown on what had occurred.

"That's too bad, luv. Luxor won't want even the hint of another scandal attached to their name."

"Tell me something I don't know."

"Well, I just wanted to offer my support before I leave the country. I've given you a high recommendation to the district manager. He'll be in on the decision."

"Thanks, I appreciate it. Best of luck to you in London. Let's keep in touch."

This appeared to be a day for visitors. No sooner had Liesl left than the receptionist sent a guy her way. He wore a courier uniform from a private company and held a sealed envelope.

"Marla Vail?"

"That's right."

"I have a delivery for you. Will you please sign here?"

She did as directed and took the piece of mail. After the man left and she slit it open, an expletive escaped her lips.

"What's wrong?" Nicole asked from the next station.

"You won't believe this." Seeing that the other stylist had a few minutes free, Marla showed her the message.

"Get out of town. Amber Connors is suing you?"

"It says that my careless use of hair dye caused her scalp to burn, resulting in hair loss and disfigurement." Marla's gut clenched. After the events of the day, she couldn't handle another blow.

"Do you remember her complaining?"

"Yes, and I removed the color and put a conditioning cream on right away." Sometimes a pink sweetener packet could help lessen the sting as well. "She'd never had that reaction before, and I'd used the same mixture on her for years."

"So what was different this time? Could she have become more sensitive?"

"Possibly, but she'd also started on a new med and hadn't told me. When I asked, she admitted she'd been prescribed a certain class of drugs." Some medications could cause people's body temperature to rise so they reacted faster to hair bleach. If Marla had known, she'd have adjusted the timing. "Even though Amber failed to provide this information, I'll still have to file an insurance claim."

"Don't worry. She won't have a leg to stand on."

Marla's next customer arrived, and she didn't have time to think about her problems until later. At home, she got occupied taking the dogs for a walk, preparing dinner, and then driving Brianna to a school function. Between her extracurricular activities and her driving lessons, Brie seemed to be handling a hectic schedule better than Marla.

Depression weighed her down. After Brie retired to her bedroom for the night, Marla waited anxiously for Dalton to return home. As expected, he'd stayed late to work on his new case.

Her thoughts returned to Valerie Weston. Had Rosana missed something in the woman's health history, similar to what had happened between Marla and her client, Amber Connors? Or had Val's death been due to an ailment no one realized she had? And what would this mean for the Friends of Old Florida annual ball? Marla wasn't sure of Val's role with the organization. She should give her contact there a call tomorrow to express her condolences. Maybe she'd learn more that way.

Spooks nudged her ankle. She stooped to pet her cream-colored poodle, amused by his jealousy when their golden retriever vied for her attention. Playing with the dogs brought her a measure of comfort.

Sleep wouldn't come, though, until she'd talked things out with Dalton.

"I hope we don't lose the fashion show gig," she said to him in bed later. "Yolanda attracts the publicity hounds when she debuts a new line. Our salon will be given credit for the models' hairstyles."

Turned on his side toward her, Dalton stroked her bare arm. "Is this designer the same person who hired you?"

"No, that was Lora Larue. She's a board member for FOFL and is in charge of producing the gala event. I bet she'll be devastated by Valerie's death."

"You said you hadn't met the deceased?"

"That's correct. Why, what have you learned about her?"

"People respected the woman. I haven't heard a negative word about Miss Weston yet."

"She shouldn't have died. How old was she?"

"Fifty-nine."

"And she has no close relatives in the area other than that sister who passed away? How sad. Had she ever been married?"

"Marla, I know the lady expired on your property, but it's my investigation. Don't you have enough on your mind?"

"I can be curious, can't I?"

"Maybe. Why is this fashion show so important?"

"It's about recognition, Dalton. That's the same reason why I'd like our salon to be involved in photo shoots. I want to believe I'm doing more than just operating a salon."

"You're serving your customers. Isn't that enough?"

"Ever since the excitement in Arizona, I have an urge for something more." She couldn't explain her restlessness, but their honeymoon adventures had left her dissatisfied with the status quo.

"Oh, yeah? I have a suggestion." His hand drifted to her belly. "We could increase our family."

"What?" His remark blindsided her. They'd already discussed this issue. "You know how I feel about having my own kids. Why are you bringing this up now?"

"You just said you're restless. And you're a wonderful mother to Brie. Having a baby would give you a new focus."

"That's exactly why I don't want more children." Sweat broke out on her brow. She'd thought Dalton and she were on the same page regarding this subject.

Marla had been through hell and back when, as a nineteen-year-old babysitter, the toddler under her charge had drowned in a backyard pool. After seeing the parents' grief, she never wanted to risk that pain herself. And until Dalton, she'd never considered herself capable of properly caring for a child. She'd gotten over that insecurity but still had too many plans to give up her life to child-raising for twenty years.

"I'm just saying we shouldn't dismiss the possibility like we have in the past," Dalton said, his tone persuasive. "Maybe it's something we should consider."

"I didn't know you felt this way. I'll think about it. Meanwhile, let's talk about Brie instead. Your daughter wanted to take the wheel tonight."

He groaned. "She's far from ready to drive after dark. That's a big step. You know how much traffic University Drive has most of the time."

"You'll have to face it sooner or later. The driving instructor will take her for the test when the time comes. She needs practice."

"Fine, I'll take her around the neighborhood over the

weekend. In the meantime, let her get a few more lessons under her belt."

Marla's hand roamed to parts of him that sprang to life at her touch. She'd rather change his focus away from troubling topics.

The next day at work, Marla found time during the day to call her friend Tally. Being a new mother, Tally would reinforce her belief that having kids wasn't on Marla's bucket list.

"Hey, how's it going?" Tally said on the other end of the line. She sounded tired, which was her usual complaint these days.

Marla cradled the cell phone by her ear in the back storeroom, her favorite place for private calls. "Have I got an earful to tell you," she said before relating her news.

"Holy smokes, you weren't kidding. Uh-oh, let me do a diaper change and call you back."

While waiting for the phone to ring, Marla stuck a batch of laundered towels into the dryer along with a fabric softener sheet. She set the dial and started the dryer before an interruption could occur. The familiar scent of chemicals in the air-cooled atmosphere brought her a sense of comfort.

"Marla, the coloring agents have arrived." Robyn carried a package into the room. Her shoulder-length, glossy brown hair swayed as she walked.

"Okay, thanks. Leave them on the counter. I'll sort the boxes on the shelves."

She'd begun that job when Tally called again. "So what's this about Dalton wanting you to have kids?" her friend asked in a hushed tone. She must have put Luke, her almost four-month-old son, down for a nap.

"He knows how I feel about having children. We talked about it before we agreed to get married. So why bring it up now?"

"Brianna will be going to college in a couple more years.

Maybe he's experiencing early separation anxiety and is thinking ahead."

"What, to start all over again with another kid? We can travel once Brianna leaves home. And she'll be back for the holidays and over the summer."

"Well, it's something you two need to discuss further."

"How is Luke? Is he sleeping through the night yet?"

"Huh, I wish. I hope to go back to work part time at the shop by the first of the year. Or not. I haven't decided what to do. I love being home with Luke."

"You could take him to work with you since you own the place." The Dressed to Kill boutique was a popular destination in Palm Haven. Tally's assistant was filling in as manager while she was on maternity leave. But her words struck fear into Marla. What if she ever had a baby? She'd never want to give up the station in life she'd worked so hard to achieve.

"I'm giving myself until New Year's to make a decision," Tally said. "Considering how you feel about kids, I hope you don't have any regrets about agreeing to be Luke's guardian?"

"Certainly not. I love Luke as though he were my own. And you're like a sister to me."

"You know we think of you as family, too. Ken and I are grateful you accepted the role. Neither of us would want to leave Luke in his brother's care. But I want to be sure you truly understand what it would mean, if anything happened to us."

"Nothing is going to happen. I'm honored that you chose me. Dalton agrees as well."

"All right. Now what's this about another client dying in your salon?"

"Not the salon. It happened in the day spa while the lady was getting a facial. I'm hoping the autopsy says she died from natural causes. Have you heard of Yolanda Whipp, the designer who has a shop on Las Olas?"

31

"Sure. Her creations are gorgeous, but they cost thousands of dollars." Tally took in a sharp breath. "Your staff is doing *her* fashion show? That's an awesome opportunity."

"Tell me about it. Now I'm afraid they might cancel."

"Why, has anyone said so? Was Yolanda the one who hired you?"

"No, it was Lora Larue. The show is part of a charity event for Friends of Old Florida, and Lora is on their Board of Directors. She's the one who approached me."

"So call her and express your sincere condolences over the woman's death. You said Valerie Weston was connected to their group?"

"That's right." Marla knew she had to make that call. She dreaded doing it, however.

"Do you think they'd cancel the entire fundraiser because of her passing?"

"I would doubt it. Maybe they'll acknowledge her death at their event, though. I'm not sure what her role was in the organization."

"You probably have nothing to worry about." A wail sounded in the background. "I have to go. Luke just woke up. Let me know how things turn out."

Marla got busy with her customers and didn't have a chance to follow through until late Thursday afternoon. But when she finally put in a call to Lora, she got the lady's voice mail. After leaving a message, she recalled the scrap of paper Traci had given her the day before. Marla had copied the phone number into the Notes section of her iPhone. Retrieving the note, she compared the number of the person who'd made Val's appointment to Lora's contact info. They weren't the same.

Anyway, what did it matter? Dalton would track down the details. He might dismiss the whole case, depending on the coroner's report.

Traci strode her way before Marla could greet her next customer. The spa receptionist wore a concerned look on her face. "I still can't get hold of Patty. What could have happened to her? Not that we need her to come in to work, but she should at least notify us if she has a problem."

"I agree." Marla didn't condone employees who were no-shows without notifying them. "Did she give any indication of something being wrong on Tuesday?"

"Now that I think about it, she did seem a bit jittery."

"Maybe she had a family emergency. Did you try sending her a text message?"

"Yes, no response. I left her a voice mail, too."

Marla frowned. "Give me her contact info, and I'll ask Dalton to look into it. This is damn strange, especially considering what happened on Wednesday."

The hours flew by and so did the weekend, and Marla forgot about her concerns for the moment. On Sunday, she finally had time to think things through while taking a walk with Brianna at Treetops Park. Dalton had gone in to work and couldn't join them.

The cooler weather was perfect for hiking along the woodland trails. She sniffed earth-scented air as they trod over the soft dirt path. Branches of live oaks spread overhead in a shady canopy. Birds sang a greeting, and the occasional creature slithered under the brush.

"So as I see it," Brie said, her brow folded thoughtfully, "you have one main concern. You're afraid the lady's death in your day spa will affect your staff's engagement at the society ball. How was she connected, again?"

"I'm not sure. My contact there is Lora Larue, a board member. I'd never heard of Valerie Weston before Wednesday."

Marla had filled in the teen on recent events. She liked telling the girl about her concerns. While Brie was her stepdaughter,

33

she'd also become a friend. It was gratifying to be able to talk to her this way in an even exchange. Marla didn't believe in holding things back, like the older generation might have done to protect their offspring. Reality intruded soon enough, and it helped develop character to face it straight on.

"It seems to me you're worrying ahead of time. Why not wait and see how things turn out?" Brianna paused to take a photo on her cell phone of a green bird that had alighted on an overhead branch. She punched a few buttons to send it along to her social networks.

"You're right. I should just chill. It's so beautiful out today. Let's head toward the lake."

As they walked across the boardwalk fielding the marsh, she surveyed the ducks and turtles under an azure sky with lazy white clouds. While the north braced for a blast of cold air, here in South Florida the days were glorious. Her shoulders relaxed, and she inhaled a deep breath with a sense of tranquility. She'd tamped down her other anxieties, about the pending lawsuit at work and her application for the educator position. Those would work out somehow, too. She couldn't be pessimistic in such beautiful surroundings.

"Can I drive home?" Brie asked, staring at a white bird with a long neck.

Marla eyed the water for alligators, but she'd never spotted them here. That didn't mean they were absent, though. "That's a good idea. You need the practice, and your dad hasn't had time to take you out this weekend." Her cell phone buzzed. "Speak of the devil, that's him. Hello?"

"Hey, Marla. Wish I could have joined you at the park, but things have taken a significant turn on this case with Valerie Weston."

"Oh? How so?" Her stomach churned. From his somber tone, she guessed she wouldn't like his response.

"We got the preliminary autopsy report. It shows she likely died from anaphylactic shock related to her latex allergy."

"What?" Marla gripped the phone tighter to her ear. "But Rosana was careful not to use latex gloves with her client."

"She wouldn't need to wear gloves. Traces of latex were found in that stuff on the victim's face."

Victim? What else did he know that she didn't? "You mean the face mask?"

"If that's what you call it. We're having the products used by the beautician analyzed."

"So you're saying one of the lotions might have contained latex? But wouldn't Rosana have known that? She told me she used different creams depending on the customer's skin analysis and medical conditions."

"We'll see what turns up. We took the jug of water she uses for the steam machine, too."

"Surely you're not suspecting this was a deliberate act on someone's part, if not Rosana's mistake?"

"I'll let you know. Meanwhile, don't count on my being home before dinner. I just wanted to give you a heads up."

"Wait, there's something I've been meaning to mention. Our new hire, Patty, hasn't been in to work since Tuesday. She's a shampoo assistant at the day spa."

"You said she's a new hire?" Dalton's voice sharpened.

"That's right. She's filling in for our regular girl who had a biking accident."

"Has anyone been in touch with her?"

"The receptionist has tried to reach Patty, but she doesn't answer her phone. We're both worried about her. She should have contacted us by now. Can you follow up? I have her phone number and address."

"Sure, text them to me when you get a chance. Talk to you later."

Marla pocketed her cell phone and resumed their walk. "Rosana wouldn't have used any products containing latex," she said after relating to Brianna what her dad had said. "How could that stuff get into a face cream anyway? Isn't it a powder?"

Brianna's soft brown eyes regarded her. "Marla, let Dad work the case."

"I hope he dusted for fingerprints. Maybe somebody else came in during the night when the cleaners were there. That's what happened with Bertha Kravitz. Her killer came in when the back door was unlocked and put poison in the coffee creamer I kept just for her."

"Don't panic. This isn't the same thing." Brianna patted Marla's arm.

"We don't know that yet. Good God, what if someone murdered the woman?" Without watching her steps, she almost tripped on a tree root when they reentered the shady forest trail. She skirted the obstruction and headed along, her sneakers crunching on dead leaves.

"This could be an error on the beautician's part. Maybe she got in a new product and didn't read the ingredients. You shouldn't jump to conclusions."

"You're absolutely right." Marla observed a squirrel leaping from branch to branch. "But just in case, I'd better make contact with the people involved in that fundraiser."

"It's Sunday. You'll have to wait until tomorrow. Let's talk about the upcoming holidays."

"Okay." Her spirits lifted. "Your grandparents are looking forward to taking you to Disney World over Christmas break."

"We have to get a tree in the next few weeks. And plan the family dinner."

Last year had been the first time Marla had decorated a Christmas tree. Previously, she'd been accustomed to lighting a menorah this time of year. Combining the holidays had been a new experience for her and one she looked forward to repeating with their extended families.

"It's our anniversary coming up, too. I'm not sure what to get your father. And I have to finalize arrangements for our holiday work party." The weight of her responsibilities crowded in on her. This was always a hectic time of year. She should let this business with Valerie go until they learned more details. Her death still could have been accidental.

But that's not what the initial reports indicated when they came in a few days later. The face cream showed components of liquid latex. None of the ingredients listed contained the substance. So how did it get there?

"What is liquid latex?" Marla asked in an undertone to Nicole at work the following Wednesday. She'd confided in the other stylist, having to share her news with someone else.

"I have no idea, girlfriend. You can look it up during your break."

Dalton's department was being mum on the case, but they'd finally released the body to Val's brother-in-law and cleared the day spa to reopen. The funeral was scheduled for tomorrow. Thursdays being Marla's late day at work, she'd be able to attend in the morning. She hoped to run into Lora Larue there and save herself another phone call. The woman had never called her back. Marla didn't know if that was a bad sign or if Lora had merely been out of town.

"Do you want anything from Bagel Busters?" Marla asked Nicole. "I'm heading over there to get our order."

At Nicole's negative shake of the head, Marla grabbed her purse and strode outside. Chilly air made her shiver. She hastened along the concrete toward the deli owned by Arnie Hartman. He'd been a friend for years. Aware he'd just returned from a vacation, she wondered if he'd heard about the commotion at her place.

37

His mustached face broke into a grin as he spotted her. Wearing his usual apron, he rounded the corner from the cash register to embrace her.

"Marla, what's been going on around here? My staff said there was some emergency next door that I missed."

She gave him a quick rundown.

"Oy, vey. It's like Bertha Kravitz all over again."

"Tell me about it. Anyway, Dalton hasn't actually said there's foul play involved. I'm trying to stay calm, but it's not easy."

"Let him handle it. He's good at his job."

"I know. How are the kids? Is everyone okay?"

He grinned at her, while the scent of garlic and onions drifted her way from a nearby table busy with patrons. Her mouth watered. She hadn't eaten much that morning.

"We're fine, thanks. Isn't this weekend your anniversary?"

"That's right. We're going out to dinner to celebrate."

"How is Brianna doing?"

"She wants to drive every chance she gets. Dalton isn't too happy about it."

"I'll bet. Here, your order is ready." He handed her a paper bag.

Back at the salon, Marla called the insurance agent about the case pending against her. He said he was still doing his research, but he didn't believe the damage to the woman's scalp was permanent. He would aim to get the case dismissed before it went further.

Hoping the guy was right, she sat at the computer by the front desk while Robyn set out a platter of bagels and cream cheese for their customers. When she put liquid latex into the search feature, a list of resources popped up. As she read on, her eyebrows lifted.

Latex was a natural milky substance derived from rubber trees. Liquid latex solutions were commonly used for special effects makeup and body paint. Flesh-colored liquid latex was applied in the entertainment industry to create scars, alien features, and other enhancements. When put on skin, the body cosmetic dried to a rubbery consistency and shrank about three percent. It was easy to apply and just as easy to peel off. Liquid latex came in different colors including metallic tints.

Marla noted the product was sold in sizes ranging from two ounces to gallon jugs. Multiple outlets sold the stuff online. Or you could buy it at party stores. In other words, the substance was cheap and plentiful, meaning anyone could obtain it.

But only one person might have acquired it in this case. It had to be someone who knew Valerie had a latex allergy and was coming in for a facial that particular morning.

CHAPTER THREE

Marla entered the funeral home in Hollywood, Florida, with trepidation. A large crowd milled in the assigned room where guests could express their condolences to family members prior to the service. Their attention focused on a man with two children. That must be Val's recently widowed brother-in-law and his kids.

Not being a personal friend, Marla didn't care to intrude, so she took a seat in the chapel once the doors opened. Comfortably upholstered pews faced forward. A maple-colored coffin with brass trim rested up front among displays of fresh flowers. On a side table sat several framed photos of Val, smiling and happy. She had vibrant eyes framed by softly layered hair. Marla's gaze rose to the electric candelabra mounted on a far wall. Its reverse V-shape pointed toward heaven.

A sickly sweet scent drifted into her nose, bringing to mind the less desirable smells surrounding death. An air-conditioned flow whooshed into the room, while fans rotated lazily overhead. Fortunately, she'd chosen a location without a draft. Nonetheless, she tugged her black blazer a bit tighter as her mood sobered.

Her thoughts drifted to her father's funeral as everyone took seats before the family members entered. A minister began the service from behind a podium. Lost in her own memories, she didn't hear much of what he said. However, her attention sharpened once people started coming forward to eulogize

Valerie Weston. When the little boy got up to remark upon his aunt, and mentioned how she'd joined his mother, Marla reached for her tissues.

She blinked away the moisture from her eyes as she followed the mourners outside and into the bright sun at the gravesite burial.

When people lingered following the service, Marla approached Val's brother-in-law. He was a square-jawed fellow with salty hair, even features, and sad eyes. A small scar marred his upper lip.

"Hi, I'm Marla Vail from the Cut 'N Dye Salon and Spa. I'm sorry for your loss." She peered down at the youngsters clutching his hands on either side. "I feel terrible about what happened, Mister . . . ?"

"Sean Knight. I was married to Val's sister."

"Yes, I gathered as much. I own the place where she . . . where it happened. Val's death was a horrible tragedy. If there's any way I can help—"

"Thank you, I appreciate the offer." He stared at the ground, a pensive expression on his face. "Val was extremely sensitive to latex. We'd known something like this could happen, but not so soon after Cathy died. It's almost like the sisters couldn't stand to be apart."

"Were they very close?"

"The girls had their differences, but their parents were gone, and the only other relatives were some distant cousins in Colorado."

"Val never married?"

He hesitated for a tad too long. "She was single. Val never had any children, so she doted on mine." Sean ruffled his kids' hair. The girl appeared younger than her brother. "Didn't your aunt adore you?"

"We'll miss her, Dad," his son said in a tearful tone.

This couldn't be easy on the children, having lost their mother not so long ago. "Val will be missed by a lot of people," Marla added. "I didn't know her personally, but she appeared to be a strong influence in the community. Did she spend all her time working for charitable groups?"

Sean shot her a sharp glance. "Why do you care? I mean, other than the obvious. The woman died under your supervision."

She stiffened. "Val wasn't my customer, but I feel responsible nonetheless. I'd just like to fill in the blanks. And I might add that we called 911 right away, but Val was gone in the blink of an eye."

His mouth tightened. "Look, I'd rather not talk about it now. In fact, I probably shouldn't be talking to you at all." With a curt nod, he moved off, the children at his sides.

Oh, great. Now she'd blown it. Was he intending to sue for negligent death? Maybe he hadn't given it a thought before she'd stuck her nose in. Would Dalton disapprove?

She scoured the crowd, but her husband's tall form wasn't evident. Usually he attended a victim's funeral. But he hadn't publicly declared this case to be murder. Maybe he was waiting for all the reports to come in.

The grounds were relatively quiet, except for their group. She didn't see any other awnings or chairs set out across the vast property. A few concrete crypts arose among the plots of land, competing for height with shady oak trees. Here and there, benches sat facing gravesites, additional memorials to the beloved departed. The place wasn't hilly and scenic like the cemeteries up north, where tall headstones stretched toward the sky. These stones were flat, needing maintenance so weeds didn't cover them. *We're all covered over in the end,* she thought.

Her heart quickened as she spied a familiar face. Lora Larue stood in a circle of people, her ample figure encased in a black dress with an inappropriately low neckline. Her bosom nearly spilled out, while the short hem exposed thighs too thick for display. The sun glinted off bronze highlights in Lora's hair, a swirl of curls framing her face. Her blue-shadowed eyes swung in Marla's direction as she approached. The woman's splash of bright red lipstick provided contrast to her pale complexion.

Marla plopped on a pair of sunglasses before greeting Lora. "Hello," she said in a subdued tone. "I'm sorry to see you again under these circumstances. Marla Vail, remember?" She stuck out her hand. They'd met in person once before, when Lora had stopped by the salon to hire her staff for the fashion show.

Lora turned away from her group of friends and accepted her handshake. "I got your phone message but haven't had the chance to return your call."

"That's all right. I wanted to express my condolences."

"Thank you. We're all a bit shocked over Val's death."

"I can imagine." How could she tactfully ask if the fundraiser would go on? "This must be a blow to your organization."

"No kidding. Val's contribution will be sorely missed."

Meaning what? Her contribution of money, or her volunteer work?

"I'd been hoping to meet her at the charity ball." Marla idly smiled at a passerby. People were starting to head to their cars. She hoped to gain more information before she had to leave. Swinging around to face the sun so Lora would be more comfortable, she waited for a response.

Lora's head lowered. "It won't be the same without Val there."

A whoosh of relief escaped Marla's lips. Thank goodness, they weren't planning to cancel the event. "What was her role in the organization? I'm sorry, but you're the only person from the group that I really know."

"Val was a major donor. She's the one who recommended your salon to us. I thought you'd met her before this."

"She was a long-term customer of our aesthetician. Evidently, she followed Rosana from an establishment east of us."

"I see." Lines creased the woman's forehead as though she were having second thoughts about her hiring choice for the ball.

Marla hastened to reassure her. "My staff is looking forward to the fashion show. We can't wait to work with the models."

"This Rosana, will she be there?"

"No, she does facials and waxing. Only our hairstylists will attend."

"People confide in their beauticians, don't they? Rosana must have known Val pretty well." Lora raised her penciled eyebrows.

"Well, yes, I guess so. They'd been together for years."

"Is it likely Rosana forgot about Val's allergy?"

Both Lora and Sean were well informed about Val's means of death. To her knowledge, Dalton had not made that information public. Had he interviewed them already?

"Rosana knew about her client's condition. I saw her customer survey form myself," Marla said, hoping to provoke Lora.

A sheen of sweat covered the woman's face, and it couldn't be due to the heat. A cool breeze swept the cemetery, making Marla glad she'd worn a long-sleeved jacket.

"We'll talk more later," Lora promised, waving to someone in the distance. "I have to go. Sean has invited people over to his house."

Not wishing to press her luck, Marla nodded a farewell. She took her leave, grateful Lora hadn't fired her from the gig and that the group still planned to carry on the event. That took away one worry.

On the way to her car, she heard raised voices that gave her pause. Two people were speaking under a shady oak tree. One was a slender brunette; the other, a towering guy with silver hair, wore a dark suit.

"What are you doing here?" the woman said, her tone hostile.

"I came to pay my respects. Val was a formidable opponent, and I admired her tactics."

"Don't think your development will go through now that she's gone, Rick Rodriguez." She emphasized his name as though it were distasteful. "Our group backs her efforts one hundred percent."

"I know that, Sue Ellen. She fought a good fight. That's all I'm saying."

"You shouldn't have come. You'll upset her spirit."

"Maybe she'll see my presence as a peace offering. Good day to you."

He stalked away, while Sue Ellen glared after him. Marla hastened along, wondering what that meant. Just another puzzle piece to add to Val's personal life, she figured.

Back at the salon, she grabbed her printed schedule from the counter where Robyn had left it and studied her client list. She had a few minutes to spare before her first customer. As she headed to a sink to scrub her hands, her stomach rumbled. It was nearly lunchtime.

"Hey, Marla, how's it going?" Nicole stopped by, a bowl in her grasp.

"I went to Val's funeral this morning. Her group still intends to put on their holiday event." Finished washing her hands, she dried them with paper towels.

"Thank goodness, right?" Nicole grinned at her.

"I'm glad we're still part of it. Val's brother-in-law was there with his children. She didn't have any other close family members."

"That's sad. I'd like to hear more, but my highlights is waiting."

"Sure, go ahead." Marla set about her own business with a heavy heart. Funerals left her depressed. They reminded her of her father's passing.

Her mood lifted as the day went on and she chatted with customers. They got talking about the holidays, making Marla ruminate about her own plans. First there was their anniversary dinner, then the charity ball, a work party, and the holiday celebrations at home. She had plenty to do. This should be a joyous time of year, not a sad one. And yet it must be sorrowful for anyone who'd lost a loved one.

The way she saw it, it was her duty to make her clients feel better about things. As she cut, colored, and trimmed, she listened with a sympathetic ear to their inner thoughts and concerns. She was gratified when each person left the salon with a smile.

By eight o'clock that evening, weariness assailed her. She arrived home to the mouth-watering aroma of homemade tomato sauce. It being Dalton's turn to make dinner, he'd done spaghetti and meatballs.

"How was your day?" He stood in the kitchen with a wooden spoon in his hand and wearing an apron.

Her mouth curved upward. "It's good now that I'm with you. Seriously? I attended Val's funeral this morning. How come you didn't go?"

"It's not officially a homicide. Besides," he said with a sexy grin, "you're my unofficial sidekick. I'm sure you worked the crowd. What did you learn?"

"I spoke to Lora Larue, the board member who'd hired my salon staff for the charity event. They still intend to put on the ball, and she didn't fire us."

"That's a plus." He stirred the sauce bubbling in a pot.

"I also met the brother-in-law. His name is Sean Knight and he has two kids, a boy and a girl. He's the one whose wife died recently from breast cancer."

"How did he appear to you?"

"Saddened by Val's passing. He said the two sisters were together now."

Marla, having put down her purse and washed her hands again, began setting the kitchen table with utensils. Brie wasn't in sight. She must be doing homework in her room, or else she was chatting on her cell phone. Did kids even chat today or merely text?

"I've touched base with both Knight and Larue," Dalton said, preempting her next question. "I wanted to find out if they knew about Val's latex allergy."

"You told them how she'd died?"

"Not initially. They thought she must have had a cardiac arrest. I asked if she'd had any medical conditions that they'd known about. Both of them mentioned her allergic condition. So I told them how she'd died. The brother-in-law wasn't surprised. He'd feared something like this might happen. Contact with latex can be hard to avoid."

"No, it isn't. Many of my stylists buy gloves without latex in them."

"Knight assumed it must have been an error on the beautician's part. I wouldn't have him believe otherwise at this point."

"That gives the brother-in-law grounds to sue us. I don't need another lawsuit on my doorstep, thank you."

His head swung in her direction, his gaze laser-sharp. "*Another* lawsuit?"

She kicked at a crumb on the tile floor. "Amber Connors is suing me for resultant damage from hair dye. She'd started on a new medication, and the bleach took too fast. I sent her to get shampooed as soon as she complained that her scalp burned."

Stepping forward, he placed his large palms on her shoulders. His gaze softened as he stared down at her. A lock of peppery hair fell across his forehead. "You should have told me."

"I know. I have too many things on my mind."

"Have you called a lawyer?"

"I notified my insurance company. The agent is investigating to see if the woman's claim is valid. He agrees it wasn't my fault since I had no way of knowing about her meds."

"Let him do the worrying." He nuzzled her hair. "You need to get out of those funeral clothes. Why don't you change into something more comfortable while I make the salad?"

"I love you." Standing on her tiptoes, she kissed him. He always made her feel better.

Two days later, they celebrated their anniversary with dinner at a neighborhood bistro. The bustling atmosphere didn't make for much quiet, but Marla liked the ambience and the food. Plus, this place was closer than a fancier restaurant on the east side of town.

"We need to give Brie some driving practice again tomorrow," she mentioned in between their salads and entrees. "Can you believe she's going to be sixteen in March?"

"Don't remind me." He gripped his wine glass and took a swig.

"Two more years, and she leaves for college. She should do well; she's a bright kid. I know we'll miss her, though. So will your parents, especially when they've finally bought a condo in the area." Dalton's parents had found a place after a long search. They'd sent her and Dalton tickets to a show at the performing arts center as an anniversary gift.

Dalton gave her an oblique glance. "We could give Mom something new to rejoice over."

"Uh, if you mean what I think you do, let's not go down that road." She sought a safe change of subject, disturbed that he'd brought up this idea again. She knew exactly what he'd meant. Were his parents pressuring him to have another child? Maybe his mom, Kate, had put the bug in his ear. Regardless, Marla would hold firm to her decision.

Getting him talking about a case would distract him. "I haven't confirmed the details with Lora, but I assume we're supposed to show up at the fashion show as instructed. Events are moving so fast. It's a week from tonight. Will you be present at the ball in any official capacity?"

He snorted, as though he knew her change of subject was deliberate. "That depends. I'm waiting on one more lab result."

"For what?"

"To see if any prints come in as a match. The tech boys had the foresight to dust the back doorknobs as well as the entry to Rosana's treatment room, among other things."

"Why is that? Oh, I get it. You think someone might have sneaked in and doctored the face cream. But who would know Val had an early-morning appointment? And who would be aware of the procedure for a facial, except somebody who's had one? How would this person have learned about Val's allergy and which products Rosana used on her?"

"All valid questions. Rosana kept a file on each customer in that room. Your staff would be knowledgeable about her practices. One of them could have snuck in and taken a peek at that file. Or another customer might have done so when the beautician left the room. Oh, I've asked your receptionist for a list of all clients who had appointments there recently and a list of staff."

"And you're just telling me this now?" Marla sat back while the waiter delivered their meals. She'd order grilled salmon while Dalton had a steak. She took a bite of fish, relishing the soft, moist texture as it slid down her throat.

Dalton's shoulders hunched, like they did when he was troubled. "We'll be issuing a statement on Monday. Somehow liquid latex got into a product that wasn't supposed to contain it and was applied to a person with an allergy. The victim died.

I don't believe this was an accident. It was a premeditated act to commit murder."

Marla almost choked on a morsel and grabbed a gulp of water to chase it down. Although she'd suspected as much and Dalton had mentioned his suspicions before, it was another thing to hear him openly state the case.

"So where will you start? I mean, in terms of interviewing people. There's a long list if you include the staff and customers, plus Val's friends and associates."

"I know. I'm going to begin with the obvious. One person of interest is that assistant who didn't show up for work. No one has heard from her, and her apartment is empty."

Marla sat up straight. "Empty, as in cleared out? Like, she's moved without telling anyone?"

"No, I mean her stuff is still there, but no trace of her exists. I don't get a good feeling about it."

"You think she was involved and then vamoosed?"

"Something like that. But we've got other possibilities."

So did Marla. Traci had said the person who'd called to make Val's appointment came from Friends of Old Florida. It was time Marla stopped by their office. Mondays were her day off, so she could drop in with the excuse of confirming details for the fashion show.

Marla found the offices for FOFL in a converted house in the Victoria Park section of town. East of the Fort Lauderdale high-rises, this pricy district boasted waterways and expensive homes, including an eclectic mixture of mansions and old Florida cracker-style houses. Its tree-lined lanes seemed appropriate for the location of a historical society. Marla had often taken a shortcut through here from Broward to Sunrise Boulevard and thought it must cost a fortune to maintain these places.

Having parked her white Camry alongside the curb, she

clutched her black Coach bag and proceeded past a cracked sidewalk to the front door of the two-story structure. Peeling paint, missing roof tiles, and holes by the windows for hurricane shutters attested to the house's age. Evidently they hadn't updated to impact-resistant windows or put on a new roof in recent times. How did the organization raise funds for building maintenance?

Facing a polished wood door, she rang the bell and heard someone from within holler, "Enter." The doorknob twisted easily, and she breezed inside. She stood in a dimly lit hallway, a staircase to her immediate left. Ahead was a series of rooms opening off a long hallway. Seeing the light on in one of them, she stepped in that direction.

A woman emerged from the doorway. She wore her dark brown hair in a ponytail and wire-rimmed glasses on her nose. A patterned top flowed over a pair of slim black pants. Her only items of embellishment were a wristwatch and a pair of pearl stud earrings. Marla felt overdressed in comparison, wearing a maxi dress with strappy sandals and turquoise jewelry.

"How may I help you?" the lady said.

She looked familiar. Had Marla seen her at the funeral? "I'm Marla Vail, owner of Cut 'N Dye Salon and Day Spa. Lora hired us for the fashion show to do the models' hairstyles. I thought I'd stop by to confirm our arrangements."

"You really should be talking to Yolanda Whipp. She's the designer in charge of the show."

"I know, but my contract is with your group."

"All right, come inside." With a gesture, she led Marla into her office. "Have a seat while I look up the paperwork. I'm Sue Ellen Wyatt, the group's secretary."

Oh, yes, now Marla remembered. She'd been the person at the memorial speaking to a man named Rick Rodriguez.

As Sue Ellen headed to a dented metal four-drawer file

cabinet, Marla wondered how she found anything among the piles of papers strewn across every surface. The air had a musty tinge, and an air-conditioner hummed in the background even though it was cool enough outside to open windows. These looked to be the old jalousie type. Maybe the hand cranks were broken.

"Did this place used to be someone's home?" she asked, curiosity overtaking her. She'd gained an appreciation for history on her recent honeymoon out west, where Dalton's uncle was restoring a ghost town.

"Yes, the history is quite interesting," Sue Ellen replied, her back turned toward Marla as she riffled through the files. "Here it is." Returning to her desk, she claimed her chair. "This house was originally built in 1915. Henry Witherspoon bought it for his wife, who operated a schoolhouse on the first floor after his death and rented rooms above to make ends meet. Eventually, it was donated to the school district."

"So when did Friends of Old Florida take over?" Marla's gaze rose to the planked ceiling. The house must be sturdy to have not succumbed to any hurricanes.

"We've been here since the 1980s. We'd like to restore the place and are trying to get it declared on the national historic register. That's Solomon's department."

"Who is Solomon?"

"Mr. Gold, the president of FOFL. You should meet him. He's just down the hall. He came in today to work on our newsletter. You'd be surprised by how many people are on our mailing list."

"Volunteers or supporters?"

"The latter, mainly. We hold events throughout the year. These days, we send the newsletter out mostly by email, but there are a few holdouts who need a stamped envelope." She waved one in the air. "That's my job. Solomon writes the newsletter, and I distribute it."

"How about Valerie Weston? Did she communicate via email? I'm asking because someone from here called our salon to make her facial appointment."

Sue Ellen chuckled. "Dear Val. She didn't like to do mundane things on her own when she could hire someone to do them for her." The woman's face sobered. "I'm going to miss her. We all are. It won't be the same around here without her strong presence. She was a fighter. Val wasn't afraid to confront anyone for what she believed was right."

"Was she in the midst of anything critical to your organization when she died?"

Sue Ellen's lips compressed. "I'm not at liberty to discuss our business, Mrs. Vail. You'd have to talk to Solomon on those issues." She glanced at the papers in her hand. "Here's your contract. You've agreed to supply at least four stylists for the fashion show, without remuneration except for associated publicity. Again, speak to Yolanda if you want to get advance notice on the type of look she's going for with her designs this year."

"Thanks, I'll do that. Does this fundraiser usually sell out?" she said, wondering at the size of the crowd. She hoped to slip into the ballroom once the show started to watch the models on the runway for at least part of the time. Yolanda's fashions were legendary. Her pulse accelerated at the thought of viewing the designer's gowns in person.

Sue Ellen turned over the papers on her desk. "Sales are going great. I'm hoping Val's friends will still come. She has a standing order for two tables each year."

"Does your organization do the ticket sales or do you hire an event planner?"

"Oh, we do them. It's no big deal. A lot of people pay via PayPal these days. You should visit our website to see all the opportunities we offer."

"I've already checked it out." Marla slung her purse strap over her shoulder and rose to leave. She'd accomplished her main purpose in coming, which was to confirm her engagement at the fashion show. "So do you know who called in Val's facial appointment?"

"Why, that was me, dear." Sue Ellen's face eased into a frown. "I don't understand why she switched her time, though."

Marla's heart skipped a beat. "What do you mean?"

Sue Ellen pointed to a large desk calendar. "I scheduled her for two o'clock so she'd have plenty of time for her lunch meeting with Rick Rodriguez."

"Two o'clock? Val's was the first morning appointment for our beautician."

"Somebody must have changed the time, but it wasn't me."

Interesting. Did Dalton know Val's initial appointment had been changed? Traci hadn't mentioned a second phone call. So who had made the switch?

"Who's Rick Rodriguez?" she asked.

Sue Ellen's face scrunched in distaste. "He's a land developer. Val was fighting one of his proposed projects."

"So she missed her lunch meeting with him that day." How convenient for the guy that Val wasn't around anymore to oppose him.

Her glance fell on a spreadsheet lying half-hidden on the desk. Sue Ellen shoved it under a pile of papers and rose to see her out.

"Thanks for coming in, Marla. May I call you by your first name?"

"Of course. It's been good to meet you. Will you be at the fundraiser ball?"

"Naturally, it's the highlight of the season for me." She spoke those words but her gaze held a hint of pain, not joy, at the prospect. Was she being sarcastic?

Marla shook her hand and then turned away, puzzled by the sudden impression that Sue Ellen was hiding something.

It's Dalton's job to investigate, she reminded herself. But inevitably, her footsteps took her down the hall toward the president's office.

CHAPTER FOUR

Marla knocked on the open office door. A gruff voice bade her to enter, and she strode inside. A heavyset man rose from behind a worn wood desk and greeted her with a quizzical frown.

"Hello, how may I help you?"

"I'm Marla Vail from Cut 'N Dye Salon and Day Spa. We're booked to help backstage at the fashion show this month. We are also the place where Valerie Weston, uh, you know." She glanced away and let her gaze flit among the organized stacks of papers on a counter and the neatly aligned collection of bird figurines on a windowsill.

"Ah, I see. I'm Solomon Gold, the organization's president. Please have a seat," he said with a sweep of his arm. His glance dipped to her wedding ring. "Had you been well acquainted with our patron, Mrs. Vail?"

"No, I'm afraid not. She was my beautician's client, although they'd known each other for years. I'm sorry for your organization's loss. I understand she was a beloved benefactor. I attended the funeral but didn't have a chance to meet you there."

He reclaimed his chair and steepled his hands on the desk. "She'll be greatly missed. Val's funding underwrote our annual ball. This event is our main source of revenue for the entire year. I don't know what we'll do without her support and enthusiasm."

"Did she come into the offices here often?"

"I don't see why that would be your concern."

"I respect her work and hope to learn more about her. I'm thinking of making a donation in her memory." *And maybe I can learn more about you in the process.*

"Well, in that case, our purpose is to preserve our historical heritage in terms of architecture. For example, we're campaigning against a developer's efforts to acquire a row of buildings from the 1930s on the Broadwalk at Hollywood Beach. He wants to replace them with a condo tower. Then there's a home built in 1925 along the New River. We are hoping to get that one listed on the national historic register."

"I get it. Your group tries to preserve places like Stranahan House," she said, mentioning a popular tourist attraction in downtown Fort Lauderdale.

"That's correct." He rose and lumbered to a side counter, where he obtained a couple of brochures. "Here is information on our organization and on ways to donate."

"Thanks." Marla stuffed them in her purse. She indicated the bird figurines by the window. "What are those? Are you a birder?"

"Not in terms of bird watching, no. One of my private interests is in preventing birds from hitting windows. They don't see the glass. Collisions kill millions of the creatures each year. Have you ever had one fly against a window at your house and fall limp to the ground?"

"I can't say that I have."

"Some of them get up again, if they've been merely stunned. Others die. It's a preventable death, if we can warn them off. There's research being done into various ways to make bird-safe windows without obstructing the view."

"That would be good." Marla gathered her handbag. While instructional, this conversation was diverting off target. Perhaps Gold meant to mislead her on purpose.

"Some larger birds have a blind spot directly ahead as their eyes are placed to the side. Songbirds don't have this gap but their frontal vision is weak. Research involves using UV light, because birds can detect it and we can't. Patterns could be built into the glass that would warn them off."

"You're very passionate on the subject."

"Yes, that's true, and I'm just as passionate about our historic buildings. I hope you'll consider joining our list of regular contributors."

"Sure, I'll read your brochure. In the meantime, I'll look forward to seeing you again at the holiday ball. Will you be coming backstage?"

"I doubt it." He gave her a patronizing grin. "I have my duties working the room. It'll be weird this year without Val being there. She was a force all her own."

"She's with her sister now and at peace."

"Yes, it's so sad. The sister left behind a husband and two children. Val was devoted to those kids. Nonetheless, I'm hopeful she left us a bequest in her will. She was dedicated to our cause and promised she'd be generous."

What's sad is how you care more about her money. "So Val never married? I'd think she would have had many men interested in her."

He shot a glance toward the door and lowered his voice. "Oh, she'd been married once. It soured her to the prospect again."

"That's too bad. Tell me, if I want to leave a donation in my will, what should I do?"

He pointed to her handbag. "The information is in the brochure. And your estate lawyer should be able to help you. Do you have children, Mrs. Vail? Actually, why is your name familiar to me?" A frown creased his brow as recognition dawned, and he pulled a business card from under a stack of papers. "Wait, are you related to that police detective?"

Marla gave a proud smile. "He's my husband. But be assured I'm here on my own. My stylists were hired for the fashion show long before Val's death. I stopped by to make sure our contract was still valid. I'm thrilled that Lora asked us to participate."

Gold snorted. "Lora had better enjoy this event. It might be our last without Val's funding. I'll have to put Howard onto finding another donor in her place."

"Howard? Who's he?"

"Howard Cohn is our treasurer. He reimburses Lora for her trips. She'll be disappointed if they're curtailed."

"Yes, Lora mentioned she travelled a lot. What exactly is her role?"

"She acts as our liaison to other building preservation groups around the country. Lora confers with them over fundraising strategies and attends special events as our envoy."

"I see." And without Val's money, Marla surmised, these trips might cease. "Surely Val's provisions, if she did indeed leave something for the group in her will, might be enough to continue Lora's trips and the annual ball."

"I hope you're right. Val had been talking recently about how pollutants contaminated our environment, and who knew which poisons caused her sister's illness? I was afraid we might lose her to a new cause."

Marla narrowed her eyes. Had he been afraid she'd change her will and leave FOFL in the dust? Her head reeling from the implications if this were true, she changed tactics.

"I spoke to Sue Ellen. She made Val's appointment at the day spa but says the initial time was for two o'clock. Do you know who might have changed it to first thing in the morning?"

Gold's wide shoulders rose and fell. "I have no idea. Why, is this significant?"

Marla wished she could tell him Val's death was being

considered a homicide but held her tongue. "It could be. If you find out, can you let me know?" She stood. "It's been a pleasure meeting you, Mr. Gold. I'll look forward to seeing you at the holiday event."

Outside, she headed toward her car while deep in thought. Wondering who had been Val's friends and associates aside from the folks in this organization, she decided it wasn't her concern. She'd accomplished what she had come to do, and that was to verify her staff's participation in the fashion show.

On the way home, she drove through Wilton Manors for a shortcut. She was heading down a main street lined with shops and restaurants when she spotted a familiar face. Was that Ken coming out of a tea room with a strange woman? What was Tally's husband doing here? And why was that gal hanging onto his arm so intimately?

Uncertain of her perception, she drove around the corner and did another pass by. The two stood in front of Ken's gold Acura, deep in conversation. Marla frowned, wondering if this was a business meeting. He could be here for any reason other than what she was thinking.

Mind your own affairs, she told herself while gripping the steering wheel. Still, after completing a few errands, she activated her cell phone and called her friend Tally.

"Hey, are you up for a visit? I haven't seen the baby in a while, and I have some free time."

Tally squealed. "I'd love for you to come over. I'm going nuts without adult company."

"Can I stop anywhere along the way for you? Do you need supplies or groceries?"

"Thanks, but I'm not helpless. Come on by. I just baked a pear upside-down cake. We can have some dessert and chat, in between Luke's feedings and such."

"Okay, I'll be there in a few." It's just a friendly visit, she told herself. Nonetheless, she couldn't shake the feeling that her sighting of Ken meant something.

Tally had moved from her comfortable house in Jacaranda to a bigger place in Weston, the hot spot for social climbers. Ken had pressured her to change locations, stating their neighborhood was deteriorating. Marla felt he just wanted to put up a wealthy front for his clients. Formerly a regional director for disaster insurance claims, he'd started his own franchise agency after making a windfall investment in a North Carolina gemstone mine.

As she pulled into their paved driveway, she admired the tropical landscaping and the colorful winter impatiens that had been planted out front. A cool gust of wind swept her skirt about her legs as she emerged into the early-afternoon sunshine. She'd stopped for a bite to eat, so with lunch done, she could linger if Tally needed help with anything.

Her friend looked hassled as she swung open the door. Her blonde hair in disarray, the baby tucked on one hip, she appeared as though a helping hand might be welcome. Without waiting for an invitation, Marla strode inside. "How's Luke? Are you getting any sleep yet?"

"Holy smokes, Marla, surely you jest." Tally locked the door and followed Marla into the kitchen. "I've made coffee if you want a fresh cup."

"I'd love it." Familiar with their home, Marla grabbed a couple of mugs from a cabinet. She helped herself to a cup from the coffeemaker on the granite counter while Tally cut slices of homemade cake.

After taking a few sips of her brew, Marla sighed with contentment. "Thanks, I needed a boost of caffeine. Here, let me hold Luke so you can relax."

"That sounds wonderful." Tally handed her the squirming bundle.

Swathed in a blue blanket, the baby lay in her arms and stared up at her. Marla's heart melted at his sweet innocence. His powdered baby scent drifted her way, making her nuzzle his cheek. His skin was the softest thing she'd ever felt. She pressed her lips gently to his forehead, drinking in this young, new life. Babies were miracles. They came from nothing, grew inside you, and came out fully formed.

"Marla, what is it?" Tally placed their plates and utensils on the glass kitchen table then sank into a seat. "You have the weirdest look on your face."

"I'm thinking how amazing it is to have a child."

Tally's penciled eyebrows rose. "Oh?"

Marla sat opposite, careful not to jostle the infant. A smile curved her mouth as she played with Luke's tiny fingers and toes. "He's so perfect. You are blessed, Tally."

"With Luke, I am."

"What does that mean?"

Tally's blue eyes darkened. "Ken has been acting strange lately."

"Uh-oh. In what way?" A lead ball settled into her stomach as she recalled her earlier sighting of Ken at Wilton Manors.

"I'm not sure. Distant. Like, he doesn't talk about his day anymore when we sit down to dinner except for a few monosyllables."

"Is he working a bad case?"

"He says things are fine but looks away when he says it. Something is wrong, but I don't know what it is. Maybe the baby is too much responsibility for him."

"Why would you think he has misgivings when you have this beautiful child? Maybe he's feeling overburdened, but he still loves you and Luke. Being a new parent is tough. You should talk this out with him, hon." Marla hoped her own doubt didn't show in her tone.

"I know, but I'm so tired all the time. I don't have the strength to confront him."

"When did this start?"

Tally ran a weary hand over her face. "A few weeks ago. It's not like him to stop talking about work, especially since he opened his new office."

"He doesn't travel anymore for disaster claims. Being stuck in the same place all day might be getting to him. And now that he owns his franchise, it could be he's feeling the weight of responsibility in that regard. Or maybe he's simply honoring the confidentiality of his clients." Marla chewed on her lower lip, debating if she should mention spotting Ken earlier that day. "Uh, how are his work hours these days?" she said instead.

Tally crossed her legs and took a gulp of coffee before responding. She looked so downtrodden that Marla wanted to give her a hug of support. "He's been working late. I phoned him just before lunch to ask him if he could pick up a few things on his way home. He said he was right in the middle of some paperwork and he'd call me back."

"What time was this?"

"Around eleven. Why?"

"Oh, you know how testy men can get when they're hungry. You should have called him after lunch." So Ken had lied. That was about the time when she'd seen him coming out of that café. Marla picked up her fork and tasted the cake while balancing Luke in the crook of her other arm. The cake was still warm, and she chewed thoughtfully. "Remember when you thought Ken might be having an affair, and it turned out financial worries were making him less talkative? He'd invested in that gemstone mine in North Carolina."

"What about it?" Tally plucked at her loose top that had baby dribble on it.

"What ever happened with that investment? Does he still

63

have it? Could the lode have fizzled, affecting his retirement account?"

"Ken hasn't talked about that mine in so long that I'd forgotten about it. Besides, I'm handling the household accounts now. I haven't noticed anything irregular."

"Then don't worry about it. But definitely tell him how you're feeling shut out and ask what's on his mind." Marla made faces at Luke. He stared back at her, indifferent to her silly antics. His arms and legs were in constant motion. His little nose scrunched, and suddenly his bottom felt warm along with an unpleasant odor. "Um, I believe Luke needs changing."

Tally laughed at her expression. "Come on, give him to me. You can follow me into his room. Do you want a lesson in diaper changing?"

"I used to babysit, remember? But a refresher couldn't hurt. The products might have changed." Marla rose to bring their near-empty mugs to the sink. Then she trailed Tally down the hall to the nursery at the other end of the house.

A grin split her face as she entered. Soft carpet muted her steps as her glance took in the crib with its colorful overhead mobile, a changing table, and a four-drawer dresser. Disney's *Cars* theme predominated, since Ken loved car shows and magazines.

Tally placed the now-wailing infant on the changing table. "Watch carefully, Marla. You might have to do this someday."

"Ugh, maybe I should wait in the kitchen."

"Don't be silly." Tally made quick business of disposing of the soiled diaper, wiping down the baby with handy wipes, sprinkling power on his butt, and swaddling him in a new disposable diaper. "There, nothing to it."

"You're a natural at this," Marla said in admiration.

"You could be too, Marla." Tally gave her an indulgent smile. "Are you really so set against having children now that you and

Dalton are settled?"

"We've talked about this. You know how I feel."

"You're a good stepmother to Brianna. You would be a wonderful mom to your own kids."

"Maybe so, but I'm not ready to go there."

Self-doubts brought an image of Tammy into her brain. Every time she saw a baby, she remembered the adorable toddler whose life had ended under her care. Although her guilt had lessened, she'd never erase the image of that child's limp body being pulled from the pool.

"He's been fed, so I'll put him down for a nap."

Tally's remark drew Marla from her unpleasant trip down memory lane. A video monitor blinked green nearby as Tally lowered Luke into his crib. His howls followed them from the room.

"Does he need to be burped?" Marla asked, unsure what else the baby needed.

"Already done. He likes to fuss for a while before he settles down."

Marla hesitated by the foyer. "I should let you get some rest. I haven't been much help."

"Nonsense, I'm always glad to see you. We don't get to meet for lunch these days."

Another reason to avoid having children. They take over your life. "Well, I'm happy I got to see Luke. He's growing so fast."

"Yes, he'll be into the next-sized clothes before we know it." Tally gave her a hug. "I appreciate your support, as always. Everything okay at your household?"

"Aside from work worries, we're fine."

"Oh, how is that case going? I totally forgot to ask you about the woman who died in your day spa. I'm sorry."

Marla waved a hand. "I won't bother you with the details. Go and get some rest while you can. We'll talk more another time."

Nancy J. Cohen

She got a chance to discuss the case again at work on Tuesday, however. The police department's announcement late the previous afternoon that Val's case was now considered a homicide had people buzzing. Questions flew at Marla as staff members came to work. Next door, the spa had reopened and reporters clamored for interviews. She instructed her staff at both establishments to remain silent.

"All we know right now is that Val died from an allergic reaction to latex," she said in her briefing to them. "Traces of the substance have been found in her facial mask. Rosana denies any involvement and I believe her. She'd been treating Val for years and knew about her medical conditions."

"So you're saying someone else put latex into the lady's face cream?" Nicole asked.

The other stylists hovered around her salon station. None of their clients had arrived yet, and Robyn had yet to put out their printed schedules. She was working the front desk, her head tilted so she could listen in.

"It looks that way," Marla replied. "Somebody also changed Val's appointment time. It had originally been scheduled for that afternoon. And the spa's shampoo girl hasn't been seen since the day before, either."

"How come your husband is on the case? Isn't there a conflict of interest?" Nicole persisted. As a mystery reader, she had a keen interest in his cases.

"Yes, but they are short-staffed this season, so he stepped in as soon as he heard the address from the dispatcher. He hasn't been reassigned yet."

Robyn brought around their schedules then scurried back up front as a couple of clients walked in. It broke up their cluster, as everyone scattered to their posts. Nicole glanced over while Marla plugged in her curling irons and blow dryer.

"Isn't latex a powder?" Nicole said, her forehead creasing

into a thoughtful frown.

Marla gave a sigh. This wouldn't be an easy day. "I researched the stuff online. It's available in liquid form, comes in different colors, and hardens when exposed to air. Makeup artists use it in the entertainment industry. It's cheap and readily accessible at online stores."

"So anyone could buy the stuff. But how would they get it into Val's face cream?"

"That's the question. Who knew she had an early-morning appointment with Rosana, where Rosana's room was located, and even where she kept the jar of cream she used on Val? For that matter, Rosana used different types of creams depending on a client's skin condition."

"So the killer would need to have access to Rosana's records," Nicole concluded.

"Yes, I suppose. But it still could be anyone, like a member of the staff, a customer, or even one of the cleaning crew who comes in at night."

"Dalton must be checking into those possibilities."

"There's one angle that's puzzling. I mentioned that Patty, the shampoo girl next door, didn't show up for work the day of Val's death. When Dalton went to her apartment, it had been emptied out. There's no trace of the woman."

Nicole's eyes narrowed. "That's suspicious. What if she'd been paid to commit sabotage and then left? Can Dalton look into her bank accounts? Maybe someone paid her off."

"I don't know if he's gotten that far in his research, but I'll suggest it to him. He should also look into who worked late the night before and who were the last few clients. Also, maybe Val got her nails or hair done at the spa and confided her medical condition to more than one staff member. No one has come forward, but I can ask people there."

"Even if this is so, nobody else would know which face cream

Rosana used on Val without accessing her records."

"Right, there is that."

Nicole wasn't the only one with questions. Marla's cell phone buzzed around eleven-thirty when she'd just finished a highlights job with a blow-out. Her next customer wasn't until noon, so she'd gone outside in the rear to get a breath of crisp autumn air. One of the nail techs leaned against a wall there, smoking a cigarette.

"Hello?" Marla noted the phone's caller ID came from the day spa.

"Hi, it's Traci. Can you come over? A lady detective is here. She says her name is Katherine Minnetti and that you know her."

"Yes, she's Dalton's partner. I'm on it."

A few minutes later, she greeted the lieutenant who wore her raven hair in a flattering style and her slim form in a chocolate brown pants suit that matched her eyes. Kat didn't bother to grant her a smile. She gave Marla an assessing glance that didn't betray her thoughts.

"Hello, Kat. Nice to see you again," Marla said in a sardonic tone.

"At another murder investigation? What happened, Marla? Were you getting bored, and so you decided to stir up trouble again?"

Was she joking? Marla couldn't tell from her stony expression.

"Oh, sure. I didn't have enough to do with the holidays approaching and all."

Kat waved a paper in her hand. "I have a list of staff members I'd like to interview. Is there a private room where we can talk?"

"Me and you, or you and them?"

Kat chuckled. "Both of the above. You can be first."

Gee, thanks. "Let's see which room is available." They entered one of the massage rooms that wasn't being used. At Kat's request, Marla ran down the list and described each one of the operators.

"And you didn't know Rosana, the aesthetician, before you hired her to work at the spa?"

"No, but one of my regular clients recommended her. She worked at a fancy salon on the east side of town."

"What induced her to move here, farther away from her customers?"

"My benefits package. It's much more generous than what she was getting. I don't allow independent booth rentals at my salon. The stylists pay me a percentage of their income rather than a fixed monthly rate. This goes for our other personnel, too. In return, I stock their products, conduct continuing education classes, and foster a team spirit rather than a competitive one. Rosana was very happy to jump ship to gain group health insurance."

Kat took notes in a purse-sized notepad. "Did you do a background check?"

"A basic one. I don't get into drug testing or fingerprinting. Her clients raved about her, and that's good enough for me. She does my eyebrows now and my lip wax." Marla observed a faint shadow above Kat's upper lip. The lady detective could use those services but Marla didn't care to offend her by suggesting it.

Kat paced back and forth, a furrow between her eyes, while Marla slid onto the massage table to sit on the edge and rest her feet. She'd worn shoes with wedge heels and wasn't used to this pair. She straightened her skirt, glancing at her watch. How could she speed this along?

"I hope you're looking into Patty's disappearance," she said, then proceeded to present her theories and findings to date.

Kat tapped her chin thoughtfully. "Your shampoo girl's

vanishing act could be unrelated to the case. She could have had a fight with a boyfriend and decided to cool off on her own."

"But then she'd have called the salon to notify us she was taking time off. You'll be following up on her absence, won't you?"

"Naturally. We'll talk to her neighbors, too, and see what they have to say."

"Meanwhile, you should look into those people from Friends of Old Florida. They might have been concerned Val would switch her allegiance to another organization after her sister died, and cut them out of her will. And then there's the builder, Rick Rodriguez. Val was supposed to meet him for lunch the day she died. According to what I learned, Val had been opposing him over a proposed development project on Hollywood Beach."

"So I've heard. Were you aware Solomon Gold, the group's president, owns some of those historic structures?"

"Oh, really? Does he favor selling them or preserving the region's history?"

"He's against selling those properties, so he agreed with Val in that regard. I still consider the beautician a more viable suspect. The victim might have discovered her secret."

Uh-oh. What did Kat know that she didn't? Marla rose to face her. "What secret is that?"

"That Rosana never filed for citizenship papers. She's in this country illegally."

"That's impossible. I confirmed her status myself."

"How so?"

"She has a valid driver's license."

Kat snorted. "Anyone can obtain a driver's license if you know the right people. Did you examine her immigration papers?"

"I didn't feel it was necessary." In retrospect, perhaps that had been an error on her part. Could this be true? Rosana had been lying about her citizenship status? And if the woman wasn't being truthful about this matter, what else was she keeping from them?

CHAPTER FIVE

Marla went back to work, troubled by Kat's revelation. How could Rosana have lied about her citizenship status? Why hadn't she applied years ago?

Wait a minute. Hadn't she married an American? Wouldn't that grant her status without the rigmarole? She yanked out her cell phone and texted Kat. Perhaps the detective hadn't looked into Rosana's family situation. Then again, on what evidence did Kat state that Rosana was here illegally? Could her marriage be a lie, too?

Troubled by a sense of betrayal, she vowed to ask Rosana about it later. Meanwhile, Marla kept busy and grabbed a bite to eat in between customers. The thought of Kat interrogating her spa personnel put her nerves on edge. So when Traci summoned her with a mysterious message, she hastened over to the spa as soon as she had a spare moment. Fortunately, the reporters who'd hovered outside hoping for a statement had already dispersed.

She was startled to see Traci with a smock on and getting her hair bleached. Her glossy pink lips split into a grin at the expression on Marla's face.

"What? I've always wanted to be a blonde. It'll go better with my blue eyes, and the guys might notice me more. Don't you think?"

"You'll look great." *Not that you needed to change your looks with that figure.* "But why did you call me over? What's wrong?"

Traci shifted in her chair at the front desk where she waited for her solution to process. "A customer came in who said she's a friend of Val. She wants to speak to the owner."

Oh, great. Did this woman intend to give Marla a dressing down for letting Val die in her salon slash day spa?

"Okay, I'll see what she wants. Where is she?"

"You'll find her in number six. Her name is Nadia Welsh."

Marla entered one of the private rooms where nails, paraffin treatments, and foot reflexology were done. Soothing New Age music played in the background, while a citrus scent perfumed the air. Vats of swirling water weren't used for pedicures here. She'd hired girls who knew a European technique employing waterless foot care. Marla had tried it herself at a salon on Las Olas and liked the more sanitary technique. None of their customers had complained about missing the foot soak.

A comfy lounge chair and a wood secretary cabinet provided the main furnishings, with a potted plant in one corner and an extra chair for visitors. From the glass of iced green tea and plate of half-eaten pastry on a rolling side table, it appeared as though the woman had raided their lounge. None of the rooms had a TV with soap operas or depressing world news to provide distraction. More than one of their clients had been so relaxed as to doze off in these chairs. The technician easily switched sides in her wheeled seat while doing a manicure.

Reclining in the lounger now was a middle-aged woman with straw-colored hair, a navy and ivory top over white capri pants, and painted coral fingernails. The nail tech smiled with a nod of greeting at Marla's approach and then got back to work on the woman's toes.

"Are you Nadia? I'm Marla Shore, the salon and spa owner."

"Hi, I wanted to talk to you about my friend, Valerie Weston."

"I'm sorry for your loss. We feel terrible about what happened."

Nadia's eyes glistened. "Val and I had known each other for years. I knew her secrets and she knew mine. I understand you're married to the detective investigating the case?"

"Yes, that's right. He's working with his partner, Lieutenant Katherine Minnetti," she added, so the woman wouldn't think there was a conflict of interest.

"I have some information you might want to pass on." Nadia winced when the nail tech scraped under her big toe nail. "You do know Val was a benefactor for Friends of Old Florida, right? She was passionate about preserving our regional history and loved those old buildings."

"Yes, I visited their offices the other day and spoke to the president. He said Val had been involved in a fight against a land developer over a strip of historic structures on Hollywood Beach?"

Nadia snickered. "Did that man tell you he owns several of those buildings, and they provide him with rental income?"

"I'd heard he owned them but not that he rented them out. Did Mr. Gold assign this project to Val, or did she take it on by herself?"

"She made her own decisions. Val loved the architecture with the rounded curves and bright tropical colors. Once she got the bee in her bonnet to salvage some old building, she went after it hog-wild. She'd butted heads with Rick Rodriguez more than once."

"The land developer? Do you think he's happier now that she's out of the way?"

Nadia shook her head. "FOFL will only pursue those issues without her. Solomon is pushing to get those 30s buildings onto the National Register of Historic Places. Lora Larue, a board member, consulted the Miami Design Preservation League, since they'd been involved with Miami Beach's Art Deco Historic District."

Marla drew over the other chair in the room and took a seat. She couldn't afford to be here too long, but this woman had some valuable information.

"Tell me about Lora. Were she and Val good friends?"

Nadia guffawed. "They worked together. I wouldn't say they were friends. They each had different dispositions, shall we say."

"Lora takes a lot of trips on behalf of the organization, from what I've been told. Do you think those will end without Val's contributions to the group?"

"I don't see why they would. Val provided handsomely for FOFL"—she pronounced it *foffle* like everyone else—"in her will, so that shouldn't be a problem."

"You know this for a fact? Val told you so?"

"It wasn't a secret. Val often mentioned her bequest to wield power. Although lately she'd . . ." Nadia cast a furtive glance at the nail tech, who pretended disinterest.

"Yes?" Marla asked in an encouraging tone.

"After Val's sister died, she'd been rethinking her purpose. She loved those old buildings, but what good would preserving them do for future generations if no one is around to appreciate their beauty? Her sister died from breast cancer. Val briefly thought about supporting medical research, but she figured pollution had to be a causative factor. We breathe poisons in the air, eat them in our food, and tolerate them in our homes in the form of radon. If we don't act more strongly to preserve our planet, new diseases will spring up to foil us."

"You sound like a believer."

"I believe in the old adage, you are what you eat." Nadia glared at her, wagging a forefinger. At her feet, the technician worked silently. She was probably used to her clients spouting off on all sorts of topics. "Unknown additives are put into our food, much of which is genetically modified. Then there are insecticides coating our fruits and vegetables. Unless you stick to organic products, you don't know what you're getting. These chemicals disrupt our systems. They're probably what cause so many of our cancers."

"I have no doubt you're right. And what about cell phone or microwave emissions? The list goes on, but you can't live your life afraid of everything you consume or use."

"No, but awareness can be raised and safety standards put in place. Val was seriously considering supporting these efforts."

"She must have been devastated when her sister passed away. Will the husband stay in the area, do you think?" Marla's cell phone vibrated in her pocket. It must be Robyn notifying her that the next customer had arrived.

Nadia shrugged. "Who knows? Sean is a nice guy. I couldn't make the funeral but I sent flowers. Poor man will have to raise their children alone."

Rising, Marla smoothed her skirt. "Too bad Val never had kids of her own."

"It wasn't in her cards," Nadia said, expressing what Marla felt about herself.

"Yet she'd been married? Did you know her back then?"

Nadia's face clouded. "Yes. Her ex was a louse. The guy was only after her money, or at least that was Val's excuse for dumping him."

"And she didn't want to take another chance on love?"

"Who says she didn't, dear? Love comes in different ways." Nadia turned her attention to the pedicurist, who'd finished filing her heels and was rubbing an exfoliate cream on her legs. "Oh, that feels good. Thanks for listening, Marla. I can see why Val liked your spa and will recommend it to my friends. But please see to it that your husband looks into the things we've discussed. Specifically, FOFL's officers."

"I'll do that. Thank you for the information." As Marla headed back to her salon, she mulled over their conversation. While she hadn't learned a whole lot that was new, Nadia's last message may have been the point of their meeting. Plus, something nagged at her. Why hadn't Val remarried? Had Dalton gone over to check out her place and speak to the neighbors?

She asked him that night after they'd retired to bed. He put down the book he'd been reading about World War II to regard her. His spice scent aroused her but she tamped down her response, waiting to see what he would share.

"Yes, I've been to her home and interviewed the staff. She lived in a Mediterranean-style mansion on the water. You'd love her place. It speaks of old money."

"Where did she get her fortune?"

"Her mother's family had a stake in Florida's East Coast Railroad. That's where the inheritance came from, but Val got her interest in history from her father. According to one of her friends, the man was a naturalist whose tales of Florida pirates, Indians, and Spanish explorers captivated her. Val's ancestry might even have included a pirate who ploughed the high seas by the Florida Keys."

"Did you know she'd been married and divorced?"

"So I heard. We looked up the guy. He lives out in California and remarried. He's not a factor."

"It's almost as though she substituted charitable works for a love life after her failed marriage. Did she have any boyfriends?"

Dalton's mouth compressed. "No one the staff mentioned. She lived a private life aside from her society functions. Oh, and the lady was an artist."

Marla sat upright. "What?"

"She painted watercolor scenes of natural Florida. Her works were quite popular at juried art shows. I can't tell which passion she held to more, saving historic buildings or painting."

"This is news to me. I'm surprised Val's friend, Nadia, didn't mention it when we spoke this morning." Marla related the gist of their conversation.

"We're already checking into FOFL's officers." Leaning on his elbow, Dalton tickled her arm when she lay down to face him.

"Sue Ellen, the group's secretary, is the one who made Val's facial appointment," Marla said. "She'd scheduled it for two o'clock that afternoon, but someone called to change the time. Will you look into it?"

"Sure, I'll check it out. It could be important."

Marla told him what else she'd learned from her visit to FOFL's offices. "Val had an antagonistic relationship with Rick Rodriguez. Mr. Gold mentioned the developer's proposal during our discussion, but he neglected to reveal his personal stake in keeping some of those historic buildings under his ownership."

"The builder is a person of interest. His path is clearer with Val out of the way."

"Not if Gold persists in opposing his project. I'm also concerned about how everyone knew Val promised a bequest to FOFL in her will. After her sister's death, the president was afraid she might make a change. That gives him a motive. And did you know Lora Larue hired our stylists for the fashion show at Val's recommendation? Lora goes on a lot of trips for the group. If they lose Val's funding, she might find this benefit curtailed."

"That hardly seems like a motive for murder."

"Maybe, but people have been killed for less. You've told me so yourself. What about that girl, Patty? Have you tracked her down yet?"

"We're working on it. Can we stop with the shop talk for

now?" His hand drifted lower, making his intent clear.

She swatted it away. "In a minute. Guess who I saw while I was driving through Wilton Manors on my way home from visiting FOFL's headquarters? Tally's husband, Ken. He was coming out of a café with some woman."

"So? It could have been a business engagement."

"I asked Tally about him later. She said he'd been doing paperwork in his office all day."

"Marla, mind your own business. You don't want to go snooping into your friend's affairs. And you certainly don't want to imagine things that aren't there."

"But Tally said he's been acting distracted lately."

"The guy has a new baby. Who wouldn't be?" His exploring fingers cupped a part of her that involuntarily reacted. "Speaking of babies, we should discuss—"

"No, we shouldn't." She sought a quick way to change the subject. "Your partner stopped by the spa to interview the staff. I don't like her implications about Rosana. She said the woman is here illegally, but Rosana showed me her driver's license. And I believe she's married to an American. Can you check into her status? I'd hate to think she lied to us."

His eyes narrowed, as though he knew she'd redirected their conversation on purpose. Thankfully, he didn't pursue it. "If she did falsify her credentials, that could be significant."

"Rosana has nothing to gain by Val's death. She'd been treating the woman for years."

"And yet someone entered the day spa and doctored the face cream, knowing exactly which one Rosana used on Val."

"Yes, and she'd be stupid to kill her own client with the smoking gun pointing right at her. The bad guy must have accessed her files."

"Kat will examine all the possibilities. She's good at her job. Listen, I'm more concerned about Brianna. She wants to drive every chance she gets. I wish she'd practice around the neighborhood more often before venturing too far."

"Did her driving instructor tell you he plans to take her on the highway next?"

That put cold water on his ardor. He rolled onto his back with a groan. "Good Lord. Not I-95, I hope. I'll forbid it until she has at least a year of driving experience under her belt. The turnpike has less traffic, or even the Sawgrass Expressway."

Marla's gut clawed with anxiety over either prospect. "Let's not think about that now."

"How about the lawsuit against you? Has it been dismissed yet?"

"No, my insurance agent is supposed to get back to me. I'm trying not to dwell on it."

"You'll see, it'll be thrown out of court as a nuisance case." He leaned over to kiss her. "I have no doubt you'll rise to the top."

"Oh, yes." She did just that, reviving their passion and erasing all further thoughts.

On Thursday morning, before going into the salon, Marla detoured to the hotel where the fashion show would take place. She needed to scout the area where her staff would be working to make sure they'd have adequate electrical outlets and such. The ritzy hotel on Fort Lauderdale Beach faced the ocean across the street on A1A.

Inside the spacious lobby, she gazed at immense crystal chandeliers, bouquets of flowers, and ornate Corinthian columns. Her heels echoed on the marble floor as she headed toward a polished wood front desk. One of the uniformed clerks smiled at her approach.

"I'm Marla Vail. I'll be working at the fashion show coming up this Saturday for the Friends of Old Florida event. Can you direct me to the location where we'll be setting up? I'd like to check out the facilities ahead of time to see what we need to bring."

"Of course, miss. Our resort manager should be able to help you." He waved to a heavy-set fellow in a suit across the grand hall. As the guy strode over at his signal, the clerk addressed him. "Mr. Kahuna, this lady would like a tour of the backstage area for Saturday's fashion show."

The man turned to her with a grin and a handshake. He had a flat nose, wide lips, and dark, expressive eyes against a tanned complexion. His longish black hair brushed his broad shoulders. "I'm Biggs Kahuna. I'll be happy to help."

"Biggs? That's an unusual name. I'm Marla Vail."

He chuckled. "Biggs is a nickname. You can see why." He indicated his rotund form.

After Marla mentioned her purpose, he gestured for her to follow him down a wide hallway. They passed double doors labeled with a ballroom name and kept going.

"That's the Starlight Ballroom where the function will take place. Up ahead and around the corner is the actual backstage area. But the section where the models get prepped is on this opposite side."

Further along, he opened a door to their left and led her through a maze of connected rooms. One held a mirrored wall and mobile clothing racks. This might be where the models got dressed, Marla figured. Or it could serve as a staging area for a theatrical performance. An adjacent space sported a row of dressing tables lined up facing wall-mounted mirrors. Each one had a swivel chair and plentiful electrical outlets.

"This is where my staff will work, I gather?" she said, bobbing her head in approval.

"That's right. The makeup artist works over there." Biggs indicated a cubicle with only two seats but generous counter space. "At least we won't have to worry this year about Miss Weston coming back here."

Marla glanced at him, startled at hearing Val's name. "Why is that?"

"With her latex allergy, you couldn't be too careful. The makeup lady warned Val to steer clear of this area."

Marla's jaw dropped. "How many people knew about her problem?" Perhaps the killer wasn't someone who'd gained this information from Rosana's files. That broadened the possibilities, and not in a good way.

"Val told most folks she met, so she wouldn't be inadvertently exposed."

"Why did the makeup artist warn Val away? Does she wear latex gloves?"

Biggs examined Marla as though she had been born in the past century. "Don't you know? Liquid latex is a staple in the entertainment industry. That stuff can cover up blemishes, reshape your face, and add special effects. It's handy for makeup people to keep in their kits."

"My day spa is where Val died. We were all horrified."

"So you must know about the substance then. Val's death was a terrible tragedy."

"Yes, it's saddened everyone who knew her."

Glancing toward the outer corridor, he lowered his voice. "New owners are coming in as of January. They'll be remodeling the property and making changes around here. I'm hoping FOFL will be able to continue this event without Val's presence. It's an important revenue-maker for the hotel."

From his sour expression, Marla wondered if his position might be at risk once the new owners took over. What would happen if FOFL cancelled their annual event? Would they have done so if Val had withdrawn her support as Nadia suggested? But now that she was dead, the provision in her will would provide continued funding, or so everyone hoped.

She tried to keep her face expressionless as she regarded Biggs Kahuna. It appeared he had a stake in Val's sponsorship. How far would he go to ensure his job security? Or was she merely being paranoid, finding suspects around every corner?

Best to pass this info on to Dalton and let him approach the hotel manager.

Marla spent the next half hour examining the space where her staff would work, calculating what tools to bring and figuring which chair she'd assign each stylist. At least they'd have plenty of room, although things could get hectic with models, dressers, and other personnel crowding the area. Her pulse rate accelerated. She was excited to meet the designer, Yolanda Whipp, and see her creations. Marla had always admired the gowns in the window of her Las Olas shop, but the prices were prohibitive. This would be the chance of a lifetime. She hoped to make enough of an impression that Yolanda might hire her for photo shoots or other events. Maybe she could even get a foot in the door for Fashion Week.

As Saturday approached, her anticipation grew. She worked through her clients at a feverish pitch, eager to be done at the salon and to head over to the hotel. Dalton had offered to drive her so he could observe the proceedings and meet the people involved. Kat would arrive later to hang out in the ballroom and mingle with the guests.

"Kat wasn't thrilled about her assignment. She's a no-frills type of person. All those society types and ball gowns aren't her cup of tea," he said during the drive over.

"I can imagine." A wry smile curved Marla's lips.

Lieutenant Katherine Minnetti rarely let down her guard, maintaining a business-like mien even at police department social functions, such as their annual barbecue. Despite Marla's efforts to get to know her better, she kept tight reins on the emotional wall she'd erected. Dalton still had no clue why she'd asked for a transfer from her former location. They got along but on a professional level.

"You look nice tonight," he said with an approving glance. "New outfit?"

"Yes, thanks, I splurged for the occasion." Marla wore a black cocktail dress with a beaded crepe overlay. Dressed for a party, she hoped to slip into the ballroom once the fashion show started. Nicole had offered to remain backstage for any last-minute hair fixes.

They gave their car to a valet. Dalton helped Marla carry in her toolbox that she'd transferred earlier from her trunk to his vehicle. She patted her handbag, which had an ample supply of business cards inside. This would be a good opportunity to publicize her establishment and perhaps gain some recognition among the town's movers and shakers.

She led the way toward the ballroom. The foyer was crowded with patrons sipping cocktails and snacking on hors d'oeuvres passed out by white-gloved waiters. Sequins and jewels sparkled in the light from crystal chandeliers. Marla's stylists would have plenty of time to do their work, since the fashion show didn't start until guests were midway through dinner. From inside the ballroom came strains of a dance band warming up for the night.

No wonder this event made money for the hotel. Finishing at a late hour, the ball probably brought in lots of overnight reservations. People wouldn't want to drive home after an evening of drinking and dancing. So hotel nights plus the food and beverage bill would add to a tidy sum. Biggs Kahuna had true cause to worry about the continuation of this holiday event.

She pointed him out to Dalton, who wandered in his direction to strike up a conversation. Marla hesitated at the door to the dressing area, while her imagination conjured Val working the crowd. The socialite must have loved this event. Being its main sponsor, her purpose had been to secure more funding for her cause. She'd been selflessly dedicated, or so it appeared. Would anyone offer a tribute to her tonight, or would things move on as her memory faded?

Someone tapped Marla on the shoulder, and she spun to face Lora Larue. The woman wore an ankle-length royal blue gown with silver beading that flattered her robust figure. Her bosom nearly spilled from a low scoop neckline, while her heavily applied makeup reminded Marla of a hand-painted doll. An exotic perfume scent drifted into her nose. Clearly Lora knew how to make the most of her generous assets.

"Marla, I'm glad you're here. I wanted to introduce you to our board members. We appreciate the work you are doing here tonight."

"It's my pleasure, Lora. I'm grateful for the opportunity and so is my staff. I've already met your group's secretary and president." She paused. "Are you always in town for the holiday ball? I gather you do a lot of traveling for the organization throughout the year."

Lora's gaze sharpened. "That's right. I'm liaison to similar preservation groups around the country."

"So what do you do on these trips? Meet with their people to exchange ideas?"

"Why do you want to know, dear?"

Marla spread her hands. "It must be a worthwhile expense for the organization to send you into the field. Otherwise, you could communicate via the Internet or phone."

Lora's mouth compressed, and her gaze grew chilly. "It's important to establish a personal connection. I find it's helpful to observe firsthand what other people do in terms of fundraising events."

"I guess you're right." Did Val look into these trips to see if they were purely business-related? Surely if her funding stopped, Lora could simply communicate with her comrades online.

To preserve good will, she changed the subject. "I can't wait to see Yolanda's creations. I've always admired her gowns in the windows of her store. You're fortunate to have snagged her for these shows each year."

Lora's face softened. "Yolanda loves doing it. She has a generous heart, even if each of her designs costs thousands of dollars. The publicity doesn't hurt, either."

A leggy, rail-thin model rushed past to enter through the dressing room door. Spotting a tall guy in a tuxedo, Lora waved him over. He had sandy hair, deep-set blue eyes, and a mouth with a bemused upward tilt. He'd just obtained a drink at one of the cash bars located throughout the area.

The man sauntered over, highball glass in hand. "You look ravishing, Lora."

"You're too kind. Howard Cohn, this is Marla Vail, our head stylist for tonight's models. Howard is our group's treasurer," Lora explained.

He examined Marla through wire-rimmed eyeglasses. "So you're the salon owner where our dear Val met her unfortunate end?"

"I'm so sorry. It wasn't—"

He gave a dismissive wave. "Your fault, I know. We'll miss her." His insincere tone said he'd miss her money more.

Lora poked him. "There's my Bigsy. I'll leave you two to chat." And she dashed off with a swish of skirts toward Biggs Kahuna, whose unmistakable large form had lumbered into view.

Bigsy? From her body language as she greeted him, Lora must be more than merely acquainted with the man. And was that a room key card he was handing her?

Bad Marla, thinking gutter thoughts. Of course, Lora would be staying the night so she wouldn't have to drive home. Biggs had probably just done her the courtesy of checking her in at the reservation desk. Never mind the way her bosom jiggled under the manager's lustful glare.

"So how did you meet Lora, Mrs. Vail?" Howard's droll tone drew her attention.

"Valerie Weston recommended our salon to her. Val had been seeing a beautician at our place for years," she explained. "Lora contacted me about working the fashion show. How did you get involved with Friends of Old Florida?"

"I've always been interested in the past. Actually, you might say I'm more interested in treasure, to be precise." He covered his mouth and gave a high-pitched giggle. "Did you know the waters off Florida are teaming with shipwrecks? Millions of dollars in silver, gold, and jewels lay at the bottom of the sea, much of it undiscovered. Spanish galleon ships alone may account for up to forty wrecks off our coast."

"Are you a treasure hunter, Mr. Cohn?"

His gaze fired with enthusiasm. "In a manner of speaking, if you consider our history to be valuable. These priceless pieces of our heritage should be preserved for future generations. Many of the wrecks are listed on the National Register of Historic Places. They're time capsules from an earlier age and contain a wealth of history. Imagine locating a vessel from the sixteen-hundreds."

"Do you dive on these sites yourself?"

He giggled again. "Not me. I'm in the banking business. But Ian over there is a certified diver." Howard waved over a lean fellow with an aquiline nose and a haughty expression. He wore a crimson cummerbund with his tux. "This is Dr. Ian Needles, one of our finest plastic surgeons. He's on the Board of Directors for FOFL. Ian, meet Marla Vail. She owns a hair salon. Her stylists were hired to prep the models for tonight's show."

Dr. Needles gave her a scornful glance. "A pleasure to meet you."

"I was telling her about shipwrecks and how you like to dive on the sites."

"Yes, the Underwater Archeological Preserves offer a fascinating glimpse into our region's history," Dr. Needles said in a snotty tone, as though Marla's interests couldn't possibly go beyond hair and nails and other frivolities.

"I've heard of the Atocha," she stated. "I've always wanted to visit Mel Fisher's museum in Key West."

"Spanish treasure ships are not the only ones sunken off our shores. Pirate vessels, slave ships, merchant transports, and Civil War ships plied these waters, too."

"So did hurricanes get most of them?" she asked, curiosity taking hold. A clock ticked in her head, reminding her that she needed to move on.

"Storms, shallow water, coral reefs, you name it. We have hazards aplenty."

"Hence all the lighthouses up and down the coast."

"Exactly." Dr. Needles pronounced his words with precision, as though doing surgery on his sentences. "I go diving every chance I get, which isn't as often as I'd like." He exchanged a meaningful glance with the group's treasurer, making Marla wonder if their shared interest in marine archaeology extended beyond the group's preservation goals.

A woman marched their way, turning heads in her wake. Yolanda Whipp, the famous dress designer, was recognizable by her blunt-cut black hair, high cheekbones, and exotic eyes. Her wide lips made a splash of crimson against her powdered complexion. She wore a colorful silk embroidered robe over a satin pants set, the top inlaid with bronze beading. Towering high heels added a few inches to her height. A wave of sensual perfume accompanied her.

Scurrying at her side was a fellow with curly red hair and an earnest expression. "All I need is ten minutes," he said in an urgent tone. "We're putting the interview in our next newsletter."

"Yes, darling. I'll catch you later, after the show. Now please let me get to work." Carrying a silver backstage box, Yolanda breezed past Marla, pushed open the dressing room door and swept inside.

"I'd better get moving." Marla turned to say a quick farewell to her companions, who then meandered off to greet some guests.

"Who are you?" the third fellow asked, forestalling her departure. "Have we met?"

"I don't think so." Marla identified herself. "And you are?"

"Andrew Fine, publicist for Friends of Old Florida. Is this your first time doing the show, Mrs. Vail?"

"Yes, it is, and I'd love to talk to you about my salon when things are less hectic." She handed him her card. "Maybe we could meet for a chat some time. I'm hoping to do more of these types of events."

"I gotcha." Andrew lowered his voice and leaned inward. "Have fun tonight. Keep your ears open and your mouth closed."

She got a whiff of cheese breath and recoiled. "What do you mean?"

"These people have secrets. They don't like you to probe too deeply."

CHAPTER SIX

Toting her supply case, Marla entered the chaotic scene where models prepped for the show. She headed over to the row of hair stations and set her purse on a counter. Her gaze took in the worn linoleum floor and the scuffed walls that she hadn't noticed on her earlier visit. Hopefully, the new owners would fix things up in the nonguest areas.

She opened her kit and confirmed it contained the brushes, combs, pins, clips, gels, and sprays she might require. She had wired tools and even a surge strip with extra outlets should they need it.

A different model occupied each station chair. Marla had brought four stylists plus herself for eight models. She'd decided to let her staff do the actual work while she supervised. In a separate alcove, the makeup artist was laying out her cosmetics. Each model would head over there for a touch-up once her hair was done.

Marla glanced at the racks of glittering dresses, wishing she had time to admire each gown. She imagined herself gliding into a ballroom in one of those creations. Bold burgundy, lemon yellow, sexy black, tropical turquoise, and luscious lime stood out among the satins, silks, and chiffons, along with sequins, seed pearls, and intricate beading. A separate rack held a dazzling array of wedding gowns. Who else but a wealthy socialite could afford these outfits? With a sigh, Marla realized this was the closest she'd ever get to high society.

Yolanda bustled about, greeting each person and keeping her tote box at hand. What was in there? Needle and thread for last-minute repairs? Jewels to go with her gowns?

"Thirty minutes per person, ladies," Yolanda shouted. "That's the goal."

Marla winced. That wouldn't give her stylists much time. "The guests have to eat dinner yet. It's still relatively early," she said, after introducing herself.

"Our show starts before the entrée arrives, to get people in the mood for dancing. The models must finish with makeup and be into their gowns by eight-thirty at the latest."

"How many changes does each girl have to make?"

Yolanda pursed her lips. "The show is divided into four segments, including the bridal procession at the end. That one requires five models. So some girls will have three changes and some will have four. You'll have mere minutes between scenes to fix any stray hairs, so make sure your people do their jobs right the first time."

Marla glanced around, noting the lack of privacy screens. Where did the models get dressed? Being professionals, they might be used to a lack of modesty.

The familiar smells of a salon met her nose as her stylists got to work. Music played in the distance from inside the ballroom. Florescent lights burned brightly overhead. A little girl wandered inside with an older woman in tow.

"Excuse me, where do you want my daughter?" the latter asked in a bewildered tone. She wore her black hair in a bun and had on a matronly dress.

"My darlings, I'm so glad you're here." Yolanda swept up to them with a wide embrace, air-kissing the older female. Her chandelier earrings swung with each movement. "Marla, would you mind fixing Juanita's hair? She's the flower girl in our bridal sequence."

"Sure, no problem." Marla sought an empty space where she could work. Hadn't there been some stacked chairs in the hallway?

She summoned one of the stagehands to help her, and then set up shop adjacent to the makeup station. After plugging in her tools, she positioned the child in the chair delivered by the stagehand. They faced a mirror propped up against the wall.

"Ringlets might look cute on her. Is she wearing a headpiece?" Marla asked the designer, who paced restlessly within hearing range.

"I have some jeweled barrettes to fix in her hair. Damn, where is that man? He should have been here by now." She gazed with an annoyed frown at the entry.

"Who are you waiting for?"

"My husband. He has my computer printouts."

Marla obtained the barrettes and placed them on the counter. She engaged the girl and her mother in conversation as she worked. The scents of hairspray mingled with perfume in the room. Cooled air whistled through a nearby vent, competing with the ever-present chatter and background music.

Nicole, busy using a dryer on a tall blonde, cursed when the power blew out.

"Try another outlet," Marla suggested once the power had been restored and everyone heaved a sigh of relief. "I have a surge strip if we need one," she announced.

"I'm done with the dryer. I can curl her hair now." Nicole picked up an iron and tested its temperature while her model sat with a bored expression.

The door burst open, and a tall, lean man with Asian features strode inside. He looked like a typical businessman in a dark suit with black hair to match. His calculating gaze surveyed the room as Dalton might for strategic entries and exits.

"Henutt, here you are at last," Yolanda cried. She pronounced his name *hee-nut.* "I need those diagrams. You can tack them up on this wall here."

He opened his briefcase and withdrew a sheaf of papers, then proceeded to tape them where indicated. They looked like sketches of the models and their series of dresses, divided into four columns for each scene in the show.

Marla angled herself for a better look. Cocktail dresses would begin the event, followed by party gowns, ball gowns, and finally the bridal collection. In the grand finale, all the models would line up together on stage. There was an empty space between the brides and the finish line. What was going to happen there?

Yolanda noticed her studying the wall. "Marla, have you met my husband? Marla Vail is our head stylist," she told the man, who'd pulled out his cell phone to squint at the screen.

Marla waved a comb in response. "Nice to meet you," she called. "I'm thrilled to be here."

The man gave her a curt nod and then pocketed his device. He helped Yolanda unpack the items from her large metal box. A couple of tiaras came out, along with diamond necklaces and other pieces of sparkling jewelry. Lastly, he withdrew another item wrapped in velvet. This he placed very carefully in a separate spot.

Meanwhile, Marla kept up a chatty banter with the child's mother while watching the couple's actions from the corner of her eye. Her hands moved automatically, using the curling iron to produce ringlets to soften the girl's face. She pinned a section of hair off her forehead while letting curls spill down the back and sides. Once done, she fastened in place the jeweled barrettes she'd been given.

"Where's the guard?" Yolanda asked her husband, with a furtive glance toward the door.

"Right behind you, ma'am," said a man in a security uniform. With his buzz-cut head of hair, erect posture, and aggressive stance, he could have been ex-military.

Yolanda whipped around, her robe swishing against her legs. "Stay here and watch these things. They're extremely valuable. Many of these jewelry pieces have been loaned to me for the night. And don't allow anyone to touch this case." She indicated the mysterious velvet wrapping.

Juanita's mother addressed Marla in a low tone. "Her husband's last name is so dumb."

"It's dumb? Why is that?"

"Because it's spelled s-o-e space d-u-m. I never knew they were married until somebody told me. Yolanda has a different last name."

"She's a celebrity. She could have kept her maiden name, or else she uses a pseudonym for her stage personality."

"Ayee, with a name like his, who would want to share it?" The woman chuckled.

Henutt Soe Dum. You have a point, Marla thought. "How long has your daughter been doing these shows? And how did she get the gig?"

"Juanita is registered with a local talent agency. She got the job through them. She's done a couple of commercials, too," Juanita's mother said with a proud smile.

"I love doing this show," her daughter said in a girly voice. "I hope to be like them when I grow up." She indicated the leggy models.

"It's a hard life," Marla replied. "They have to diet all the time."

She studied the other women. Sitting in Jennifer's chair on the far side of Nicole was a model who wore a V-necked top with jeans and comfortable flats. She had a bag at her feet. Had she brought her own dress shoes, or did Yolanda supply those, too?

Another stylist was fixing a model's red hair into a chignon.

A fourth model had her wavy, brown hair teased in sections while the stylist applied spray. Each hairdresser worked fast, creating magic and glamour out of ordinary hair.

"I know a guy who does body sculpting for a hundred dollars," the makeup artist said to Yolanda's assistant, who'd stopped by to confer with her. "You should try it, honey. He could do wonders for you."

"No, thanks, I like myself the way I am." The young woman headed for the clothing racks, where she proceeded to remove the dress tags. She recorded each one in a ledger before stuffing the tag into a manila envelope. Her black painted fingernails matched her leather bustier and skirt. "Uh-oh. We're short the peach and white," she hollered to Yolanda.

"I can't imagine where it might be. I checked everything last night. You'll have to take the least glitzy dress and have the assigned model wear it twice," Yolanda responded.

"What size is this one?" The assistant fingered a coral creation. "Maybe it'll fit her."

"Do you have food? I'm starving," one of the models called. She wore a white tank top over black skinny jeans and had a crescent moon tattooed on her neck. From her stick-thin figure, Marla was surprised she ate much at all.

"Sandwiches are over there, babe," a stagehand said. He rolled a round table out into the hall from a storage area among the warren of rooms.

"Excuse me?" the girl retorted. "My name is Ashley Hunt, bozo. Not 'babe.' Show some respect."

"She's the top model," Juanita's mother whispered in Marla's ear. "I don't know why Yolanda uses her all the time. She's a nasty piece of work."

"Maybe so, but I'll bet those gowns look divine on her."

Marla glanced up as two more models strolled in, one with black curly hair and another with straight chestnut hair down to her waist. Now what? She hadn't expected any others. Her stylists were all occupied with their second round. She'd have to take on at least one of these girls herself. With a second glance at the wall diagrams, she realized the scenes called for ten models each, except for the final segment. If she'd been observant, she would have noted that earlier. Five stylists for ten models meant they'd have two each, not counting Juanita.

"You're finished," she told the child. "Good luck tonight. I bet you'll be great."

"Thank you, miss." The child stood, grinning at her image in the mirror before her mother led her away to the makeup lady.

I should ask that person about liquid latex, Marla thought. *She might know about the substance that killed Val.*

Unfortunately, her schedule didn't leave a moment to spare. She signaled one of the newcomers over just as a handsome young man entered the room. He had a camera bag slung across one shoulder and a large camera in his hand. Without a single greeting, he started snapping photos. As he aimed his lens, he stepped backward in her direction.

"Watch where you're walking," she warned.

"Oh, sorry." He spun around to face her. "I'm always amazed when I'm back here. All these gorgeous women, you understand. It numbs the brain."

"Do you work for Friends of Old Florida?" she asked with a smile. She could understand the sentiment, afflicted by sensory overload herself with so much going on.

"Heck, no. Yolanda hired me. I'm Jason Faulks, the event photographer. And you are?"

"Marla Vail, owner of Cut 'N Dye Salon." She handed him her card. "I'm always looking for photo shoot opportunities, so please recommend me if anyone needs a stylist for a special event or advertisement."

"Sure thing, doll." He took a few pictures of the models being prepped and paused to whistle at Ashley Hunt, chowing down on a sandwich and chips. "She'd kill me if I took a photo of her stuffing her mouth like that."

"You're right. I doubt she would appreciate it. So tell me, have you done this show before?" she asked to distract him. Maybe she could gain some information in the process.

He nodded. "Several years in a row. I can't wait to see what Yolanda unveils this time. She always makes a big splash in some way."

"I'm excited to be here. I was afraid they might cancel our participation after Valerie Weston's death."

That got his attention. "How is that?"

"Val died in my salon. I feel terrible about it."

His gaze sharpened. "I can imagine. Rumor has it she died from a latex allergy."

"That's so, but our beautician knew about her condition and had been treating her for years. My husband is on the case. He's a police detective."

"Really?" He looked like he wanted to say more but Yolanda's spouse made a move to leave. "Yo, I'd better snap the diva and her husband while they're together."

Moving off, he took a shot of Yolanda and Henutt grinning for the camera. Henutt's smile looked like a crocodile grin.

Marla turned her attention to the model who had plopped into her chair. The woman chewed gum while studying herself in the mirror. Marla examined the girl's hair, mentally configuring the best arrangement for her facial structure. Then she got to work, sectioning off long strands and using the curling iron at a frenetic pace. She fastened the coils of hair up with a multitude of hairpins. When she was done, she stood back to admire her masterpiece.

Satisfied, she glanced at the other models in nearby chairs. One girl had her short hair pinned up in back in an elegant fashion. Another brunette had her long hair twisted into a braided design. Their upsweeps were artistic creations. Marla's chest swelled with pride for her stylists' work.

Her inner antennae alerted as Dalton entered visual range. He strolled among the players, nodding to this person and that, pausing to speak to the security man guarding Yolanda's valuables. Noting that Marla was free, he sauntered her way. In his dark suit, he looked rakishly handsome. With a surge of affection, she regarded his angular features, firm jaw, and steely gray eyes that brightened as he neared her.

"You look harried," he said, his mouth curving upward.

"We haven't had much time to do each model. What's going on outside?" The band was playing in earnest now. Thumping music vibrated through the place, making her raise her voice.

"Cocktail hour is over. People have sat down to dinner. Unfortunately, Kat couldn't make it. She got a call on another case and is following through on it."

"That's too bad, but you can manage without your partner. After all, you have me."

"I know." He responded to her statement with a quick kiss.

"Have you learned anything new?" she asked him, aware of his keen powers of observation and his skill at interviewing people.

"I've asked around about Val Weston. She held a lot of respect. Her presence is missed."

"No one here has said a word." Marla related the conversations she'd had so far. "I only talked about her with the photographer because I brought it up."

Leaning inward, Dalton spoke in a low tone so as not to be overheard. "Steer clear of Yolanda's husband, will you? He's under investigation."

"For what?" Marla sucked in a deep breath. It felt good to take a break, even for a few minutes. She hadn't realized her shoulders had been so tense. A glance at her wristwatch told her they were getting down to the wire.

"We suspect the man has a connection to the Asian mob. It's been suggested he might be using his wife's store to launder money."

"No way. Would Yolanda know about it, do you think?"

"She may not be aware. It makes me wonder if Val stumbled onto something about him that led to her death, but all of this is supposition. Just be careful around the guy."

"All right. So what now?"

"I'll be in the ballroom. You're coming out later to watch the show, right?"

"Yes, we're almost done here. Then it'll be a matter of touching up the models' hair in between their runway walks and helping the brides with their veils. My staff can handle it. I want to see Yolanda in action."

He nudged her, a teasing glimmer in his eyes. "Maybe we can catch a dance or two."

"We'll see." Her parched throat needed a drink of water. As soon as he left, she wandered toward the stash of food and grabbed a water bottle. The cool liquid eased her thirst.

Her pulse accelerated at noting the makeup lady wasn't occupied. Marla strode in her direction, determined to obtain some useful information. She struck up a friendly conversation, casually veering the topic toward Valerie Weston.

"I know everybody loved her, but not me. She didn't like to get her hands dirty," Joyce Underwood said with a grimace.

"What do you mean?"

"She hired out every little job. I couldn't believe what she asked of me. Could she employ me in advance to make her look good at her funeral?"

Marla stared at her. "She really said that? Did she anticipate dying any time soon?"

"How would I know? Maybe she had a premonition. I told her I didn't do that kind of work." A shudder wracked the woman. "Ugh, can you imagine? I mean, they do use makeup artists just like they have hairstylists in mortuaries, but that's not for me. I prefer to work on live people."

"Me, too. Did Valerie ever come back here before the show?"

"Oh, no. She was too busy out front, working the room and getting folks to donate money for the cause. I have to admit she was skilled that way. And she didn't dare risk coming backstage with her allergies and all."

"I understand most people knew about her sensitivity to latex?"

"She was quite verbal about it. I warned her to steer clear of this area myself, just in case. I'd heard she died from a reaction to the stuff. Is that true?"

"Unfortunately, yes. Would you know anything about liquid latex in particular?"

"It's popular in the film industry for special effects. I don't normally keep the stuff in my kit, though. Other people use it for all sorts of enhancements."

"Her case has been declared a homicide. Do you know anyone who might have had a grudge against Val?"

"Like me, you mean?" Her expression darkened. "Val and I attended the same high school. She stole my boyfriend and ended up tossing him away. I might have married the guy if we'd stayed together. Instead, I fell for the next jerk that came along. Our marriage lasted six miserable years before we got divorced. If not for Val, my life might have been better."

"Did you resent her enough to kill her?"

Joyce snorted. "Certainly not. If I hated her that much, why wait until now?"

"Good point." Although, every murderer had a trigger, Marla thought. Something might have happened more recently to provide incentive. However, she went on as though she believed the woman. "So who else might have done it?" she asked in a sweetly innocent tone.

Joyce's glance flickered toward Ashley Hunt. "Can't say, luv."

You can't or you won't? Marla didn't press for answers. She wished the lady good luck for the evening and wandered off to pack her supplies.

Yolanda bustled about barking orders, her jewelry glittering. A guy wearing an earpiece intercepted her.

"You can't change the order last minute like this." He thrust a bunch of papers at her. "I won't do it. We've the lighting set and everything."

"Very well, we'll stick to the original plan. But next time, I'll want to work with someone more flexible." The designer lifted her chin and stalked away. "Girls, it's eight-fifteen," she called to the models. "Hurry and get dressed."

Marla glanced at her stylists. Nicole was finishing an updo on a girl with reddish-blond hair while one more model sat in front of a mirror with her hair being done in a braided design.

Oy, it was hot. Marla wiped beads of sweat from her brow. Either the temperature had risen as the room got more crowded, or the pounding music—along with the strong scent of hair products in a confined space—was getting to her.

Yolanda approached, her face harried. "It's almost time. We're on right after the fundraising speech. I'm going to throw up." She tapped Marla's arm. "I'd like to introduce you on stage, so be ready behind the curtain after the grand finale."

Marla gulped with sudden stage fright. "Okay, thanks." Her gaze swung from the woman's expensive designer watch to the diamond necklace she wore around her neck and rose to inspect Yolanda's hair. "Uh-oh, some of your hairs have come loose. Let me fix it."

She sat Yolanda down in a chair and fluffed her layers, curling

101

a few ends that had flattened.

"Thank you, darling." Standing, Yolanda flashed her a smile. "I have to go." She pressed on an earpiece, speaking to the stage manager from what Marla could gather.

In the middle of the room, the models tossed off their street clothes in full view of everyone. Breasts got exposed as bras were cast aside. They all wore thongs and flesh-colored tights.

"Line up as soon as you're ready," Yolanda commanded, a sheaf of notes in her hand.

Marla spoke to each of her stylists. Two of them would leave. Nicole and Jennifer would remain backstage for touchups. She could slip inside the ballroom now and find a corner from which to view the event. Before the finale, she'd enter the backstage area.

A model wearing a cream confection with rosettes and a gathered bodice teetered past in a pair of stacked heels. She began the line as directed. Other girls fell into place behind her.

Marla hastened into the hallway, leaving her box of tools with Nicole for safekeeping. She glanced up and down the corridor. On the right, steps led to the immediate backstage area where a black curtain obscured the view. Music blared from the ballroom. She hesitated, enjoying the blast of cool air that refreshed her. Speaking of refreshing, she should use the restroom before the show started. The fundraising spiel would be going on now.

She passed guys wearing headsets rushing to and fro, carts stacked with table linens, and piles of stacked chairs. The aroma of roasted beef drifted her way from the kitchen at the far end, causing her mouth to water.

Completing her business in the restroom, she washed her hands and headed out toward the ballroom.

Tiered crystal chandeliers dimmed inside the vast hall while spotlights aimed at the runway. A man at a podium on stage spoke about making tax-deductible contributions to the organization. Marla surveyed the round tables filled with guests that stretched from one end of the room to the other. Her nose sniffed food again, and her stomach growled. She should have grabbed one of those sandwiches earlier, but nerves had kept her appetite at bay.

She couldn't spot Dalton at the darkened edges of the room. She'd have to look for him later. Hopefully, he was somewhere nearby, watching the show same as her.

The announcer's voice boomed in the cavernous space. "Now let's welcome the woman in charge of this spectacular event, the great fashion icon, Yolanda Whipp."

CHAPTER SEVEN

Yolanda came sweeping onto the stage with a radiant smile to a round of wild applause. After giving a brief introduction, she signaled the band to play a lively overture. As she segued into the prescribed segments, her voice resonated throughout the ballroom. She described each model's outfit in lavish detail. Two girls began the cocktail dress sequence by walking down the runway together. At the tee on the end, they crossed places and strutted back toward the stage, finally vanishing behind the curtain.

Marla imagined them tossing their dresses to the assistant and donning the next outfit in a rush. Meanwhile, Yolanda described the next scene of party gowns. This involved a single model walking alone. When one girl was halfway back, the next one appeared from the side curtain and began her stroll. Everything ran smoothly, and the audience looked as entranced as Marla felt. If only she could afford one of those dresses!

Scene Three included ball gowns. Again, each one of the ten models strode alone down the runway. Cameras flashed all around. Marla caught a glimpse of Jason Faulks among the media crowd. Her mouth widened into a grin. This event would be splashed across the community news boards by tomorrow, and hopefully her salon's name would be listed.

Finally, the flower girl paved the way for the bridal procession. Bubbles blew onto the stage, from which emerged each of five models to pose alone at various spots along the runway.

Their gowns glittered and so did the tiaras on their heads. Gauzy veils completed the look. Marla could only shake her head in awe. And here she'd thought her wedding dress had been special. These were worthy of royalty, and likely the prices were, too.

"But we're not finished," Yolanda announced, after the last of the models disappeared behind the curtain. She nodded at the band, which played a flourish. "I am pleased and excited to introduce my latest development, a signature headpiece. This unique creation not only changes color with the mood of its wearer, but it can read your brain waves and transmit them to a receiver for biofeedback. Behold our top model, Ashley Hunt, wearing this glorious achievement, a blend of fashion design and technology for tomorrow's future."

Ashley appeared in a ravishing black sequined gown. Her hair had been let down, and a jeweled hairpiece crowned her head. Marla jostled forward so she could get a better look. The thing was made up of tiered black ridges studded with turquoise and black diamond-like stones that glittered in the light's reflection. Exclamations of awe came from the audience as camera bulbs flashed.

The model didn't exit, remaining at Yolanda's side as the brides and other girls in their long gowns reentered the stage to take a final bow together. Yolanda read each person's name and thanked the various people who'd made her show possible. Her voice cracked when she mentioned Valerie Weston.

"Although Val is no longer among us, I'm sure she is watching over us now. She was an inspiration to us all with her generosity. Val would have loved this show. I don't know how we'll go on without her."

Would the ball continue without her underwriting? Or did her will include a provision for the group as everyone expected? Marla had meant to ask Dalton if he'd contacted Val's attorney.

Still not catching a glimpse of him among the throng, she added it to her mental list for later. Hopefully they would hook up once the lighting improved and she could see clearer.

Glancing at her watch, she gasped. How could it be ten o'clock already? She'd been there since five. And these people hadn't even finished dinner yet.

"I'd like to thank Marla Vail from Cut 'N Dye Salon, for the hairstylists who made our models look so amazing tonight," Yolanda said. "Marla, please come out now."

Oy, vey. Marla had forgotten all about waiting backstage. Her heart thumping, she hurried forward. She'd take the steps in front leading up to the dais.

"And Joyce Underwood is our expert makeup artist. Please join us so we can acknowledge your contribution. Of course, I wouldn't be here without the support of my dear husband, Henutt."

As Yolanda rattled off more names, Marla climbed a short flight of stairs onto the stage, carefully watching her footing so she wouldn't trip. Then she turned to face the hot, bright spotlights. Joined by the others Yolanda had mentioned, she smiled at a round of applause.

Finally free, she reentered the ballroom proper to search for Dalton as the lights brightened. The dance music resumed and guests headed for the dance floor. She didn't encounter her husband but ran into Solomon Gold giving a dressing-down to Andrew Fine, the group's publicist.

"What were you thinking in that article?" the organization's president said, his eyes blazing. "One would think you were on the side of the developers."

"Sometimes preservation isn't in the best interest of the community, Sol. You have a personal stake in this site, so you're biased."

"You're being paid to slant pieces in our favor, buddy, not

side with the enemy."

"Rick isn't the enemy, man. Sometimes sacrifices have to be made for the sake of progress."

"I agree, if conditions warrant it, but not in this case. Soften your slant, or you might find yourself looking for another job."

The publicist marched off, a scowl on his face. Gold's gaze swung to Marla, who craned her neck as though searching for someone. "Marla, your gals did a splendid job tonight."

"Thank you, Mr. Gold. I'm looking for my husband. He was here earlier, but I don't see him anywhere."

Gold cleared his throat. "Can you do a favor for me? Tell the detective to look into Andrew's paper trail when you have a chance."

"Why is that?" She kept her expression sweetly innocent.

"His recent articles have favored the building developer's efforts to acquire those historic structures on Hollywood Beach that I'd mentioned earlier. Andrew is supposed to drum up support for our organization, not the opposite."

Maybe Rick Rodriguez is greasing his pockets. She didn't voice her thoughts aloud. "Don't you own some of those buildings?"

"I do, and I appreciate their historical value. I could sell and make money, but preserving our heritage is more important in this case." He pointed. "Speak of the devil, there's Rick now. Have you met the guy?" Gold pulled the man over and introduced them. "I see someone I have to greet. Please excuse me." He wandered off, leaving Marla alone with the land developer.

"I understand you and Val were at odds over certain projects," Marla said to Rodriguez after they'd exchanged conversational platitudes.

"She put up a good fight," the man said with a tinge of admiration. He looked like a fighter himself with a crooked nose, hooded eyes, and broad shoulders. His tux seemed an ill fit, as though he'd feel more at ease on a construction site than in a society ballroom.

"Did you butt heads often?"

"We had our differences. I stand for progress. Val stood for saving old structures that cried to be torn down."

"She believed in preserving our region's heritage. What's wrong with that?"

"It's okay if you're talking about a significant property, like Whitehall in Palm Beach, the home of Henry Flagler. His estate has inestimable value as a piece of our area's history."

"But not a row of buildings from the 30s on historic Hollywood Beach?"

"Look, Mrs. Vail, I've already had this argument. I can't say I'm sorry Val is gone. She was a thorn in my side. So is this group's president. Mr. Gold has his own biases."

"So why are you here tonight at a fundraiser for their organization?"

He sneered. "Many of the city's movers and shakers are here, that's why. I can work the room same as their crowd. Gold isn't thinking straight, or he might have asked me the same question. Either he's blinded by his own selfish interests, or he's been dipping into Dr. Needles's concoctions."

"What does that mean?" Marla leaned forward to better hear him over the band's loud tempo. The music's thumping vibrations shook her to the bone.

"You didn't hear it from me, but ask Ashley Hunt if you want to know more. Good evening, Mrs. Vail. I have to circulate."

Marla meandered through the crowd, wondering where Dalton had gone. She'd call him on her cell phone once she found a quiet zone. She sought Lora Larue to thank the woman for including her in the show, but Lora was engaged in a cluster of friends. Marla could send her a thank-you note later, perhaps with a small gift of appreciation.

Meanwhile, she headed backstage to collect her gear. These fights weren't hers. She had enough to deal with on her own without getting involved in preservationist issues.

The dressing room resembled chaos with the models changing into their street clothes right out in the open. Yolanda's assistant checked off each gown on her list, hanging it properly and reapplying the dress tag. Other personnel bustled about, including stagehands carrying equipment back and forth.

Marla sent Jennifer and Nicole on home with her hearty thanks. Then she sought Yolanda to let her know she'd be leaving. "I'm going to head out," she said to the designer. "This has been a blast. I'm glad we had the opportunity to participate. Please keep me and my stylists in mind for future events."

Yolanda's face crinkled into a smile. She had a small mole above her wide lips that Marla hadn't noticed before. "I will. And here's a little something for your trouble. You can divide it among your girls." Yolanda reached into a hidden pocket of her robe and handed over a roll of bills.

"Please, that's unnecessary. You weren't even the one who hired me." But Yolanda insisted, so Marla stuffed the gratuity into her purse. She'd divide it among her stylists on Tuesday. "Thank you from all of us. It's very kind of you."

"My pleasure, darling." Yolanda turned away, pausing when a blood-curdling scream pierced the air. "Oh, my God, what is that?"

Without hesitation, Marla sprinted toward the sound. She came to an abrupt halt further back among the maze of rooms where people formed a semi-circle. They faced a man slumped against the wall, a screwdriver-type tool sticking from his chest. Crimson stained his dress shirt.

"It's Jason Faulks," Marla said, recognizing him. "Is he dead?"

"I think so," squeaked a trembling woman in a housekeeping uniform. She must have been the person whose shrieks had summoned them.

"Stay calm, the police will want to talk to you. That goes for everyone here. And stop taking videos, please." Horrified that some of the onlookers were filming like they had at her day spa after Val's death, Marla personally knocked down a few of the people's raised arms.

"What's going on?" Dalton's voice thundered from behind.

With a whoosh of relief, she spun to face him. "It's about time. Where have you been?"

"I was interviewing folks." His gaze swung toward the object of people's fascination. "Oh, no. Don't tell me you've found another one."

She gave a hysterical half-laugh. "Not me. That maid was first on the scene."

Dalton was already pulling out his cell phone. He barked a few orders to the crowd and then stepped aside for privacy while he called for assistance.

Marla's glance returned to the photographer who wouldn't be covering these events any longer. And speaking of coverage, where was Jason's camera? His camera bag lay open on the floor, but a quick glance told her it was empty. The camera had been too bulky to fit in a pocket.

She scanned the area, wishing the onlookers would disperse but knowing the cops had to get their statements and contact info first. The space was cluttered with furniture needing repairs, heavy-duty cleaning equipment, extension cords, and other miscellaneous items that would make a search difficult. Her stomach sank. It also meant Dalton might not be home for hours.

Exhaustion made her shoulders sag. She turned away, intending to look for a seat on which to wait, but Ashley had already claimed the only viable chair in the vicinity. Marla's eyes narrowed at the way Dr. Needles knelt by her side, holding her hand in an intimate manner. They exchanged a brief but intense dialogue before he rose and left.

Sirens wailed in the distance. Backup would arrive soon. So would other detectives. This may not be Dalton's jurisdiction, but since some of these people were involved in his ongoing investigation, perhaps it would justify his presence. She hoped the same team didn't show up who'd dealt with the wedding murder. Marla had been a bridesmaid at her friend Jill's ceremony when the matron of honor got fatally stabbed with a cake knife.

"Marla, isn't it?" Ashley said, approaching. "Do we have to hang around?"

"If you'll give your name and phone number to one of the cops, then you can probably leave. Did you see anything relevant? Like, did you notice Jason coming back here?"

"Not at all." A tear streaked down the model's face. "I can't believe this happened. Jason covered a lot of my events and always caught me at my best angle."

It would be about you. "I don't see his camera. You wouldn't know where it is, would you?" Marla eyed the large bag at the model's side. She could fit a host of things in there.

"I have no idea. Sometimes he wore it on a strap around his neck."

"It's not there now." Had someone stabbed him because of what he'd caught on film? "I saw you speaking to Dr. Needles. What was he doing back here?"

Ashley looked startled. "Um, he . . . why do you care? And how come you haven't left already? All the other stylists are gone."

"I'm waiting for my husband, Detective Dalton Vail."

Ashley's mouth gaped. "You're married to *him?*" She pointed to Dalton, who cut an authoritative figure as he interviewed witnesses.

"That's right. I gather you and Dr. Needles are friends? Or do you have a professional doctor–patient relationship?"

Ashley lifted her chin. "If you must know, Ian has been treating me for back pain. I injured myself during a rehearsal when a loose board on a runway made me trip and fall. I'd been seeing him for a cosmetic procedure and mentioned my injury. He offered to help."

"It looks as though you've made a good recovery." Marla didn't miss her familiar use of the doctor's first name. She opened her mouth to ask another question but was drowned out as other officials crashed the area.

"Here's my card," she told Ashley. "If you think of anything important, please call me. I can pass your information along to my husband."

Dalton was apt to be here late, and Marla didn't care to wait around that long. She should leave him their car and hail a taxi. She'd stepped forward to tell him when a howl of anguish froze her in place.

"My masterpiece is gone!" Yolanda hollered. "Thief, thief! Someone has stolen my priceless crown."

Marla rushed over. "What do you mean? Your jeweled headpiece is missing?"

"Yes. Oh, I am going to faint. Someone call my husband."

"Calm down. It has to be here somewhere. Maybe you misplaced it."

"I did not. I'd put it inside its case and got distracted same as everyone else."

"Where's your personal guard?" Marla peered at the crowd.

"He went over when he heard the screams from that stupid maid. That's probably when somebody stole it. My assistant isn't here either. She left to load the gowns into the van."

"What use could the crown be to anyone else? It's your signature item. Or are those stones worth money? I thought they were lab-made crystals."

Yolanda gave Marla a cold glare. "My invention has garnered interest from other parties, including the military. It has ramifications you wouldn't understand. Help! Help! Somebody find the thief."

Marla stepped back to let others minister to her. She studied the throng with suspicion. During the commotion, anyone might have snatched the case with its precious cargo. It was a decent-sized item that would be difficult to hide. Had the thief stashed it nearby, intending to return for it later?

She commenced a search but gave up shortly thereafter, too tired to continue. It wasn't her job, anyway. The thought briefly crossed her mind that the murder might have occurred as a smokescreen for the theft. Was Yolanda's invention so precious that someone would kill for it? Or was this merely a ruse to collect insurance money? She should suggest Dalton check into Yolanda's finances.

Standing on her tiptoes, she scanned people for the guard's buzz-cut head. He seemed to have vanished, as had the young assistant. Maybe they were both involved somehow.

Another thought made Marla pause. Val had been an acquaintance of Yolanda's. Had the benefactress discovered something suspicious about the designer that had led to her death?

She sent Dalton a text message that she'd grab a taxi and meet him back home. This new ripple would add hours to his stint here, assuming the local boys didn't mind his presence.

Outside the main lobby, the last crowd of guests lingered while waiting for the valet. She caught one of the young men and asked him to call a taxi for her.

"Hey, Marla," said a sultry woman's voice at her elbow. "What's the matter, your date stand you up?"

Marla whirled, her stomach plummeting at the sight of the

redhead smirking at her. What was *she* doing here? "Well, bless my bones, if it isn't Carla Jean Hatfield. What's a sales rep from Luxor doing at a society ball?"

Carla Jean smoothed down her emerald and black beaded dress as though to emphasize her status as a guest. "The company sent me to make sure we got credit for the products you used backstage. I grabbed several copies of the program to show where we were listed." She patted the bulging tote bag strapped on her shoulder. "You might have snagged the spotlight with your work tonight, but don't think that puts you ahead of me for the educator position." She must have noticed Marla's look of astonishment. "That's right. I'm in the running, same as you."

Marla recovered her composure. "We're not in a race. The best person will get the job. It's not our decision to make." She shivered in the night air. The temperature had dropped considerably. Or could it be the icy tone from the other woman that sent a chill her way?

This would be a tough call. Carla Jean was always in the top ten sales positions. So why was Marla even being considered?

"It surprises me that you're the competition," Carla Jean said, as though reading her thoughts. "Luxor was impressed by your work at the trade show, and you get high recommendations. But I don't see how they can view you as a contender when you're involved in one scandal after another. You'd better be careful, dear. The higher-ups won't tolerate any taints on their image, especially after the trade show disaster."

Marla's blood seethed as a wild thought entered her head. Maybe the sales rep had orchestrated Val's murder to cast her salon in a negative light. The publicity from this latest incident would generate even more sensational press. Could Carla Jean be behind the nuisance lawsuit as well? Her attempts to discredit Marla might have no bounds.

"Oops, there's my car," Carla Jean said with a dismissive wave. "Nice seeing you."

Yeah, right. In a sour mood, Marla took a cab home. She let herself in the house quietly, checked on Brianna asleep in her room, and petted the dogs who'd roused at her arrival.

Too wired to go to sleep, she sat at her computer in her nightshirt to check email. Her eyes widened when she saw what popped up on the screen. Jason Faulks had sent her a message? When was this? The time stamp said nine forty-five. That was before the fashion show had concluded.

He'd attached two jpg files along with his email, which said exactly nothing. How peculiar. She opened the first picture. It showed Yolanda's spouse, Henutt, conferring with another guy in a hotel corridor. The second shot showed two middle-aged men together. Marla thought the features of one of them looked familiar but couldn't place him. Why did Faulks send these to her? Did he mean for her to show them to her husband, a homicide detective?

CHAPTER EIGHT

Marla mentioned the photos the next morning while she prepared Sunday brunch in the kitchen. Still fatigued from last night's events, she'd thrown on a pair of jeans and a sweater and a smidgen of makeup. She flipped blueberry pancakes on the electric griddle while Brianna set the table. Dalton, already seated, separated the sections of the *Sun Sentinel* and sipped from a mug of fresh-brewed coffee. The dogs, having completed their business outside, roamed the kitchen sniffing for morsels of food.

"I have news," she began. She put down her spatula and grabbed her cell phone. "Jason Faulks sent me a couple of photos last night. I noticed them after I got home and checked my email. Here, I can show you."

Dalton squinted at the images as she displayed them. "Weird. I recognize Henutt Soe Dum but I'm not sure about these other guys. How about sending me copies so I can add them to my case file?"

"Are you involved in Jason's murder investigation? Doesn't it fall under another jurisdiction?"

"Yes, but our departments are cooperating since our cases are connected."

"What happened, Daddy? Why did you get home so late?" Brianna, still in her pajamas, regarded him with curiosity.

He gave his daughter a brief summary. "I didn't expect theft to be added to the puzzle."

"Do you think Jason's murder could have been a smoke-screen?" Marla asked. "Like, somebody wanted to distract people's attention so the thief could steal Yolanda's headpiece?"

Dalton grimaced, his coffee cup poised midair. "They could be unrelated acts. Or maybe Jason took a shot of the thief without realizing its significance. The fact that a screwdriver was used to kill him indicates a crime of opportunity."

"A screwdriver? Ugh." Brianna turned back to setting utensils on the table.

Marla remembered various bits of equipment lying around the storage areas. "You're thinking one of the guys in the photos stabbed Jason because of his snapshot?"

"It's a possibility. These photos must mean something important for Jason to have sent them to you. And that would explain his missing camera." Dalton put his cup down with a worried frown. "Uh-oh. I have a bad feeling about this."

"What's wrong?" Brianna brought over a pitcher of orange juice that Marla had handed her.

"We didn't find a cell phone on the victim. That might have been taken along with the camera. And if the killer checks for outgoing calls, he might target you next."

"Oh, great." Marla felt as though a big red bull's eye had just been painted on her forehead. "I assume you'll try to track his phone?"

"Yes, but I'm more concerned about you. You're already involved by virtue of Val's demise happening at your salon, and now this. Whatever is going on, you need to lay low."

"No problem. I'll be too busy at work and preparing for the holidays to do anything else. Just solve these cases so we can enjoy the season, will you?"

Despite her words, when Monday rolled around Marla decided to pay a visit to Yolanda's boutique. She didn't get there until two o'clock, after meeting Dalton's mother for lunch and completing some chores. The glitzy establishment on Las Olas Boulevard had drool-worthy window displays.

Inside, gowns in every color embellished with beads, crystals, pearls, and other exquisite design elements met her awed gaze. She dared to examine one price tag. Five thousand two hundred and eighty dollars. Whoever bought this dress probably would not wish to be seen in the same garment twice.

Hmm, maybe Marla should look for a consignment shop in the vicinity . . . not that she had an occasion to wear such frivolity. Besides, princess-type ball gowns weren't her style. Oh, but she did like that flowing chocolate brown strapless beaded creation that molded to one's body. Dalton would love it on her, although he'd likely be more eager to divest her of the dress.

"May I help you?"

The shop girl's inquiry splashed cold water on her daydreams. Marla studied the employee, whom she recognized from the fashion show. The young assistant wore her black hair in a short, spiky style. The stark color was too harsh for her pale complexion. Her black leather mini-skirt, tank top, thigh-high boots, and silver nose stud added to her overall gothic look.

"Hi, is Yolanda here?"

"She's stepped out for a moment. Is she expecting you?"

"No, but I'll wait for her. Or you can notify her that I'm here. Marla Vail, remember?"

Another woman bustled forward from a back room. A middle-aged lady, she wore a tape measure around her neck and a conservative skirt ensemble.

"Are you *the* Mrs. Vail? Stacey, I'll take over now. You can help count inventory. Hello, my name is Eve Grimes. I'm the senior sales associate."

Marla shook the older woman's hand, not wishing to disavow her of the notion that she was an important customer. "Um,

I'm looking for a dress to wear at a holiday party."

"Any particular color or style? Keep in mind that we do our own alterations, so if you find something and it's the wrong size, we can make adjustments."

"I'll take a look around. I want something fairly simple." Marla glanced at the glass display cases by the cash register. One of them held designer costume jewelry and another had beaded evening bags. Toward the back of the store were a variety of shoes. Likely they had the proper undergarments hidden away somewhere.

"I attended the fashion show," she said to the clerk, hoping to gain information while Yolanda was gone. "Her headpiece is amazing. Did she find it yet?"

"Sorry, I don't know what you mean. I was off yesterday. Yolanda brought the gowns back then and returned the borrowed jewelry this morning. We haven't had a chance to touch base."

"Oh, well you should ask her about it then. Or maybe Stacey can fill you in, since she was there." Marla pretended to examine various dresses Eve offered to her, resisting the urge to try them on. "Does Yolanda's husband come into the store often?" she asked in a casual tone. "I met him last night."

"He stops by now and then. How about this red dress, dear? It would look ravishing on you with your coloring."

Marla couldn't help admiring the short, beaded number. It was gorgeous, but where would she wear it? "That's a possibility. So tell me, is Yolanda the sole owner of the store? I'm a businesswoman myself," she admitted, even though it might disavow the saleswoman of the notion that Marla was a renowned socialite.

Before Eve could respond, the chimes over the door tinkled. Marla glanced up at Yolanda's breezy entrance. Too bad. She might have been able to squeeze more info from the clueless clerk. Clueless about Marla's identity, but not about the owner, perhaps.

"Marla, what a pleasure. I didn't expect to see you in my shop." Yolanda strode forward and embraced her like they were old friends.

The designer's genuine warmth surprised Marla. She grinned in response. "I was looking through your lovely creations. I have some parties coming up, and I couldn't resist coming here after drooling over your gowns Saturday night."

Yolanda poked her. "Don't let the prices frighten you. I'll give you a discount." She stashed her purse behind the counter with the cash register.

Eve excused herself while her boss took over. She disappeared behind a curtain into the rear to join the younger woman counting inventory.

"Did you ever recover your headpiece?" Marla asked, stating the first thing on her mind.

Yolanda's brow folded. "Unfortunately, no. We searched everywhere, even in the van in case someone had inadvertently packed it away."

Close up, Marla could see her heavy application of makeup. She wore a lime green patterned dress with matching high heels that gave her a few extra inches of height. With her slash of bright red lipstick, she reminded Marla of a brightly colored parrot.

"I'm sorry. Is it that the stones themselves are valuable or the technology? You'd said something about the piece having military applications."

Yolanda sighed, wringing her hands. "I suppose someone could pry the stones loose, but individually, they are worth nothing. My creation contains several thousand of them. They're made of magnesium aluminum and coated with my proprietary chemical ink. This causes them to change color in response to the wearer's mood."

"So how is it worth more than an expensive mood ring?"

Yolanda chuckled at her ignorance. "My dear, besides changing color, the stones can measure brain waves. Your brain is constantly generating an electrical field. My stones are highly conductive and act as a wireless transmitter of your brain patterns. It's great for biofeedback. But think about military interrogators using such a device. Even something as small as a cell phone could be used as a receiver."

"So your crown is a glorified lie detector?" Marla had trouble understanding the significance of the theft.

"That's a simplified way of putting it." Yolanda paced back and forth, while Marla leaned against the counter. "Biochemical inks are finding more uses today. These chemicals can change color based on the pollution in the air or the temperature of your skin. The healthcare industry is also interested in possible applications. Imagine if you could transmit your health status via your clothing."

Marla knew of color-changing tee-shirts but had never considered them anything other than a novelty. The thought of bad guys getting hold of a brain-wave reader was scary. They might even miniaturize the tech so people who put on a pair of eyeglasses wouldn't know it was transmitting. Or what if they learned how to reverse the signal to influence someone's brain pattern? Good God, you'd have mass mind control.

"What did you intend to do with this device?" she asked Yolanda.

"My primary goal is to sell it as a fashion accessory. It's an exquisite design. And the mood-changing factor appeals to people. It would be my signature piece. But I might also license it for research in certain arenas."

"So who do you think stole it?"

Yolanda glared at her. "Anyone who hopes to make a profit.

121

It could easily sell on the black market. My husband is on the lookout. He'll know if it comes up for sale."

Marla ignored her implication that Henutt had access to the black market. "Wouldn't a collector of eclectic items also be interested? Maybe it's destined for a secret stash somewhere."

"Henutt has a wide ring of associates. He has them sniffing in various corners. If anyone can recover my treasure, he can do it." Her wide mouth curved with pride. "You should talk to him, Marla. He was interested to learn about your salon."

"Oh? Why is that?" Dalton's admonition that the guy might be associated with the Asian mob and using his wife's shop to launder money came to mind. She glanced around, wondering how he might benefit. Did he buy the fabrics and accessories for his wife's store with his excess cash? Or maybe he funded the labor force overseas that made these creations?

"Your stylists do a lot of haircuts, right?" Yolanda wagged a finger at her. "Sometimes he buys the cuttings. I don't mean the long banded pieces like you'd snip off for Locks of Love, but hair from the floor."

"What for?" Marla couldn't think of anything more gross.

"Henutt has connections in China where they make wigs. It's quite a profitable business. You'd be surprised at the extent of the industry there. Didn't you know that's where most of your hair extensions are made? Well, aside from India."

Marla's heart thudded in her chest. Valerie Weston's sister had cancer and might have needed a wig. Had Val done research into where the hair originated? Maybe she'd discovered some irregularities that led back to Henutt. It was a wild supposition as a murder motive, but as Dalton repeatedly said, people had been killed for less.

"So are you saying that I could make money by selling cut hairs to your husband? And he, in turn, would sell them to wig makers in China?" Marla grimaced at the notion.

"It could be a good source of income." Yolanda swept her arm in a broad gesture. "Then you could come in here and buy any gown you liked."

"Thanks for the tip. I'll think about it. In the meantime, I'd better get going on my errands. I really enjoyed working with you, Yolanda. I hope we can do it again sometime."

Her thoughts troubled, she scooted out of there, forgetting until later that she'd meant to mention Jason's death and show Yolanda his photos, including the one with Henutt. Now she'd have to return to the shop another time. Then again, Dalton had warned her against getting involved in his case, especially when Jason's killer might be on to her. If Henutt was involved in something shady, she could be digging her grave deeper by speaking to his wife.

Back home after completing her errands, she let the dogs out and made herself an energizing cup of coffee in the kitchen. While waiting for it to heat up, she called Dalton.

"I stopped by Yolanda's shop to thank her for letting me work with her," Marla said to explain her visit before mentioning the gist of their conversation. "Who would want to buy discarded hairs from a salon that have fallen onto a dirty floor? We usually throw them away. Can you imagine using it to make wigs?"

"Maybe Yolanda's suggestion is an excuse for Henutt to get closer to you, so he can learn what you know."

"I suppose that's possible."

"You didn't show her the photo of Henutt that Jason sent you, I hope?" Dalton said, disapproval in his tone.

"I forgot about it."

"Good. It's always possible Henutt stabbed Jason because of that photo. He might not have wanted to be seen with the other guy for some reason. It's bad enough the killer knows you have those photos. You don't want to be bandying them around town."

"Why not? Somebody might recognize one of those other men."

"Let me deal with it."

"Could Val have caught onto Henutt's schemes? She might have done research into wigs for her sister's sake and discovered something unsavory about his Chinese connection."

"It's possible she might have uncovered an item of importance, although not necessarily related to Yolanda's husband. When I went to her house to interview the staff, her employees said the place had been broken into recently. Val's home office had been ransacked. She didn't report the incident since nothing was stolen, but it made her nervous."

"Did you speak to her estate attorney to see who inherits her stuff?"

"He's on vacation for the holidays. But the brother-in-law, Sean, said Val had told her sister that she would be leaving a bequest to Friends of Old Florida. The remainder, plus her personal property, goes to her sister's children now that Cathy is dead."

"Is Sean serving as executor?"

"No, apparently it's the same person who's currently serving as her trustee. The attorney should be able to provide more information. I've asked his secretary to try and reach him so he can call me, but he's overseas."

"Didn't Val have any other relatives?" How sad to be so alone.

"Nobody whom she would appoint to such a significant role."

Marla thought about Tally and Ken, who'd asked her to be guardian of their child if anything happened to them. She'd also been named as their successor trustee. Ken had a brother who was a chemist but the guy was a bit of a flake. Tally didn't trust him to give her son the love he needed. Marla hoped to hell their faith in her would never have to be tested. And speaking of her friend, Marla needed to call Tally to check up on her.

"So, will you be home for dinner?" Marla asked, anxious to get off the phone.

"I should be able to leave by then. Love you, sweetcakes."

She thrilled to his endearment. "Love you, too." She hung up, glad to focus on personal issues and leave the crime investigation to her husband.

The rest of the day she spent calling Tally, working on bookkeeping tasks, and consulting with her mother and Dalton's mom regarding arrangements for Hanukkah and Christmas. Marla couldn't believe the first holiday was three days away. Meanwhile, she had her salon party coming up on Friday, gifts to wrap, more greeting cards to send out, and myriad other things to do. Her heart rate accelerated at the frantic pace of it all.

Her good intentions to steer clear of Dalton's affairs went awry on Tuesday at the salon, when the same friend of Val's entered and accosted her.

"Marla, do you have a minute?" said Nadia, an eager look on her face. The forty-something woman clutched a large handbag under her arm.

Marla, in between clients, nodded with a smile. "Sure, I'll step outside with you." She could use a breath of fresh air. Pine and cinnamon scents emitted from their holiday decorations as she headed for the exit. They passed an electric menorah shining with blue lights on a bed of silver tinsel at the front desk. A miniature Christmas tree stood at the other end.

As soon as they were alone, Nadia withdrew a wrapped parcel from her purse. "I received this in the mail. It's from Val."

"What? How is that possible?"

"She must have mailed it before she died, or else she'd left instructions for this to be sent to me in the event of her death. A note inside said I should turn it over to the police if anything bad happened to her."

Marla took the item, sank onto the bench in front of her salon, and opened the packaging. Inside was a bound book with a black leather cover.

"It's a journal that appears to be written years ago," she said, flipping through several of the browned pages.

Nadia pointed at the typewritten text. "I don't know why Val sent it to me. Your husband might find it useful for his case. You can give this to him, can't you?"

"Yes, and I appreciate your trust in us." Marla wanted to delve into the book to see what secrets lay hidden inside. Why would Val keep this item until her death? Could this journal be what the intruder had meant to find at Val's house?

This discovery opened a whole host of new questions. Marla didn't have time to take it to Dalton now, though. She showed it to Nicole in a spare moment, noticing other people's eyes light up when she mentioned Val's name. Aware of the potential for gossip, she hastily stuck the book inside a drawer at her station until closing time.

Dalton was late getting home from work after all, and by the time she got around to mentioning the journal, they were both ready for bed. She'd taken Brie to dance class and forgotten about the item until she and Dalton were alone.

"Why don't you copy it before you turn it in?" he suggested, tickling her arm as he lay beside her. "I wouldn't mind having you glance through the book. You might find something significant."

"Thanks, I'm eager to see what's in it. The journal must be important for Val to have kept it stashed away. How is your investigation going? Was there a particular reason why you had to stay late?"

"We've been looking into the FOFL board members. Some interesting details have come to light. But let's not talk about work now. I'd much rather relax." His fingers roamed south, showing her what he had in mind.

It wasn't until Thursday morning that Marla finally had time to sit with Val's journal on the family room sofa. This was her late day into work, and also the first night of Hanukkah, so she had until one o'clock to accomplish her tasks. But she'd awoken early to send Brie off to school and kiss Dalton goodbye before he left the house.

She wore a bathrobe against the chilly weather since another cold front had come south. Resting the journal in her lap, she opened the first page. The book was titled *Florida Escapade*. It appeared to be an account of a young man's 1934 trip through the Sunshine State. The author's name, Warren Brookstone, didn't ring a bell.

Warren had been twenty-eight at the date of the entries. A naturalist, he and two of his friends had traveled to Florida in search of adventure and a slice of paradise. Marla frowned as she flipped through the pages. Why were only two of the men present in the final photos? What happened to the third guy? Did he leave the expedition at some point?

The pages were browned and brittle and the corners crumbled at her touch. Afraid they'd fall apart before she read much further, she closed the book and headed for the bedroom to get dressed. At least the author had typed his manuscript. Had he tried to publish it?

She detoured to her home office and did an online search for a book by that title. Nothing by this author popped up. So Warren must have kept it for personal reasons. But who was he in relation to Valerie Weston? And how did she acquire the forty-page journal?

She'd have to deal with those questions later. After getting dressed, she put her brisket in the oven and commenced making the side dishes for tonight's family dinner. She hadn't booked any clients past six, so she'd scheduled the meal for seven o'clock. Brie would set the dining room table when she came home from school.

It was trash day so she took some additional garbage out to the curb and waved to Susan Feinberg, two doors down. Susan waved back. She was a consulting editor for a women's magazine as well as a popular blogger. Fortunately, Susan could work from home.

That could be me, Marla thought every time she saw the woman with her two young children. They were the same age at thirty-seven. It merely confirmed Marla's resolution not to get tied down with kids or to experience the years of worry that came with them. Caring for Brianna gave her enough gratification. She didn't feel the need to expand her family.

Finally having cooked the dishes for later and refrigerated them, she stuffed the journal inside a large handbag and headed for the local office store. There she had a clerk make a print copy of the typed manuscript. She had the guy scan entire pages of pictures rather than each photo individually, or it would have taken hours. As it was, she left to do her other chores and rushed back to pick up the completed order.

She dropped the original off to Dalton on her way to work. "Here," she said, thrusting the package at him. "I have a copy that I'll look through later. Good luck with it. I researched the author's name online and came up empty."

Dalton, seated at his desk with papers strewn across its surface, thumbed through the journal pages and paused at one of the photos. "This guy looks familiar."

Craning her neck to examine the picture, Marla uttered a cry. She opened her cell phone and retrieved one of Jason's photos. "See these two men in the photo Jason sent me? There's a resemblance between the man in the journal and this fellow."

She felt the pair could be related by their rectangular-shaped faces, light-colored hair, and deep-set eyes.

Dalton frowned, examining first one photo and then the other. He pointed to the picture Jason had sent. "Now I recognize him. That's Howard Cohn, the group's treasurer."

"You're right. I didn't connect this photo to him earlier." She'd only met the guy once, and Jason's picture showed him at an angle. "He must be related to the man in the journal."

Dalton's mouth compressed. "See what you can find out when you've read Warren's account. There has to be something important to Valerie Weston in the story."

Or perhaps in these photos the author included. "Will you show Howard the picture Jason took? He could identify the other man in the picture with him."

"I don't want to tip Cohn off yet about what we know. We might find the connections we need in the journal without going further."

"Can you tell me what you've learned about the board members?" Marla asked with a surreptitious glance at her watch. It was already noon and she hadn't eaten lunch. She'd have to pick up a sandwich at Arnie's deli on her way to work.

A rap on the door forestalled his response.

"Hey, Dalton, do you have a minute? Oh hello, Marla. I didn't realize you were here." Detective Katherine Minnetti hovered in the doorway, looking stylish in a pencil skirt, cream sweater with gray pearls, and heeled pumps.

"I'm just leaving," Marla said, gathering her purse.

Through the open doorway, she spied the police captain speaking to another cop she knew. She'd encountered nearly everyone in the department by now and didn't want them to think she beleaguered her husband with personal visits.

"Thanks for bringing in this evidence," Dalton said in a hearty tone so his voice would carry.

"Sure. How's it going, Kat?"

"Just fine, Marla." Minnetti wore her ebony hair in a French twist. She looked more like a savvy businesswoman than a detective.

"Do you have plans for the holidays?" Marla asked in a friendly voice, curious to see what melted Kat's frost.

"I've signed up for the duty shift. No sense in depriving my fellow officers of time home with their families."

"That's generous of you." She almost blurted out an invitation to their Christmas dinner but hesitated at the glower on Dalton's face. "Well, I have to be going. Nice seeing you."

After muttering her farewells, she fled the station. She always felt awkward going there anyway, even though the guys made her feel welcome. Kat was another animal. She'd been transferred there without an explanation and wouldn't discuss her background.

Wait a minute, I have an idea. She'd send Kat a gift certificate for a cut and blowout for the holidays. If she could get Kat in her salon chair, she'd worm the woman's secrets out of her.

Meanwhile, what could Dalton have learned about FOFL's board members? Dying with curiosity, Marla pondered the possibilities as she slid inside her car and started the engine. Who else besides people from the volunteer organization could have been involved with Val?

At work she greeted everyone, stashed the sandwich she'd bought in the refrigerator, and headed to her station. She opened the top drawer to stuff her purse inside and paused. Hadn't she left her favorite pen on top? She dug inside, finding it buried beneath the spare hairbrushes, ticket book, color key, breath mints, hair clips, and extra makeup she kept there.

Could someone have gone through her stuff?

She glanced around, noting the familiar faces. A shiver crawled up her spine. She kept client notes in this drawer with hair formulas and sensitivities. Remembering how the killer might have accessed Rosana's notes about Val, she vowed to keep the drawer locked hereafter.

She fit her bulging purse inside. She'd stuck the copy of the journal into her handbag, not wishing to leave it in her car. Now she locked the drawer, feeling less secure about her environment despite their security system. Then again, it could merely have been another stylist looking for a tool. They often borrowed each other's implements.

Busy at work for the next several hours, she lifted her head when a car alarm went off in the parking lot. "What's that?" she called to Robyn at the front desk.

"I dunno. Don't see anybody. Must be a fluke."

Her nerves jittery, Marla dashed outside. She peered at the scattered cars parked on the asphalt lot. It was after five, and most workers had left for the day. The darkening sky made it difficult to discern details.

Was it her imagination, or did that noise sound as though it were coming from the direction of her vehicle?

CHAPTER NINE

The alarm deactivated as Marla approached her car and tapped on the remote. Her Camry appeared intact, but the parking lot lights weren't too bright in this area. Peeking inside, she noticed the office store bag on the rear seat. Had a thief been going for that item? The holiday season was rife with shoplifters and thieves stealing things from cars.

Maybe Dalton could get fingerprints off the car's body. Then again, no crime had been committed. Kids could have come by looking for easy loot to steal.

Or might somebody be after the journal, the same reason why Val's house was invaded? She couldn't think about it now. Her family was coming for dinner in just a short while and she had to finish up at work.

Finally home by six-thirty, she rushed to heat the food, put the shamash and first night candles into her menorah, and pour oil into her electric fry pan to make latkes. Brianna had finished her chores and was in her room doing homework. Dalton hadn't come home yet.

Marla, wearing an apron, bustled about the kitchen blending the potato pancake mix. She'd taken shortcuts with tonight's meal, but that was permitted, considering she'd had to work all afternoon. Ma was bringing desserts, and Dalton's parents were bringing a salad.

Hanukkah was never as big a deal as Christmas. Nonetheless, Marla had attempted to bolster the holiday. At the very least, it warranted a special dinner.

The lights on their tree twinkled from the living room. She still hadn't gotten used to decorating a Christmas tree, but she could see how collecting ornaments through the years and hanging them together would be a joyful family activity.

She should put on a CD with Hanukkah music to make things more festive. While the oil was heating, she did just that. As the strains of "I Have a Little Dreidel" played, she thought about how an oil lamp had started the holiday. While Passover remained her favorite religious occasion, this one also held fond memories from her childhood. Thus she let her mother explain what it meant to Dalton's parents after dinner, when they gathered around the menorah.

Anita was happy to oblige. "In the early days, the Syrians—under the leadership of a tyrant named Antiochus—defiled the holy Temple in Jerusalem and abolished the practice of Judaism. Jews were given a familiar choice: conversion or death. But a resistance movement grew strength, led by Judah Maccabee. His forces liberated the Temple from Syrian armies. To purify the Temple, the Jews lit the eternal lamp that is in every synagogue to this day. But there was only enough oil to last for one night. Miraculously, the lamp burned for eight days. Hence, Hanukkah is known as the Festival of Lights. It symbolizes freedom from oppression."

"That's why the menorah has eight branches," Marla concluded, "plus this top one called the shamash candle. We use it to light the others. Each night, we add another candle from right to left." She handed out copies of the blessings, and everyone read them together as Anita did the honors and lit the candles. Normally, the kindling was done from left to right so the newest candle got lit first.

They stood around in harmony, staring at the flames. Marla felt a swell of affection for her extended family. Religion didn't matter in her book as long as you cared about each other. The power of love surpassed all belief systems.

"So this is why we eat potato pancakes," Brianna said to her paternal grandmother. "They're fried in oil."

"Jelly doughnuts are another traditional food," Anita added with an affectionate smile. "But usually I forego that treat because they're too fattening."

They exchanged small gifts, saving the larger gift exchange for Christmas, and played the dreidel game, which Anita taught to everyone after passing out silver foil-wrapped chocolate coins known as *gelt*.

With all the hustle and bustle, Marla completely forgot to tell Dalton about the near break-in of her car until she heard his exclamation in the garage the next morning.

"How did you get these scratches on your door?" he called.

She let the dogs in from the backyard, locked the patio door, and rushed through the kitchen to the garage entry. Pressed for time, she still had to give Brianna a ride to the bus stop and finish the breakfast dishes before leaving for work.

"I meant to mention it to you last night, but it slipped my mind. I heard a car alarm go off in the parking lot at work last night. It turned out to be mine. It was too dark out for me to look closely except to note nothing had been stolen, and then I was in a rush when I got home." Her mouth curved downward when she saw the damage. "Oh, crap."

"Did you see anyone in the vicinity?"

"Nope. Whoever did this must have been scared off by the alarm. See that empty shopping bag? I figured it was a crook looking to steal Christmas gifts." Chilly air swept in from the open garage, and she shivered, wrapping her arms around herself. "But then again, I could have sworn somebody searched through my drawer at work. Things weren't the way I had left them."

"Really?" Dalton frowned at her. "What would someone be after?"

"Possibly the same thing they wanted at Val's house—the travel journal. It's in my handbag. They wouldn't know mine is a copy and you have the original. Have you read any of it yet?"

He laid a hand on her shoulder. "I haven't had time. You'd better be more careful. I don't like this. Your safety has been compromised."

Yeah, and I'd better not remind you that Jason's killer has my number.

"I'll watch my back. I've been meaning to read that book, but tonight is our holiday party at work and tomorrow I'm booked solid. I might not have time until later on this weekend."

"That's okay. Maybe I'll get a chance to take a look today."

"You never told me what you'd learned about the Friends of Old Florida board members. Come in for a minute. You still have time to get to work." She cast a glance at her car. Now she'd have to pay a visit to the body shop.

Dalton followed her back into the kitchen. "Solomon Gold is having renovations done on his properties by the same companies he recommends to the city for restoration work. It makes me wonder if he's getting kickbacks by means of personal services."

Marla washed the dishes while listening. "So you think he has a company low-ball the competition, and when they win the bid, they do free work for him on his private property as a bonus?"

"That's a likely scenario. If Val found out, it could explain why she was bumped off, but not Jason Faulks."

"That's assuming the two cases are connected, and that the monetary rewards to Gold and these companies are substantial enough to warrant murder. What else have you learned?"

"Gold supported Val's efforts to block Rick Rodriguez's

corporation in their quest to develop beachfront properties into condo towers. He's the one who tipped me off that the organization's publicist, Andrew Fine, is writing articles slanted in Rodriguez's favor."

"He told me the same thing."

"It's more than supposition on his part. According to Kat, who's been looking into the paper trail, Fine's bank account shows some generous deposits lately."

"So he could be accepting bribes from Rodriguez. Why would he jeopardize his position with FOFL that way, not to mention his integrity?"

Dalton shrugged. "He could need the money for some reason. We're digging deeper."

"What else has Kat learned?"

"The secretary's ticket sales reports from last year don't jive with the actual bill from the catering department at the hotel."

"Meaning what? That she fudged on the number of seats sold to give the impression attendance was higher?"

"Her group paid the catering bill per their contract. Sue Ellen claimed three hundred people attended at two hundred fifty dollars per seat. In actuality, when Kat checked with the hotel, they said they'd charged for two hundred guests. That leaves a discrepancy of twenty-five thousand dollars. Do you think anyone from FOFL would go around counting seats? The way those tables were placed this year, the ballroom appeared filled."

"So you think Sue Ellen siphoned that money for herself? If so, she could have been doing this for years."

"Maybe Val caught on, and Sue Ellen had to get rid of her."

Marla couldn't imagine the timid secretary doing such a vile deed, but she'd known folks before who'd hidden their true natures beneath a meek exterior.

"If all these people had reason to resent Val's interference, why did she send Nadia this journal? How does that tie into things?"

"Who knows? I have to go to work. We'll compare notes again later. Be careful, you hear? Someone has their eye on you. And you might want to report those scratches to the insurance company. Tell them it was vandals." He kissed her and then left.

Marla got too busy to think about the journal, between clients at the salon and their holiday party that night at a favorite Italian restaurant. She was pleased Nicole brought Kevin, the hunky EMT from the fire department whom she was dating. Having introduced the couple, Marla observed their glow of happiness with a sense of pride. Ignoring the lively music, loud chatter, and clanging dishware in the background, she sat in her chair at a long table in the restaurant surveying her friends and colleagues. Dalton still hadn't gotten any new leads on Patty, the missing shampoo girl from the day spa. Marla hoped something bad hadn't happened to her, although it appeared she'd cleared out on her own.

As they opened gifts exchanged through their Secret Santa tradition, she wondered where Val had celebrated the holidays each year. Most likely, she'd spent them with her sister's family. It must have been a terrible blow to lose her only sibling. Had Val really been considering changing allegiances and cutting Friends of Old Florida out of her will?

Marla's thoughts segued again to the journal whose significance remained obscure. She had to make time to read the thing. So Saturday morning, while fatigued from the night before, she bounced out of bed early. Brianna was sleeping in, having made plans with friends for later, and Dalton had decided to go into the office.

Snuggling up on the couch with a mug of coffee and the journal, Marla began turning pages. She quickly got engrossed in the story.

My friend George and I vacationed in Miami during February 1934. Thoroughly fed up with civilization, its artificialities and complications, we were bored with the monotony of our existence. An overpowering desire for a new environment and for the freedom of unconfined space, for adventure, swept over us. Both George and I had experienced these symptoms of wanderlust before, and we'd usually found a temporary cure by escaping to the simple life of the outdoors. This was what we needed on this occasion.

It was at this propitious time that Ralph appeared from the north in a dilapidated Ford piled high with camping equipment. We questioned his presence and discovered another restless soul willing to do anything and go anywhere within reason, as long as it was away from people and the hustle and bustle of modern life.

Our tropical surroundings influenced our imaginations. We remembered stories we had read as children about South Sea Islands and Robinson Crusoe, and we pictured ourselves inhabiting a similar small island.

Our dream showed us living in a hut constructed from palm thatch and sunbathing on a beach with no other humans in sight and only scattered clusters of palm trees for company. Being severed from worries, toil, and turmoil that defined civilization would prove an idyllic existence. Such were the fantasies that passed through our minds, and so tempting did they become that we decided to make them materialize. We agreed to find our tropical paradise among the Florida Keys.

Marla put the book down. So the other guys were named George and Ralph. If their last names weren't given, how could she find out who they were? The captioned photos didn't provide any clues, at least not to her. Dalton might be sharper at picking up nuances.

Sipping her coffee, she read on. The boys took a car ferry to Key West and from there headed northward.

We spent an entire morning in a fruitless search for nonexistent beaches on low-lying and swampy islands, which were nothing but

138

breeding places for mosquitoes and other insects.

Another afternoon spent repeating this experience left us feeling that such a place as our imaginations had pictured was not to be found anywhere in the state of Florida. And so we put the thoughts of an island from our minds and began to think of finding a substitute, some desolate and wild spot that would satisfy our extreme taste in this regard.

An inkling of an idea sprang into Marla's mind. What if these young men, searching for their personal Shangri-La, had discovered something more than they'd bargained for? The trio might have come across a dead body that washed ashore and hadn't wanted to get involved. Or maybe they'd hit someone on a deserted roadway one night and had fled the scene. Good God, she sounded like Nicole, who devoured mystery novels and suspected a crime under every stone.

Perhaps the young men had discovered something more valuable, like oil in the swamp. Or was black gold only found in Texas? Val had guarded this journal for some reason. Perhaps it disclosed a dark family secret she'd wanted kept buried or a treasure map to a hidden lode.

Something had happened on that journey. Marla felt it in her bones. Only two of the men had made it out of Florida's swamps in the end.

Brianna stumbled into the room, ending her reverie. Marla put the pages aside and refocused her attention. "Good morning, honey. You woke up early."

"I have to study for a test before I go to Randy's house. It's on Monday."

"I'll make you breakfast. What will you have?" She didn't need to leave for work until eight-thirty and still had a half hour to spare.

Her time became occupied until later that morning. She'd stuffed the printouts into her purse, hoping to have time to read more later, and locked it in her drawer at work. But as one customer after another walked in, Marla barely had time to breathe.

However, when Ashley Hunt entered the salon asking for her, she made time to speak to the model. "Hey, Ashley, what can I do for you?" Marla asked, approaching the young woman upon the receptionist's summons.

"Do you have a minute? I don't want to be overheard."

"Sure, let's go sit on the bench out front." Marla grabbed a jacket on her way. Once seated facing the parking lot, she waited for Ashley to begin the conversation.

Ashley avoided her gaze, staring at the discount store across the asphalt. "I know you're married to that detective, and I have information for him. Do you know Dr. Needles?"

"Yes, I met him at the party. You said he's been treating you for a back injury." She remembered them huddled together. What was Ashley about to reveal?

The model tossed a lock of blonde hair off her face in an angry gesture. "Ian hasn't been returning my calls. I know he's in town. He has to be avoiding me. When I suggested we move in together, I didn't think it would spook him that much."

"Whoa, are you saying that you two are a number?"

Ashley glanced at her through long lashes. "Let's say his interest in me isn't purely professional. I don't deserve to be treated this way."

"How long have you been together?"

"For over a year. He had the most soothing touch when I told him about my back injury. I know it was hard for him to resist me. He implied he'd do more at our next examination if I was interested."

Marla's throat squeezed. "Wait, are you saying that he . . . that his hands wandered?" How could she pose the question so as to be more tactful?

"Men always want me. Who wouldn't with my figure and looks? Ian is an attractive man and a rich surgeon besides. I decided to have a fling with him. Maybe he could buy me the jewelry I wanted and a condo on the water."

"Did he . . . touch you inappropriately during your examination?" The breeze picked up, whipping a scrap of paper along the sidewalk. A trio of people exited from Arnie's deli down the strip, laughing and chatting on the way to their car.

"As I said, Ian gave the merest of hints about what he wanted to do. His fingers know how to move in just the right manner to turn a girl on."

"Is this what you came here to tell me?"

"Hell, no. If he's going to drop me without so much as a word, I'll need another doctor to write my prescriptions. Ian has been pretty liberal about giving me what I want, although he hasn't offered any break on the price."

"Is this related to the back pain from your injury?"

"I still suffer from bouts of pain, and the meds help. Ian has a lot of patients, but not all of them look as though they've got a real problem like I have. Do you get my drift?"

"Yes, I do." Marla had thought the authorities cracked down on pill mills, at least with clinics. Could private practices have escaped their notice? Maybe Val had stumbled upon the doctor's disreputable activities and threatened to expose him.

"With your permission, I'll mention your name to Dalton as my source of information," Marla told Ashley. "He may want to contact you."

"I don't mind as long as my involvement is kept confidential. Ian has a temper when he's angry. I wouldn't want him to learn I'm the one who ratted on him. But he's not going to get away with ignoring me."

"Thanks for coming here, Ashley. I appreciate your trust."

For an instant, a look of vulnerability entered the model's

eyes. "I figured you'd be a good listener." Smoothing her skinny jeans, she rose. "I hope we work together again. Your stylists are very talented. Maybe I'll come here next time I need a trim."

Marla stood and smiled at her. "Please do. And unlike Dr. Needles, I'll give you a professional discount."

As soon as Ashley left, Marla scurried through the salon and into the rear storeroom where the cool breeze wouldn't chill her skin. She took out her cell and phoned Dalton.

"That's an interesting development," he said in his wry tone after she'd related her conversation with Ashley. "This is between us, but the doctor is being investigated for possible prescription abuse. The sexual harassment is a new angle. I'll have Kat check into any possible complaints against him."

"How do you feel Val fits into this, if anywhere? Did she threaten to expose his unethical practices? And how would she have learned about them?"

"She knew a lot of people around town. She might have heard things."

"Even so, it doesn't explain her connection to Warren's journal or to the men in Jason's photos, except for Howard whom she'd met through FOFL." Marla still knew so little about Val's personal background. "Are the staff still present at her house? If so, I should pay them a visit. They might be more willing to talk to me than the authorities."

"Kat and I have already interviewed them."

"So? I'll approach it differently. Besides, I really would like to learn more about Val. She couldn't have been as saintly as people painted her." Val had been a painter, Marla remembered. Maybe she could catch a glimpse of Val's artwork. "The staff might be able to tell me how Val came to acquire the journal."

A brief silence fell. "All right. You could be useful."

"I'll stop by tomorrow. You're taking Brie to the hockey game, so that will give me something to do."

"Just be careful. Val sent the journal to Nadia. That means she didn't trust anyone else who was close to her."

Sunday morning, Marla drove east toward the Intracoastal. She turned left onto one of the bridges off Las Olas Boulevard toward a series of islands housing wealthy mansions and private boat decks. Yachts in every size docked along the waterways that made Fort Lauderdale the Venice of the South.

She couldn't imagine the lifestyle of these people, who cruised on a whim, planned parties, and lived the high life. It wasn't for her. She was driven to have a purpose, and a large part of it was helping women look good. Marla liked to think of it as her calling. It empowered people when they looked their best and gave them confidence.

Lord knows she'd needed that boost herself when she was married to Stan. If not for Tally urging her to go to cosmetology school and eventually leave him, she might still be stuck in the bored wives' club. Once she'd gotten out from under his domineering thumb, she'd grown and thrived. She owed Tally her life in that regard.

Did Val have anyone whom she could rely on? Her friend, Nadia, seemed like a nice person. Hadn't Nadia said she and Val knew each other's secrets? What did that mean?

Hopefully Val's staff would be willing to talk. She glanced at the residences along the street, shaking her head in wonder at each magnificent house. As she neared the Intracoastal, they grew in grandeur. While part of her envied the residents who lived there, another part of her knew she wouldn't be happy in such an enormous place. Her house was comfortable and cozy.

She pulled into a circular driveway in front of a two-story Mediterranean-style villa. The garage was separate and had its own upper level, presumably extra living quarters or perhaps housing Val's art studio.

A gray-haired fellow in a staid suit opened the door at her summons. Once she introduced herself, he bid her to enter.

"You may wait in the green parlor. I'll get Mrs. Dale, the housekeeper. She'll speak to you."

He bustled off after leaving Marla inside a delightful room facing the landscaped rear grounds that she could see through a series of French doors. Potted plants decorated the airy space along with white wicker furnishings. It looked like a pleasant room in which to cozy up with a cup of coffee and an iPad. Imagine if she lived in a place like this. She could decorate each room differently. Maybe she'd get used to it after all.

A matronly woman clad in a black dress and white apron joined her. She had wary brown eyes and pursed lips with a dash of coral lipstick. Her graying black hair was fastened into a bun at her nape, while her ample figure indicated she frequented the kitchen.

"I'm Mrs. Dale, the housekeeper. How can I help you?"

Marla plastered a sympathetic smile on her face. "I own the salon and day spa where your employer, uh, passed away. I'm sorry for your loss."

"As you should be. I can't understand how something like this could have happened."

"Liquid latex was found in the face cream Val's beautician used on her, and it wasn't listed in the ingredients. The substance would not have affected anyone else. I suspect the same person who added the latex made sure Val had the first appointment of the day. The secretary at Friends of Old Florida initially made her appointment for that afternoon. Would you know who called in and changed the time?"

The housekeeper sank into a chair and indicated Marla should do the same. "I have no idea. This is the first I've heard of these matters."

Marla raised an eyebrow. "I assume the police detective filled you in."

"He came by to question us, but he wouldn't share the details of Miss Val's death."

"Did any of the household staff attend the funeral?"

"The brother-in-law didn't invite us. He explicitly told us he wouldn't be happy to see us there. We decided to hold our own quiet memorial at home."

"Do you live in this house?"

She nodded. "So do Cook and Mr. Lawson. He's the butler who let you in."

"You must have been devastated by Val's passing. Why wouldn't Sean want you at the funeral? You would have been like family to Val."

Mrs. Dale twisted her hands in her lap. "We were indeed, poor thing, especially after Miss Cathy died. The sisters were close, but Mr. Knight resented how Miss Val had inherited the bulk of their parents' wealth, including this house."

Why would the parents leave more to one sister than the other? Did they feel Val, being single, needed the money more? Or didn't they like the brother-in-law? In that case, they could have kept the money in trust for Cathy and her children, which is what Marla presumed they'd done.

"Val could have evened things out in her will, if she didn't believe her parents had been fair," she commented.

Mrs. Dale peered at her. "What's your interest in this? You're asking very personal questions."

She gave a sheepish grin. "I'm married to Detective Vail. Sometimes I help him with his investigations. And I feel bad about what happened to Val. I didn't know her as well as my beautician, but I'd like to honor her memory by getting better acquainted now."

"I see." Mrs. Dale compressed her lips. "I can tell you that

Miss Val was a generous employer and a friend. She was really quite shy, more so than people believed. She'd hole up in her studio for hours. Painting brought her peace."

"Did either of her parents have artistic talent?"

"No, but Miss Val got her love of history from her father. He filled her imagination with stories of pirates, Indians, and Spanish explorers. Would you believe she went to garage sales looking for old diaries written by Florida pioneers?"

"Really?" Marla rummaged in her handbag and withdrew the copied pages in her possession. "Is that how she got hold of Warren Brookstone's journal? I've made a copy."

Mrs. Dale's face paled as she noted the papers in Marla's hand.

CHAPTER TEN

"How did you get that journal?" Mrs. Dale demanded.

"Val must have left instructions for this book to be sent to a friend in the event of her death. The friend, one of our customers, thought I should pass it on to my husband."

"Oh, my. I never guessed . . . I never thought—"

"Wait. *You* mailed it to Nadia?"

Mrs. Dale gazed out the window. "I was following Miss Val's wishes and figured Nadia already knew what was inside."

"Nadia did admit she and Val knew each other's secrets. Do you know what this is about, Mrs. Dale?"

The woman's lips compressed. "All I'll say is that Miss Val felt torn after she read that book, but she wasn't at fault for her father's sins."

Ah, now we're getting somewhere. "Who is the Warren fellow who wrote it? Was it someone Val knew?"

"Warren was her father. Miss Val took on her mother's family name after her divorce. Once she'd read those pages, she was glad of her choice."

"Did her father share this book with her while he was still alive?"

"No, Miss Val discovered it while sorting through his things after he died."

Marla squirmed with impatience, wishing to get to the heart of the secrets. "What happened during his early trip to Florida?"

Mrs. Dale plucked at her apron. "Something nobody wanted

to talk about, then or now."

Marla tried another tack. "I take it Val's dad married into wealth?"

The housekeeper nodded, her expression easing at the safer topic. "The mother was a Weston. They made their fortune from Florida's East Coast Railroad in the 1890s. Miss Val didn't have an easy childhood, trying to live up to her parents' expectations. Her sister, Miss Cathy, was better suited in that regard. Miss Val tried to please them once by marrying, but it didn't work out. She claimed the guy was only after her money and got a divorce."

"I hear the former husband remarried and lives in California."

"He did all right for himself. I often wonder if Miss Val's the one who did him an injustice."

"How so?" Marla leaned forward, her shoulders aching from inactivity. She wanted to rise and pace the room but maintained her seat so as not to disrupt the flow of conversation. Mrs. Dale seemed eager to talk, as though she couldn't trust the other staff members enough to confide in them.

Mrs. Dale's gaze darted toward the door. "You might ask her friend Nadia that question."

Marla let a weighty pause come between them. "Why did Val give this book to you for safekeeping rather than the trustee of her estate?"

The housekeeper gave her a narrowed glance. "She wasn't too happy with him, that's why. At first, she loved the guy like an uncle, but lately she'd begun to suspect he hadn't fallen far from the tree."

"Meaning?"

"Like father, like son."

Marla gritted her teeth in frustration. Mrs. Dale wasn't going to give up any names. About to whip out the photos on her cell phone that Jason had sent, she had a better idea.

"I'd love to see an album of Val's childhood to get a better sense of her personality. I can see Val was much beloved and I'm sorry I never truly got a chance to know her. I already told Friends of Old Florida I'd make a donation in her memory."

"That's kind of you." With a sweep of her skirt, Mrs. Dale rose. She marched over to a console, opened a drawer, and withdrew a heavy album. "Miss Val was into scrapbooking in her younger days, another manifestation of her artistic talent. She was really quite good." Beaming with pride like a parent, she showed Marla the large tome.

Impressed by Val's creativity, Marla turned the pages displaying photos of birthday parties, childhood milestones, family trips, and school events. A particular face ballooned out to her in one photo with all four family members. Yes, that guy was the spitting image of the man in Warren's travel journal. So Val's dad had been the author.

"Thank you," she said finally, closing the album. "I appreciate you taking the time to talk to me. This has been insightful." True, although Marla had more questions than answers.

"I'm sorry I can't be more helpful. I'll see you to the door, Mrs. Vail."

Marla rose obediently and followed the woman toward the vestibule. "How long will you and the others be allowed to live here?"

"The trustee has hired us to maintain the place until it's sold and to prepare the contents for auction. He's giving us all references. You needn't worry on our score."

"I forgot his name. It's Mister . . . ?"

"Sorry, I'm not at liberty to say. He's mentioned that Miss Val remembered the staff in her will. She was always thoughtful of us."

"So I gather." Aware she'd overstayed her welcome, Marla bid the woman farewell and headed for home. She had a few hours of quiet time to spare. She'd put them to good use by delving further into the journal.

After taking the dogs for a walk so she could get some exercise, she settled onto the family room sofa with the stack of printed pages. She began reading at the spot where she'd left off. The three friends, having yet to find their idyllic spot, had camped out overnight.

Early morning found us in the town of Homestead and on individual searches for information. This we did more through force of habit than with the expectation of receiving a good lead regarding our fantasized island. However, the unexpected sometimes happens, and it was Ralph who returned with good news.

He'd learned that about sixty miles from Homestead, at the extreme tip of the wildest and most desolate part of Florida, rested Cape Sable. Upon settling the state, the Spaniards had planted here an immense grove of coconut trees. These trees had been perpetuated and cultivated for many centuries until a forest extended for miles bordering a beautiful sandy beach. This lonesome site was seldom visited by human beings.

Marla took a break to get a cup of coffee. Then she read on as the boys made a difficult but uneventful drive that came to a less than satisfactory halt. The details fascinated her, as did the boys' bravery in exploring the unknown.

The only water we saw along the way was in drainage canals. At one time, we had a very narrow escape that might have had serious results had our guardian angel not been with us. Racing along the road at breakneck speed, we sped around a curve. George and I gave a simultaneous yell of warning.

A dozen feet ahead of us was a canal bridged by two narrow planks just wide enough to accommodate our tires. By a quick application of the brakes, which nearly put our heads through the windshield, Ralph managed to bring our car to a quivering stop, mere inches from the waterway. Our crossing was an extremely cautious one. We put another canal behind us and finally came to the widest of them all. This one was filled with racing water of a greenish, unhealthy color. We had reached the end of the road and took to our feet.

Equipped with our hatchet and two stout clubs for protection, we paraded single-file along the narrow and barely discernible trail that paralleled the canal. We passed pools of discolored and slimy water to our left. As we continued, these were replaced by treacherous-appearing mud. Gaunt, sun-whitened trunks of dead trees grew from this slimy ooze as if nurtured by its foulness.

Soon we came to an immense forest of ghostly remains. Some of these trees were twisted out of shape as if they had died in terrible agony. The roots of these once mighty monarchs resembled thick, entwined masses of sleeping snakes. From the few branches that remained, streamers of Spanish moss hung like so many shrouds.

When we reached the point where another canal intersected the one we had been following, we halted. The turbulent waters rushing together in the middle of the streams made it impossible to wade to the other side. We touched bottom with a long stick and found it to be well over our heads.

None of us was able to swim well enough to risk battling the rough current. Even had we been able to do so, the thought of hidden alligators would have deterred us. A boat was out of the question. We wasted no further time in contemplating the impossible and hurriedly began to retrace our footsteps to the car.

Her mood dampened, Marla put down the pages in her hand. Although she hadn't read anything significant to Val's case yet, the quality of the writing impressed her. Warren's vivid descriptions made her feel as though she was there in that awful swamp.

She picked up her cell phone, needing comfort, and called Tally. She'd meant to check on her friend earlier anyway.

"I hope I'm not disrupting your Christmas preparations," she said when her friend answered. "Can you believe the holiday is two days away? We're still celebrating Hanukkah."

"How did your dinner party go?" Tally inquired.

"It went fine. Brianna likes lighting the menorah. And her parents didn't make the mistake of blowing out the candles like that year your husband did it." They shared a laugh. "How is Ken, by the way? Is he taking any time off for the holidays?"

"No, if anything, work is keeping him later. It's a busy season."

Marla heard the flippant remark with concern. She sensed more going on there. Should she pry? Had Tally learned the real reason for her husband's late hours? Torn between loyalty to her friend and not wishing to stir a hornets' nest, she decided to keep silent on the matter.

"How is little Luke? Is that him I hear fussing in the background?"

"I just laid him down for a nap. I've some more gifts to wrap and then I'm going to rest. How's the murder case going? The lawsuit with the disgruntled client?"

"All right." Marla kept her tone light. "I'll let you go. We should make a date to get together with the guys after the holidays. If your plans for New Year's Day fall through in the meantime, you can join us here. We're having a few people over for a low-key party."

"Sure, Marla. Thanks for calling."

Marla hung up, a sour flavor on her tongue. Tally was usually so talkative and much more interested in Marla's investigative activities. Troubled over what might be going on at her friend's house, she picked up the papers again and read on. The boys' exploration for a spot of paradise continued. They bought supplies in Miami and then headed north toward Fort Lauderdale. Discovering a dirt road that ran parallel to the ocean, they took the less-travelled path.

The sight that greeted us when we had driven a short distance brought forth cries of enthusiasm and joy. The sky blue waters of the ocean and a wide expanse of beach stretched into the far distance. In the middle of this panorama of beauty, sitting in splendid isolation, was a rugged log cabin. It seemed to have been built to order for our benefit. A few lonesome coconut trees stood romantically outlined in the reflected glory of the setting sun.

We approached the door that stood invitingly open. When we entered, it was to find a scene of disorder. Rubbish littered the cement floor. Piles of empty tin cans, old newspapers, sand that the wind had blown in through holes between the logs, and a varied assortment of odds and ends covered every inch. Spider webs stretched overhead, and their disturbed occupants scurried around in great excitement. Thousands of fast-moving ants moved everywhere. Where there had once been windows, now were yawning gaps.

But this sight did not discourage us. Without bothering to make inquiries regarding the place's ownership or to consider that we might be trespassing upon private property, we rolled up our sleeves and began to clean house.

Marla's pulse accelerated. She felt on the brim of discovering something important. Had these men found an item of significance in this isolated cabin? Buried treasure? Old letters between lovers? An important political document lost to time?

The inner garage door banged open, and she set the pages down. Brianna rushed to greet her with a radiant face. The teen's long braid swung as she approached. "Dad let me drive home. I did good, didn't I?"

Dalton gave Marla a quick kiss after she'd leapt up at their arrival. "Yes, you were great. I was a nervous wreck, though. I fear the day when you get your own car."

"It's an anxiety every parent has to confront," Marla said in a soothing tone. "You'll get through it." *We'll worry ourselves sick, but we'll manage. There's no choice.* "I've been reading the journal. I got to an interesting part where the boys found their idyllic location at a log cabin on the beach. I have a hunch that's where they discover something relevant."

"Sorry to interrupt." Dalton sounded regretful.

"Don't be. How was the hockey game? I assume you ate lunch there?"

"It was great." Dalton stared after his daughter, already on her cell phone while walking to her room. "She met some kids from school that she knew. One of them was a boy who gave her the look."

"What look?" Marla asked with a smile, as though she didn't know what he meant.

"You know. What if she wants to start dating? She's way too young."

"Kids hang out in groups these days. It'll be a while before she goes on a real date. Besides, you're jumping the gun. Driving lessons are enough for right now." She tilted her head. "I've set the table for Christmas dinner. Have you confirmed the time with your parents?"

"Yes, they'll be here. Let's hope nothing calls me away, although Kat will be on duty for the holiday. So what have you accomplished today?"

"I went to Val's house and spoke with her housekeeper." She sat down at the kitchen table while he claimed a chair opposite. "Mrs. Dale said the staff had been employed by Val's trustee to prepare things for auction. The housekeeper didn't mention the guy's name, but she said Val wasn't happy with him lately. She'd considered him like an uncle but recently had begun suspecting he hadn't fallen far from the tree, whatever that means."

Dalton nodded as she concluded her recital. "The attorney is due back from vacation this weekend. I'll stop by to see him tomorrow. He'll give me the man's name."

"What about the bank where Val had her accounts? Wouldn't the trustee be listed there?"

"The account is in her name, not the trust's. Kat is tracking down Val's investment accounts."

"Listen to this. Mrs. Dale admitted that Val's dad wrote the journal. Warren Brookstone was Valerie's father."

"Interesting. I hadn't gotten that far in tracing her family history, especially since her ties relate to the wealthy Westons."

"She took her mother's maiden name after getting a divorce. The housekeeper hinted that something in this journal convinced Val she'd made the right choice."

Dalton frowned. "I still can't guess how Jason Faulks enters the picture. One of the photos he sent you shows Henutt Soe Dum and another man. The second picture shows Howard Cohn speaking to someone at the charity ball."

"We know Howard must be related to one of the guys in the journal. They look too much alike. Why do you think Jason was interested in them? Could he have been more than a society photographer? Perhaps he was working on an investigative piece and stumbled onto something relevant."

"You could be right. Kat is checking into his background. Meanwhile, Detective Monroe from Fort Lauderdale is in charge of that investigation. I'll have another chat with him to see what he's learned."

"Assuming Jason's death is related to one of the photos he sent me, that still gives us Yolanda's husband as a suspect. Did you ask him for the identity of this other person?"

"He claimed it was a guy he barely knew and stopped to greet." Dalton thrust his fingers through his hair. "I'll ask Monroe to have his cyber team search Faulks's computer files. The photographer must have left notes somewhere."

"I should have asked Mrs. Dale if Jason had ever visited Val at her home. That would provide a connection between them." She rose, too fidgety to sit still.

"By the way, Kat tracked down the girl from your day spa."

She stared at him. "You found Patty and didn't call me? You know we've been concerned about her."

"I was waiting until we had more solid info." His mouth compressed. "Your former assistant used her credit card in Wellington, where she'd recently set herself up in a new rental apartment. The landlord said she'd paid cash for her first month's rent and the security deposit."

"So did Kat interview her?"

"Yes. When threatened with being considered an accomplice, Patty admitted she'd been paid to mix a substance into Val's face cream. It was supposed to be a prank."

"How could that be a prank? Did Patty think causing Val to have an allergic reaction would be a mild scare?"

"She didn't think. The money tempted her. A man on a phone hired her and left a bundle of cash for her cooperation."

"Patty must have added the substance the evening before, probably after Rosana left for the day. She would have had access to Rosana's files, too."

"It's likely the killer already knew Val's allergic tendencies."

"That's true. But the bad guy would need to know which particular cream Rosana used on Val's face."

"Patty's the one who changed Val's appointment. She called Val and said Rosana wouldn't be available that afternoon, and would Val mind coming earlier in the morning."

"Then Patty must have changed the time on our computer schedule. I didn't realize she had those skills."

"She got scared after Val died and abandoned her apartment here. But the guy who hired her must have been tracking her movements because he contacted her again. We got nothing on those calls. Likely he used a burner phone each time."

"What did he want?" Marla asked with a sense of dread.

"He asked her to do one more thing, or he'd rat her out. So early one morning, when Robyn was the only person in the salon and she went next door to get your usual order from the deli, Patty ran inside and searched through your drawers. The man was after the journal."

"Then when she didn't find it, Patty tried to break into my car?"

"That's right. It's unfortunate she made the wrong choices. I don't think she's inherently a bad person, but now she'll probably end up serving some time."

Marla sank back into her seat. "She got greedy. That's what happens to people who yield to their dark side."

She fell silent, wondering who might have hired Patty. Knowing it was a man narrowed the field. Her suspicions swung to Henutt Soe Dum. Jason had sent her his photo for a reason.

"Has any progress been made in locating Yolanda's headpiece?" she asked. "I'm wondering if Henutt stole the thing and sold it to his overseas friends. His wife said it could have military applications."

Dalton glanced at her. He'd started sorting the different sections from the *Sun Sentinel* on the table. She'd bought the newspaper on her way home, aware he liked to do the Sunday crossword puzzle. "Henutt wouldn't have had to take the risk. He could merely copy her blueprints if he wanted to pass them on to his associates. But I don't think his goals are so political. He's in the game for profits."

"I should ask Yolanda about the guy in the photo with him. Maybe she'd recognize the other man. I don't believe it was a random encounter like Henutt claimed. But if he didn't take her signature crown, who did?" She opened her eyes wide and leaned forward as an idea surfaced. "Heck, why didn't I think of this before?"

"Think of what, sweetcakes?"

"I ran into Carla Jean Hatfield at the fundraiser. She's in the running beside me for the educator position at Luxor Products.

When I asked what she was doing there, she said she'd been sent by the company. They wanted to make sure Luxor had been given credit for the products I used backstage on the models."

"Did you use their products specifically?"

"Yes, and I notified Luxor, hoping they'd be pleased with the extra publicity. I would have sent them a program myself had I thought about it."

"So they sent Carla Jean to verify your claim. What's the big deal?"

"Did they send her, or was she lying? Where's my phone? I'm going to send Luxor a text. I have a wild idea, but I need confirmation before I act on it."

Marla sent a message to the district manager. Despite it being Sunday, she got an answer within minutes. She responded with another text. A few minutes later, she put down her phone with a broad grin. "So I asked if they'd sent Carla Jean to the ball. The manager said no, and what did I have to report? I told him everything had gone well, and I would mail him a copy of the program."

Dalton's brow furrowed as he regarded her. "I still don't get what you're implying."

"Carla Jean had a huge handbag that didn't go at all with her cocktail dress. I paid no attention to it at the time, but what if she's the one who stole Yolanda's invention?"

"A sales rep for a hair product company? What would she want with the thing?"

"Same as any thief. To sell it and make money."

"Sell it to whom?" He put down the newspaper section he'd been holding.

"Perhaps to a hair accessory firm. I think we've been looking at this the wrong way. It's not a military group or another country who's interested in the brain-wave applications. A smart company could reverse-engineer the invention and mass-produce similar copies. It would be a popular novelty item that could bring in substantial revenue."

"But why would Carla Jean risk her position that way?"

"Sales reps work hard. They're always on the road. Being an educator would mean even more travel. Maybe she's hoping to acquire enough money to retire instead."

His eyes narrowed. "Oh, yeah? We need to discuss that traveling part."

"Put that aside for the moment. What if I'm right? How can we investigate this angle?"

"*We* are not going to investigate anything else right now. I'll tell Detective Monroe your theory. He can pass it on to his property unit."

Marla's heart thumped with excitement. If she was right, not only could they recover Yolanda's proprietary headpiece but she'd gain the upper hand regarding the educator position.

So why did this latter prospect make her feel hollow instead of joyous?

CHAPTER ELEVEN

Monday morning, the day before Christmas, found Marla scurrying to complete her final chores. She'd already set the dining room table for their dinner party the next day, wrapped the last of her gifts, and dropped Spooks off at the groomer's.

She missed her former neighbor Goat, who'd owned a mobile grooming service. He'd moved out of town to be near her friend, Georgia Rogers, whom he'd met when Georgia stayed with Marla to work at a beauty trade show. Georgia was the sales rep for Luxor Products who had helped her procure a job at the show as assistant hairstylist. Had it been only two years ago? Gosh, so much had happened in that time. She really should call Georgia to catch up.

A germ of an idea sprang into her mind. Could Georgia get information on Carla Jean? Marla didn't trust the cops to follow up on her theory. Property crimes never got the attention they deserved. If she had some leverage, she could bargain with Carla Jean.

After completing a few more errands, including last-minute food shopping, Marla returned home. She put away the groceries, let the dogs outside to the fenced backyard, and took a moment to relax. Gripping her cell phone, she settled onto the couch in the den and dialed Georgia's number. Her friend's familiar voice came on the line.

"Georgia, it's Marla. I wanted to wish you a Merry Christmas."

"Omigod, how are you? It's been forever."

"I know. I'm sorry I haven't kept in touch. I miss you guys. Are you still with Goat?"

Georgia gave a low chuckle. "He's moved in. We're talking about getting married."

"That's terrific! You'll have to invite me."

"Of course. So what's going on with you? Anything new to report?" Her voice changed to a teasing tone. "Like, any buns in the oven yet?"

"Huh? Oh. No way." A flush heated Marla's skin. "I have enough to do watching over Dalton and Brianna."

"Just thought I'd ask. How's the salon?"

"We opened a new day spa next door." Marla proceeded to fill her in on the particulars, eventually getting around to the current case.

"Sorry, I haven't met Carla Jean," Georgia replied when Marla asked.

A wave of disappointment swept her. There went her idea of leverage. She'd been hoping Georgia might have heard some gossip about the woman that would put Carla Jean in an unfavorable light. "Is there any way you can find her address for me? I might pay her a visit."

"Sure. We have a directory of all the sales reps. Hold on a minute." After retrieving the data, she shared it with Marla. "Please don't mention where you got this info."

"My lips are sealed." They chatted for fifteen more minutes before Marla hung up. It felt good to catch up with an old friend. She needed to pay more attention to the people closest to her. That said, she phoned her mother and Dalton's mom to confirm details for the next day.

An hour later, she pulled up to the curb outside a townhouse supposedly owned by Carla Jean Hatfield. The unit sported a ubiquitous sand color with white trim and had a detached garage out back. It shared the row with four other homes of similar design. Flowering hibiscus shrubs, graceful palms, and colorful crotons decorated the lawns. A dog barked nearby as Marla stepped from her Camry.

Fortune shone upon her because the Luxor sales rep was at home.

"Who is it?" Carla Jean called from behind the closed front door after Marla rang the bell. A shadow crossed the peephole.

"Marla Vail. I have something to tell you."

"Really?" Carla Jean swung the door wide. "What is it, Marla? I'm surprised you could spare the time from your busy schedule." She flicked a speck of dust off the teal top that she wore over a pair of black denims. A beaded necklace hung from her neck, matching the bracelets on her arm.

"Monday is my day off," Marla explained. "And besides, it's a holiday. Is that why you're home and not out in the field?"

"It's a quiet time for me in terms of travel. What brings you here?" Carla Jean lounged in the doorway.

"Can I come in? I won't take much of your time."

"Sure." A puzzled frown creased her brow. "Have a seat in the living room, but please try to be brief. I just got in a large order that I have to send to the main office. It's often more expedient for me to process orders from home."

Marla sat on the cocoa-colored sofa while Carla Jean shut the door and joined her. She took an armchair opposite.

"I've been thinking about how odd it was that you showed up at the Friends of Old Florida fundraiser. Why did you say you'd come? Oh yes, the company sent you to make sure they got credit for the products I used backstage. But they knew I could send them a copy of the program, so you didn't need to be there. And would they really spend two hundred fifty dollars to buy you a ticket?"

"What are you implying?" Carla Jean's eyes grew wary.

"I believe somebody else sent you, only it was to steal Yolanda's signature headpiece."

Carla Jean shot up from her seat. "How dare you."

"You have to admit it makes sense," Marla continued in a calm tone, hands clasped in her lap. "Who else would benefit? Surely not a collector, who'd stash the item in a safe somewhere. A military group? A research consortium? Another country after our technology? Or a hair accessory company who could potentially make thousands of dollars on such a novelty item?"

"You're crazy, you know that?"

"But I'm on the mark, aren't I? Their offer must have been tempting. Steal Yolanda's crown of achievement, and get a bonus that would allow you to retire. Did you already hand it over to them?"

"I'm not going to tell you anything."

Marla's pulse raced. She must be on the right track. And then the proper leverage popped into her mind. It fit so perfectly, she didn't know why she hadn't thought of it earlier.

"Yes, you will. And if you still have it, you'll give it to me to return to the proper owner. Or you'll tell me who has it. In exchange, I promise to withdraw my application for the educator position."

Carla Jean gaped at her. "You'll do what?"

"I won't compete with you. You can have the job." Or had she misjudged the situation? Had her competitor already turned over the stolen goods and received her payout? In that case, Carla Jean wouldn't care about her generous offer.

As for Marla, it seemed a relief to give it up. Maybe the traveling part wasn't for her, after all. She didn't really want to leave her family, and the salon kept her busy enough. She'd rather gain Yolanda's approval and do more work with the designer.

"Do you mean it?" Carla Jean asked in a small voice. She

sank into her chair with a slumped posture.

"Yes, I do. So what's the scoop?"

Carla Jean didn't meet her eyes. "All right, I took the thing. I got paid half up front and half upon delivery. Except the company changed its mind. You were correct, it was a hair accessory firm. But a lot of their stuff is made in China. My contact said they hadn't realized the designer was related to Henutt somebody, and this guy had Chinese connections their company didn't care to cross."

"So they backed out of the deal."

"They let me keep the initial payment as long as I promised to keep my mouth shut. But now I'm stuck with the item. What do I do with it?"

"You give it to me. I'll return it to Yolanda without mentioning your name."

"I don't want this Henutt person coming after me."

"He's Yolanda's husband and may be involved with the Asian mob."

Carla Jean covered her face with her hands. "Oh, God."

"Give me the headpiece, and you'll be finished with it. But you have to make me a promise, too. You'll be honest with your customers and do your best if you win the educator position."

"Sure, Marla. Wait right here." The sales rep stood and hurried from the room. A few moments later, she returned carrying a bundle in a plastic bag. "Here you go."

Marla peeked inside to verify it held Yolanda's invention. The stones sparkled from its nest in the velvet case. "You won't regret this. You're making the right move." She rose and gathered her purse.

"If it means anything, I'm sorry I stole it." Carla Jean walked Marla to the door. "I'm not really a thief, but I'm getting tired of the same old routine. I'd hoped with the money, I could retire."

"Make retribution by being a better person and a great teacher. You might find that to be enough of a change. Goodbye, Carla Jean. I'll see you around."

As she got into her car, Marla's spirits lifted. She'd done a good deed in relieving Carla Jean of this burden. It had helped her, too, to see her rightful path. The educator position was not the answer to her restlessness. Her family shouldn't suffer because she felt dissatisfied. She'd have to set herself a new goal.

Glancing at the sack on the seat beside her as she drove downtown, Marla considered what she would say to Yolanda. Would her shop even be open since tonight was Christmas Eve? People might have parties to attend and would want to pick up their dresses, or so she hoped. At least traffic was light heading east.

Shoppers were engaged in last-minute gift buying along Las Olas Boulevard as she scurried on foot toward Yolanda's boutique. In the window on one side was a magnificent bridal gown worthy of a Disney princess, while the other held a turquoise sequined creation and a lovely beaded rose dress. Marla's envy level climbed for the women who could afford to shop here. But then again, where would she wear these things? She didn't have society balls to attend, although a short number would look good at next year's Taste of the World benefit.

A door chime tinkled as she entered. Yolanda glanced up from the cash register where she was ringing up a sale. Her elder assistant stood helping another lady some distance away.

Gripping the plastic bag in hand, Marla approached. She waited until Yolanda's customer left before greeting her.

"Hi there. I see you're busy, but I need a moment of your time."

"Sure, darling. What's up?" Yolanda's eyes gleamed as she viewed the bundle in Marla's grasp.

Marla whipped out her cell phone and accessed the photo of Henutt and another man that Jason had sent her. She showed it to the designer. "I need for you to I.D. this fellow with your husband."

"Where did you get that picture?" Yolanda shot a nervous glance toward the curtain at the rear.

"Jason Faulks took it at the ball. Now he's dead. I'm curious as to why Jason emailed this photo to me before he was killed."

"I recognize him." Yolanda pointed to her husband's companion. "But why did the poor photographer send *you* the picture?"

"Probably because I'm married to Detective Vail, and Jason knew I'd show it to him."

Marla weighed how much to tell Yolanda. Was the designer aware of her husband's possible involvement with the Asian mob? Did he launder cash through her store with her complicity? She scanned the array of colorful gowns inside the shop. Where did these luscious fabrics come from? The sequins, beading, and pearls? And what about the shoes, evening bags, and lingerie? Did Henutt's money buy the accessories?

"I need information," she stated flatly. "Please, Yolanda. I'll make it worth your while if you give me a name. I have something you want in return."

Yolanda's crimson mouth formed a pout. "Very well. It's Gabriel Stone. He's a funeral director in Parkland." She mentioned the name of his place but it didn't ring a bell.

Gabriel. How appropriate for someone in the death business.

Wait a minute. Did this guy ice the victims from Henutt's mob hits? Or was her imagination taking flight in an unsavory direction?

"And how are the men connected?" Marla asked with infinite patience.

"They're friends. I've met him before. Gabriel is a personable guy for someone in his line of work."

"Why do you think Jason sent me this particular photo?"

Yolanda spread her hands. "How should I know? You could ask Henutt."

Was Yolanda truly innocent about her husband's activities? "That won't be necessary, but I might have a chat with his friend." Marla lifted the bag she held. "Here, I believe this belongs to you."

Yolanda gave an exclamation of joy upon noting the contents. "Good Lord, where did you find it?"

"Someone took it who realized they'd made a mistake. I promised not to reveal their identity, but be assured it had nothing to do with politics or military applications."

"Well, that's a relief." Yolanda's face eased into a smile. "I'm grateful to you for recovering this piece. It could have been dangerous in the wrong hands. I have to lock it up. Please wait here a moment." She disappeared into the back area.

Meanwhile, the sales associate named Eve came to ring up her customer. Marla stood aside and surveyed a display case with expensive costume jewelry. The necklaces were a bit elaborate for her taste but she liked the earrings.

"How much are these?" Marla asked once the customer had left. She pointed to a pair of smoky crystal stud earrings.

Eve took them out and laid them on a velvet cloth. "They're only forty-eight dollars a set. Lovely, aren't they? We also have them in clear crystal, blue topaz, and citrine."

Marla held them up to her bronze highlighted chestnut hair and glanced in a mirror. They sparkled in the light. "Oh, gosh. I love them." They'd look great on Brianna and on her mother, too. You could dress them up or down, depending on what you were wearing. "I'll take all four," she said, giving in to impulse. She still had time to put them under the tree. They'd planned a gift exchange for tomorrow. Between Hanukkah and Christmas, she'd go broke, but these earrings were irresistible and in her price range.

Yolanda chose that moment to return. "I'll give you a discount," she said upon learning of Marla's pending purchase.

Marla handed over her credit card then stood by while Eve wrapped her boxed items in festive tissue paper, subtly labeled each one's color, and put them into a logo bag.

Marla took the package and thanked the woman, who turned to greet a new arrival. She was about to make her departure when Yolanda tapped her arm.

"Tell me, has any progress been made in finding Jason's killer?" Yolanda asked in an undertone so her voice wouldn't carry.

"That's another jurisdiction from my husband, so I wouldn't know."

"But he's in touch with their department, yes?" Yolanda brushed a stray lock of raven hair off her face. She wore her sleek hair in an attractive chignon.

"He doesn't share details of his cases with me."

"When did you say the photographer sent you this photo?"

"I didn't, but the time stamp put it before his murder."

Yolanda's face folded into a frown. "How peculiar. I cannot fathom what it might mean."

"Me, neither. That's what I'm trying to learn." Marla paused to retrieve the other picture. "Jason also sent me this one. I recognize Howard Cohn here but not the other man."

Yolanda squinted at the photo. "Sorry, darling, I can't help you there. He doesn't look at all familiar to me."

"Tell me more about Howard. You know these people from your society functions. What was his relationship to Val, aside from their association through FOFL?"

"He and I are not well acquainted. Isn't he the group's treasurer? Maybe their fathers knew each other. Both older men would have run in the same social circles."

"I understand her father's love of history rubbed off on Val. Is there any truth to those pirate tales he used to tell?"

"How should I know? Warren did well for himself, marrying into the Weston family. Theirs was a blessed union."

"Too bad Val's marriage didn't last."

"Look, I was grateful when Val invited me to participate at FOFL's annual ball, but I never pried into her affairs."

Marla shifted feet, tired of standing. But as long as the information mill was forthcoming, she wouldn't quit. "Did you know Val was an artist? I wonder if she exhibited her work."

"Sure she did." Yolanda jabbed a finger in the air. Her nails were painted blood red. "She'd get a booth every year at the Las Olas arts festival in exactly the same location. I could see her from inside my shop. She faced in this direction. From what I gathered, she did a decent trade in sales. People loved her watercolors of natural Florida."

"So she was positioned directly across from your place?" Did the event organizers assign locales, or had Val requested that spot? Marla would have to tell Dalton to check into this angle. Perhaps Val wished to keep an eye on Yolanda's establishment. But why? So she could note Henutt's comings and goings?

"Actually, it's not my shop that captured her interest," Yolanda said with an astute gleam in her eyes. "She had a contract with the gallery next door. They had exclusive rights to sell her work. She let slip once to me that she wasn't thrilled with the arrangement."

"Do you know those people?"

"Not really. They get a lot of tourist business. It's too bad they've lost one of their popular artists. I imagine Val's work has soared in price since she died."

Hmm, how much more would her paintings be worth with her dead? Watercolors weren't as valuable as oils, to Marla's meager knowledge. And paintings of nature scenes wouldn't be uncommon. But then, she knew little about the art world.

Yolanda poked her arm as another customer entered the shop. "I have to go. Thank you again for returning my precious crown."

"I'm glad I could help. Please keep me in mind for future events. I'd love to work with you on other projects."

Marla sauntered outdoors and into the gallery next door. A fortyish woman in a sweater and skirt ensemble bustled forward from a counter where she'd been wrapping a framed picture.

"May I help you?"

"I'm wondering if you have any work by Valerie Weston. I saw her paintings at the last arts festival and fell in love with them, but I didn't have enough money with me to buy anything."

"My name is Henrietta. This way, please. We have Val's works along this wall."

"I'm sorry for your loss. That must have been a blow for you. Had her style been popular?"

"Oh, yes. She had the perfect eye for detail. Visitors adore her watercolors."

"Are you the proprietor, Henrietta?"

"No, that would be Mr. Belorski. He's not in today."

Examining the display of Val's works, Marla had to admire them. They conveyed the tranquility of the Everglades, the fragility of the beach at sunrise, the majesty of a moss-draped live oak. "One of these would look great in my day spa," she said, handing over a business card. "Val was our customer when she had her unfortunate episode."

"That's terrible. I read about it in the papers. Such a tragedy."

"It's only fitting that I buy one of these to remember her by. How much is this one?" She pointed to a pleasing scene of a hammock surrounded by sawgrass and populated by birds.

Henrietta checked the tag. "That would be seven hundred and fifty dollars."

"Whoa, it costs that much?"

The saleswoman clucked her tongue. "I told you her works were popular."

"That's beyond my budget. But I am glad to see her work will find a home."

Marla followed the lady toward the exit. They passed a section depicting framed photographs. Some of those nature scenes were stunning in their reality. Maybe these were more affordable. She liked the portraits, too, wondering about the people this artist had captured.

Wait a minute. She halted abruptly to peer more closely at the photographer's name. A gasp of surprise escaped her lips. "What are these?"

"They're by an artist who's also recently deceased. Jason Faulks. Poor man. The fellow got stabbed at Yolanda Whipp's fashion show. She owns the shop next door, you know."

Marla's pulse accelerated. Here was a connection between the two victims. She had to tell Dalton.

"I've met Mr. Faulks. I didn't realize he had an artistic bent. I thought he did wedding and graduation photographs, that sort of thing."

Henrietta gave a snort of laughter. "Jason was an artist in his own right. Yes, he did take society photos to earn his bread, but he does . . . or he did . . . quite well with his work here."

"Who handled the contracts for Jason and Val? Was it you or your boss?"

"That would be Mr. Belorski." Her voice lowered. "You won't tell him we've been talking, will you? He urges us to have the utmost discretion about our artists. I probably shouldn't have told you so much about them."

"I'm grateful you did. Were you here the last time Val came into the gallery?"

Henrietta cast her gaze downward. "I can't say anymore. It

171

could cost me my job."

"Why should it? Any customer is going to want to learn about an artist."

"Val wouldn't have been with us for much longer. Oops, I shouldn't have said that." Henrietta clapped a hand to her mouth.

"What do you mean?" Had Val considered pulling her works from the store? And if so, for what reason?

"Please forget what I said. Good day to you, Mrs. Vail. Thank you for stopping by," Henrietta said by rote as she showed Marla to the door.

Feeling sure Henrietta had been on the verge of spilling the beans, Marla swallowed her disappointment and left. How much did the saleslady really know, anyway? If there were shady goings-on, would she shut up and put up to keep her job?

Someone ought to have a chat with Mr. Belorski. It couldn't be mere coincidence that two of his artists died within a short time of each other.

CHAPTER TWELVE

Christmas Eve loomed, and Marla didn't have time to ponder the meaning of her visits to the Las Olas shops. Dalton had promised to get off work early. They were invited over a friend's house along with Brianna that evening. Since it was still Hanukkah, she'd light the electric menorah but forgo the candles. It wouldn't be safe to leave them burning in her absence.

Focused on family, Marla pushed aside thoughts of a querulous nature while they enjoyed the party that night and prepared the following morning for company.

Brie rushed into the living room bright and early on Christmas Day, still in her pajamas and eager to open presents. Dalton had educated Marla on their traditions. She was happy to participate and give their lives meaning again. Holidays could be sad and lonely when you'd lost a loved one. Now theirs was joyous again, thanks to her. She glowed with warm satisfaction as she watched them tear into their gifts. Dalton grinned like a kid as he unwrapped the tablet computer she'd bought for him.

"I know you have a laptop, but this can be more convenient to carry around," she told him. "Now you and Brie will each have your own."

Marla hadn't been a technology fan until she'd received her first iPhone. Then Brie's grandparents gave her stepdaughter a tablet computer, and she'd seen what that device could do. Now Marla was a convert to the electronics age.

Dalton's gift to her was more traditional. Her jaw dropped as she opened the box in her hand. A diamond circle necklace sparkled in its embrace. "I love it," she said, taking it out and holding it up to the light.

"You've made our family whole again. A circle represents us, bound together for eternity." He came over and gave her a kiss before fastening the jewelry around her neck.

But that wasn't all. Brianna's present for her was a pair of white gold knot earrings that matched perfectly. Marla wasn't necessarily a jewelry person. She had a collection of costume trinkets that went with her outfits for work. Otherwise, she wore very little adornment except for earrings and her wedding ring. But she appreciated value nonetheless. She'd add these items to the few fine pieces Stan had given her. That had been one good thing about her ex; the attorney had good taste in his gifts for women.

They had a few presents each, having saved some from Hanukkah to open this morning. Dalton's other gift made her frown in puzzlement. "A slow cooker recipe book? Why this?"

"You can always use another cookbook. And I thought you might like this one. You can cook slowly on your days off, unlike those quick five-ingredient recipes."

She twisted her lips to smother her mirth. "My dearest, that's not what this means. I don't own a slow cooker. It's an electric type of pot that you plug in and let food simmer all day while you're at work."

His face flushed red. "Well, how would I know?"

"My mother has one. Would you mind if I rewrapped this and gave it to her?" Besides, she got most of her recipes off the Web now. They had enough books crowding their shelves.

Anita was thrilled with the gift and the others they gave her when the expanded family met to celebrate the combined holiday Marla called Christmakkah. She was relieved Ma had broken up with her boyfriend Roger. She couldn't stand the fellow with his huge appetite and boisterous manner. He had raised Ma's spirits, though. Anita seemed okay on her own but lacked a certain *joie de vivre* she'd had in his presence.

Her brother Michael had come down from Boca with his wife and kids. They mingled with Cousin Cynthia and her family while Marla chatted with Dalton's parents. Kate and John were busy decorating the condo they'd purchased in Delray Beach. Their house in Maine had yet to find a buyer, but in the meantime, they'd decided to become full-time Florida residents.

"I'm so happy to see the joy you've brought my son," Kate told her in an aside. "Now that you guys are settled, maybe you'll consider adding to the family. You're a great mother to Brianna. Isn't it time you thought about your future?"

Marla almost choked on her tongue. "Um, we're okay as we are. I have enough to do with my salon and all."

"You could cut back on your hours. You own the place, for heaven's sake."

"And that's exactly why I have to be there to supervise. Oh look, my cousin Julia is here. Please excuse me." She scurried away, her heart pounding. Likely Kate had put the bee in Dalton's bonnet about having more kids. Thankfully, he hadn't brought it up again.

Marla greeted the new arrivals with air-kisses and a warm welcome. She'd turned to go into the kitchen to check on the food when the phone rang. She dashed into the study to answer it and have a moment alone to regain her peace.

Dalton's cousin Wayne was calling from Arizona to wish them a Merry Christmas. Before she went to summon her husband, she glanced at their desktop. Yesterday's mail sat there untouched. She'd forgotten to open it in her rush to get everything ready for today. One return address stood out. She recognized her insurance company's name.

After handing the mobile receiver to Dalton, she returned to open the envelope. As she scanned the contents, she stretched her mouth in a smile.

"Good news," she said when she'd rejoined their company and Dalton had hung up. She waved the paper in her hand. "Amber Connors dropped her lawsuit against me in the spirit of Christmas, or so my agent says. He believes she realized her case didn't hold water."

"That's wonderful," Dalton replied with a broad grin. "I'm glad it's over. That should ease your mind."

"Tell us about your case concerning the woman who died in your day spa," Cousin Cynthia urged as they sat around the dinner table.

Marla had served the food buffet style. Her various relatives had contributed to the meal so she didn't have to make everything. She'd hoped to avoid talk of work but now that the topic had been introduced, everyone peered at her and Dalton with curiosity.

The dogs barked in the backyard as a pregnant silence fell over the assembled guests. She would let the pets in later, after she'd put the food away. Since Spooks had once eaten half the broccoli cheese casserole she'd made for Rosh Hashanah, she wouldn't let the animals anywhere near the kitchen when unattended.

Dalton cleared his throat. "We have a lot of leads. We're still working on it."

"Oh, I have news that I totally forgot to tell you," Marla said. "Yesterday, I visited Yolanda's boutique after I went to see Carla Jean." And she related most, but not all, of what she'd learned from her conversations with the Luxor sales rep, Yolanda at her store, and the clerk at the art gallery next door. "Keep this quiet, okay?" she warned her relatives. "Dalton's case is still open, and so is Jason's murder."

"Hey, Marla. Did you say you're giving up the educator position?" Brie spoke from where she sat wedged between her paternal grandparents. "I hope you're not changing your mind because of me and Dad. We wouldn't want to hold you back."

Marla's eyes misted. "It's not that, honey, but you're a sweetheart for thinking that way. I've decided I don't want to be away from home, even for short trips, without you or your dad being with me. And I don't really need that type of career change."

"No, what you could use is another sort of focus," her mother mumbled. Anita and Kate exchanged a knowing glance across the table.

Marla's lips firmed. This type of pressure was exactly what she did not need. "Let's get back to the point of what I was saying. Carla Jean confessed to having stolen the headpiece to sell to a hair accessory company. They turned on her, afraid that Henutt's Chinese associates might not appreciate the theft. So Carla Jean was stuck with the goods."

"And you gave her a viable alternative. Good thinking; I'm proud of you." Dalton beamed at her, and then his face sobered. "I'll talk to the property unit and make sure they list the missing item as recovered."

"Don't mention any names, please. That goes for all of you. I promised Carla Jean her role would remain confidential, aside from sharing her info with Dalton."

Brianna's eyes radiated enthusiasm. "So you returned the headpiece to Yolanda. And then what? She mentioned the gallery next door?"

The kid was too enthralled by their cases, Marla thought. They needed to steer her attention to soccer, the acting classes that she took now instead of dance, and her driving lessons.

Or not. Pretty soon she'd qualify for her driving test and then Dalton would go ballistic.

"I gave Yolanda the headpiece in return for information about the man in the photo with Henutt. She said he's a funeral director from Parkland and his name is Gabriel Stone. Dalton, you'll follow up on that lead, won't you? Why would Jason take that particular photo unless it meant something?"

He speared her with an intense gaze. "We have yet to learn the answer to that question. You said you'd showed Yolanda the other picture."

"Yes, that's the one with Howard Cohn. He's the treasurer for FOFL," she told her relatives. "Yolanda didn't recognize the other guy in the picture. We got to talking about Val, and I mentioned how she was an artist. You heard the rest."

"Isn't it odd that Ms. Weston would get a booth at the arts fair every year facing Yolanda's boutique?" Cousin Cynthia inserted. She'd taken an interest in Marla's crime solving ever since a saboteur had tried to derail Taste of the World one year. As that event was Ocean Guard's annual fundraiser—Cynthia's pet charity—she had sought Marla's help. They'd made a good team in catching the miscreants involved.

"I'm not sure Val wanted to keep an eye on the dress designer. She exhibited her paintings next door at the art gallery. Maybe she was watching that place, instead. She wasn't happy with them for some reason."

Dalton shifted his position. "I find it interesting that Jason Faulks had his pictures for sale at the same establishment. This has to be more than a coincidence. You did good work, Marla."

A warm glow spread through her at his praise. "Thanks. I hope you'll share what you find out about them." Doubtless he'd want to pay a visit to the art gallery himself.

"All right, people. Enough shop talk." Anita rapped a spoon on her water glass. "Let's hear what the children have been doing lately."

The conversation drew on into the evening until everyone finally took their leave. Marla rinsed the dishes and loaded the dishwasher while Brianna helped clear the table. Dalton dried the more fragile serving pieces. They finished dissecting their views of various family members until done. With a sigh of exhaustion, Marla removed her apron and hung it on a hook by the inner garage door.

Dalton embraced her for a long kiss. "Thank you for being a wonderful hostess, mother, and wife," he murmured, nuzzling her ear.

Relishing his strong arms around her, she planted another kiss on his lips. "And thank you for being a wonderful husband. I love how our combined families can get together now."

"Too bad my Arizona contingent can't be here. Speaking of family history, I'd like to take a look at that journal. I haven't had a chance to read it before now." He glanced at the clock. "It's only eight."

"What, no football on TV tonight?"

"Oh yeah, let me see what shows are on." His eager expression made her smile as he headed into the family room.

Shaking her head over the male predilection for the TV remote, she aimed for the bedroom and a well-deserved rest. Maybe she'd curl up with Warren's journal herself. Things had been too hectic for her to concentrate on it lately, and soon New Year's would be here.

She bit her lower lip as she changed into her nightwear. Normally, they made plans with Tally and Ken for New Year's Eve, but her friend hadn't said a word about it. Marla had invited the couple for the next day instead, but even then, Tally said they couldn't come. It was possible they didn't want to go out because of the baby, but wouldn't Tally have said so? Her silence on the subject puzzled Marla.

Not wanting to get a babysitter for their child was an excuse she could understand. That's probably it, she determined. Tally could at least have given her the courtesy of telling the truth, though. As a new mother, she shouldn't feel ashamed of being tied down.

After removing her makeup and saying goodnight to Brianna, Marla curled up in bed with the copied journal in her lap. She smoothed a hand reverently over the top page. Here was a valuable piece of Val's history. Too bad she didn't have any children to inherit it.

Marla read about the three men's explorations along the beach where they'd discovered the log cabin. They made camp there for the first night and were awakened early the next morning by a rap on the door. Two uniformed men questioned their presence and gave the order for their eviction.

Determined to track down the owner and get permission to remain, they headed into town. It appeared the city owned the property. Warren visited the proper department and obtained a conditional promise to use the cabin. But he had to obtain the approval of the troop scoutmaster for which it had been erected. Once this was done, the boys settled into their new lodgings.

Before nightfall, we had put our house in fair order. With the aid of a saw, hammer, and nails we'd had the foresight to obtain, Ralph and I utilized pieces of logs and lumber we found in the vicinity to construct frameworks for three cots. Across these we stretched the pieces of canvas we'd bought in town for that purpose. George had also been busy. He made an attractive kitchen nook in one corner and artfully decorated it with a cook stove, a miscellaneous assortment of pots and pans, and a good supply of canned goods.

We had done a fair day's work and went to sleep on our comfortable cots for a well-earned rest. This night, however, was not meant to be an uneventful one.

Shortly after we extinguished our light, I heard the patter of little feet over the cement floor. Bags and papers that we had left there rustled as rodents searched for food. One of the disturbing pests got into a large tin can we were using for refuse and started a tap dance, or so it sounded. But we were tired and did not stay awake for long.

I awakened suddenly around midnight. When I heard something being dragged along the floor, I realized it must have been the noise of our trap being sprung that had interrupted my sleep. I stopped the snores emanating from George's direction by jabbing my fingers into his ribs. He was very much disgruntled when I called his attention to the disturbance and asked his opinion regarding its source.

He told me to stop annoying him with nonsensical matters. If I wanted to investigate, I could take his searchlight. His suggestion met with my agreement.

So I climbed out of bed, gingerly placed my stockinged feet upon the cold cement, and illuminated the floor in front of me. Cautiously, I inched toward the disturbance. One glance at our prisoner, and I gave a yelp of surprise. It was a furry, white-striped animal. I immediately knew its presence called for an expeditious departure from the premises.

Marla's lips curved in mirth. She could imagine their distress at finding a skunk in their company. If it were her, she'd make a hasty departure as well. Her eyelids were growing heavy but she read on.

I shot out of the cabin like a bullet out of a gun. George and Ralph nearly fell over me in their anxiety to escape the offensive odor beginning to pollute the air. Before we reached the car, our feet were full of painful burrs. We hated that skunk more than ever for having caused such discomfort. As we piled into the car, it became evident none of us would get much sleep that night.

However, it was not George's nature to sit helplessly by and be denied his due rest. He meant to remedy the situation.

He found an old sack nearby. Gripping it, he approached the cabin with Ralph and me trailing him, but not too closely. We all held our noses as we drew near the scene of our hasty exit. Ordering one of us to dig a deep hole, Ralph grasped his nose tighter and dashed into the cabin. I scooted away, having appointed myself the official grave digger.

Because George had retained the searchlight, I stumbled over ridges of sand and into numerous depressions as I hurried through the moonlit night to finish my job before the undertaker approached with his nauseating burden. I literally made the sand fly after I reached a sufficient distance from our home. But then my shovel hit something solid. Curious, I dug around the edge. In the faint light from the moon, it appeared to be a wooden chest.

"Dalton, listen to this," Marla said when he entered the room. And she related the gist of the passages she'd just read.

"Sweet. What happens next?" He unbuttoned his shirt, momentarily distracting her with his admirable physique.

She glanced down. "I want to read more, but I'm getting tired."

"Just read enough to see what's in that chest." With those parting words, he disappeared into the bathroom.

Marla's eyes grew round as she read on. "No way! They found treasure at the end of the proverbial rainbow. The chest was filled with gold coins."

Dalton reappeared, toothbrush poised in his mouth. "What?"

"They figured it must have been cargo from a wrecked Spanish ship, or perhaps one that pirates had plundered. Maybe this is where Warren got his wealth, instead of living off his wife's fortune as everyone believed." Had Val read this story and realized what her dad had discovered? Had the boys found more loot and left a map to their buried stash?

"You could be right. We should look into wrecks in this area." Dalton headed into the bathroom to complete his bedtime rituals. When he returned to crawl under the comforter, he gave her his special smile. "Why don't you put aside the journal for now? I have something else in mind to do." His fingers tickled her arm.

She put the book on the nightstand and turned toward him. The rest of Warren's tale could wait. Whatever had happened to him was over and done. The present had priority, and so did showing her husband how she felt about him.

Wednesday morning, Marla was midway through her initial rush of clients at work when she got a text message from Dalton to call him. As soon as she had a moment alone, she followed through. "Hey, what's up?" She stood outside facing the parking lot and breathed in the crisp December air.

"I have bad news," his somber voice said. "Nadia Welsh has been found dead."

"No, I don't believe it." She walked over to a nearby bench and sank onto the seat.

"A car hit her while she was out for her morning jog. The driver didn't stop. A pedestrian saw the accident and called for help."

"That's awful. Poor Nadia. What a terrible way to go."

"She had a note in her pocket to call you and a message with a letter missing. Looks like P-I-blank-A-T-E-S. Does that make sense to you?"

Marla, still in shock, couldn't think straight. It took a few minutes for her brain to register what else he'd said beyond Nadia being dead. "Could it mean Pilates? It sounds as though she worked out to keep fit. Maybe she took a class or belonged to a sports club."

"I'll need you to tell me everything you know about her and what she'd said to you."

"Nadia claimed she and Val knew each other's secrets. Do you think that's why she was killed? The murderer figured she might know something about him?"

"This could have been a hit-and-run accident. There's no evidence it was intentional."

"I'm sorry. You're saying she was mowed down in broad daylight, the driver didn't stop, and it could have been an accidental oversight?"

"The person driving could have been texting. His moment of inattention could have caused a death. It's happened. He got spooked and ran. The crime tech boys should be able to tell the make and model of the car, so that will help us track down the guilty party."

"Meanwhile, you might want to see if Nadia took Pilates classes. Let me know what you learn." She rang off, distressed by this horrible news. Moisture filled her eyes. How many more people would die before this case got solved?

Why Nadia, and not her? The bad guy knew she had the journal. Was he keeping hands off because she was a cop's wife?

He'd hired Patty to do his nasty work before. Perhaps he didn't care to get his own hands dirty. Actually, that wasn't true. He might be the one who'd stabbed Jason at the gala. But that had been a crime of opportunity. Nonetheless, she should still watch her back.

Her thoughts wandered to Friends of Old Florida. That group was involved in this somehow.

Hey, wait a minute. Hadn't Howard Cohn mentioned he researched shipwrecks for a hobby? She should talk to him about wrecks off the coast of Fort Lauderdale. And there was also the issue of his resemblance to the guy in the journal, not to mention Jason's photo. It all tied together, even though she couldn't make sense of it.

Kat Minnetti gave her another piece of the puzzle when she strolled into the salon later that afternoon. The detective wore a sleeveless navy dress, her layered black hair stylishly arranged. She pursed her lips upon spying Marla at her station.

"Have you got a minute?" Kat said after they'd exchanged pleasantries.

"Sure, what's up?" Marla couldn't warm to her, feeling Kat wasn't totally open about herself. But Dalton trusted her, and so Marla did as well. Still, she'd rather his partner was more forthcoming. Remembering her intent to give Kat a gift certificate for the holidays, she set herself a mental reminder to mail it along with a greeting card.

She led the lady detective toward the rear where the storeroom was empty of personnel for the moment. Marla leaned against a counter while Kat paced back and forth.

"You were right about Nadia belonging to a health club. She was a member of KB Fitness over on Nob Hill Road."

Marla was happy one hunch had been correct. "So did you talk to them?"

"I haven't had a chance to go over there yet. Dalton wanted you to know."

"Thanks for relaying the information. Good call on tracking down Patty, by the way. It's too bad you couldn't trace her contact, though."

Kat's mouth tightened. "At least we know how the liquid latex got into the victim's face cream."

"And Patty was responsible for changing Val's appointment time. But you were wrong about Rosana's immigration status." Marla tried to keep the chastisement from her tone. "She'd married an American and had the proper documents. Dalton verified it. Rosana feels bad enough about what happened. I wouldn't want her to quit because her credentials are in doubt. She's had enough of a drop in her clientele list after this affair."

"Well, she's not to blame. Patty's confession proved that much."

But you were hasty in jumping to conclusions, Marla wanted to add but didn't. "So is that all you came to tell me? That Nadia belonged to a health club?"

"The crime scene techs are still working the scene. I went to her house. According to neighbors, she lived alone. Were you aware of her personal situation?"

"Not really. She was a friend of Val's. I'm not her stylist, so I didn't know much about her."

Kat stopped and pierced her with a stare. "Didn't you wonder why Val left instructions for the housekeeper to send Nadia the journal instead of the trustee to her estate?"

"Did you finally track him down?"

"Your husband must have forgotten to tell you. The trustee is Howard Cohn, treasurer for Friends of Old Florida."

CHAPTER THIRTEEN

Marla couldn't fathom this news. So Howard Cohn was Val's trustee. He was the man she'd regarded as an uncle but had come to distrust for some reason. And Howard was a banker. His establishment was likely where she had her accounts.

Marla mused over this development after Kat departed and while she worked on her afternoon customers. She considered the resemblance between Howard and one of Warren's friends in the journal. What if the older fellow was Howard's dad?

They could find out easily enough if his name was George or Ralph. She texted Dalton to ask him. Her pulse accelerated. They could be on to something. If Howard's father was involved with Warren, their discovery in the past might have led to Val's death in the present. Was it the cache of gold? But why would anyone kill Val over that issue today? The buried treasure would have been divided among the three guys long ago, unless they'd left a stash for pickup later.

Then again, if Val and Howard's fathers had been friends, this could explain how Val chose Howard to be her trustee. She'd regarded him as an uncle. Now that statement made sense. So why had she begun to disapprove of him? Could it relate to this journal that Val had found among Warren's possessions?

She sniffed burning hair and hastily moved the curling iron she was using on a client's head. *Pay attention, Marla. You already have a job. Let Dalton do the investigating.*

187

But if Howard was involved, that didn't explain Henutt's photo that Jason had sent, or Jason's connection to Val through the art gallery. The roles of the FOFL board members still had to be determined as well as the developer's interest in getting Val off his back. And what about Lora Larue's relationship to the hotel manager?

This last one was easy to check on. She'd seen Biggs Kahuna give Lora a room key and had assumed he'd merely saved her time checking in. But had she been a registered guest?

Thursday morning, Marla paid a visit to the resort while she had the morning free. She didn't have to be into work until one. Slipping the reception clerk at the front desk a twenty-dollar bill, she smiled sweetly at him. His name, according to his I.D. tag, was Hugh.

"Can you tell me if a certain guest was registered here on Saturday, December fifteenth? We met at the ball for Friends of Old Florida. I don't need her contact info or anything, but I'd like to know if she stayed here overnight."

The clerk gave a furtive glance at his colleagues before bending over his computer keys. "Let me take a look. What's her name?"

"Lora Larue." She spelled it out.

"I'm sorry. I don't see anyone with that name listed here for that date."

"Could she have registered under another name perhaps?"

"I would have no idea, miss. I don't see anyone by the name of Lora with a different spelling, either."

Marla lowered her voice and leaned inward. "I saw Mr. Kahuna hand her a room key. I'd assumed he was saving her the trouble of checking in at the front desk."

The man's face reddened. "Oh. Well, that's a different story. She wouldn't have checked in, ma'am. I really can't say anything more."

She stared at him for a long, hard moment. "I get it. Thanks for your help, Hugh. This has been illuminating."

Stepping outside, she squinted in the bright morning sunshine. So Lora Larue and Biggs Kahuna had some hanky-panky going on. Had Val detected their relationship and threatened to expose them?

Someone, and she couldn't remember who, had mentioned that Lora might be more concerned about her trips being curtailed. Did Lora have the same arrangement for accommodations at the other hotels where she stayed? She could save money that way. Or not, since the organization that sent her as field liaison probably paid for her trips.

Returning to her car, Marla considered her next move. She should go home and work on bookkeeping but couldn't let this case rest. She wanted to help Dalton wrap things up so he could enjoy New Year's without any burdens.

So she drove to KB Fitness on Nob Hill Road. Doubtless Kat had been there already, questioning the personnel and members, but maybe Marla could learn something new. A short while later, she approached the front doors.

"Are you a cop?" the lithe blonde who greeted her said from behind a reception counter, after Marla asked about Nadia Welsh.

"No, I'm not. You've probably been talking to a lot of people today about Nadia. I was a friend of hers, and we were mutual friends with Valerie Weston. I don't suppose Val ever came in here?" She glanced at a workout room filled with gleaming machines and sweating patrons going through their paces. Lively music played on a soundtrack, competing with the splash of water from somewhere beyond. Her nose sniffed a faint eucalyptus scent.

"You're not the only one who's mentioned her recently. Val's death shook everyone up. I can't say that I knew her on a personal basis, though."

"People here were acquainted with her?"

"Yes, she was a friendly sort. I believe Ms. Weston supported some historical group."

"Friends of Old Florida."

"Right. This other lady from their organization hits us up every year for gift certificates. They do raffles at their spring tea party." She scrolled through a file on her computer. "Here she is. Lora Larue."

Marla raised her eyebrows. "Lora? Is she a member here?"

"Yep, although she doesn't come in very often. Lora said she travels a lot for business. That must be cool. I'm stuck in this same spot day after day."

"Would you know if she and Nadia took a Pilates class together?" Marla wondered if Kat had learned about their connection at the sports club.

"You'll have to ask the instructor." The blonde checked their daily schedule. "Sandy has a session finishing in ten minutes. Go past the machines, and you'll find the workout room back there." The receptionist smiled as a couple of young women approached. "Hello, how may I help you?" At their inquiry, she directed them to the membership office.

"I should let you get back to work," Marla said with a wave. "Thanks for your time."

Sandy was a tanned woman with a pert expression and a lean form who wore her auburn hair in a high ponytail. Marla hated athletic instructors. They always made her feel like a slouch.

"Hi, I'm Marla Vail, a friend of Nadia's," she said to introduce herself. The rest of the class had dispersed, leaving her alone with the Pilates instructor.

Sandy's face sobered. "I heard about her death. A detective came here and questioned us. It's a terrible tragedy. Imagine going for your morning run and being hit by a reckless driver. I hope they catch the guy."

"Me, too. Tell me, did Nadia appear worried about anything the last time she was here?"

"She'd been upset after that other lady died. They'd been together for a few years."

"Which other lady?" Did she mean Val, or was she referring to Lora?

"You know, her girlfriend." Sandy's eyes narrowed. "Were you *that way* with Nadia?" Her glance fell to Marla's wedding ring. "Oh, I guess not. Maybe you don't know."

Marla's blood ran hot and cold. "Hold on. Are you saying Nadia was gay?"

"You couldn't have been a good friend if you weren't aware of her nature."

"I'm sorry, but which girlfriend do you mean? Lora Larue? Or their mutual friend, Valerie Weston?"

"Why *are* you asking these questions, Mrs. Vail?"

"I'm married to the detective on the case. You might have met his partner, Katherine Minnetti. I'm involved because Val died at my workplace. I own a hair salon and day spa."

"I see. And you're doing police work now?"

"No, I need answers for myself. If it's relevant to the case, I'll tell my husband. So who was Nadia's significant other? I presume that's what you mean."

"Why, Val of course. They kept things discreet so as not to ruin Val's reputation, but Lora knew about them. She and Nadia were both in my class. The last time I saw them together, Lora said something to Nadia that made her storm out in tears."

Marla pondered this for a moment. "Could Lora have been jealous? Was she that way, too?"

Sandy erupted in laughter at her suggestion. "Not her. You really don't know beans about these people, do you?"

"So why don't you enlighten me?" Marla pressed her lips

together, annoyed that she had to pry the answers from Sandy. But she was more annoyed with herself that she hadn't detected this trait in Val earlier. Why had the housekeeper mentioned nothing about Val's persuasion? Was it because she didn't know?

Sandy packed up the last of her belongings. "These tales aren't mine to tell, but I have a suggestion. You could sign up for my class and catch Lora then. Or are you two already acquainted?"

"Yes, we are. Lora hired my salon staff to work Yolanda Whipp's fashion show at FOFL's annual ball."

She pictured the plump woman in the Pilates class. It wasn't a pretty image but at least Lora tried to keep in shape, however infrequently. Another visit with the FOFL board member was in order.

After taking her leave from Sandy and heading toward her car, Marla considered whether she should drive to the police station to tell Dalton her latest news, or save it until later. She hated to disturb him at work. Instead, she texted him the following message:

Did you know Nadia was gay? I learned it from her Pilates instructor. It appears Nadia and Val were an item, and Lora Larue knew about them. Lora and Nadia were in the same Pilates class.

There, that should keep him busy. An urge to discuss the case with Tally hit her. Her friend had always proven a wise sounding board whose perspective brought Marla fresh insights.

She also yearned to see Luke. The thought of holding his soft body and smelling his sweet baby scent drew her in their direction. Maybe Tally had been a bit curt the last time they'd spoken because she was feeling shut in. A new mother could feel deprived of adult company. Marla should make it a point to call more often.

"Sure, Marla, I'm home," Tally said when she phoned. "Would you mind picking up some diapers on your way? I've been stuck here and haven't gotten out, and Ken is staying late at work again."

"Okay." Marla got instructions as to what brand to buy. She intended to question Tally about Ken's movements to ensure he was paying proper attention to his family. He'd hear from her if he wasn't. Her fierce protective nature extended to her friends.

Her resolve weakened when Tally dumped Luke in her arms so she could put away the diapers and the cute outfit Marla couldn't resist buying while in the baby store. She couldn't believe how costly some of the things were in there. Was Ken feeling the financial pinch from having a child? Or was his interest diverted elsewhere for reasons she already suspected?

Marla kissed Luke on the forehead, holding his softness close. He made smacking sounds with his lips, scrunching his eyes as she peered down at him. His facial expressions were fascinating to watch. Swaddled in a blanket, he squirmed as though eager to break free. Tally would have her hands full whenever he started to crawl. When did that happen? She knew practically nothing about a child's stages of development. If she was to be a proper godmother, perhaps she should buy a book on the topic. Or she could just ask her friend.

"Here, I'll sit him in his stroller so you can be free. I've made some coffee." Tally led her into the kitchen that had various dishes lying on the counter. They were clean but not put away.

"So how are things?" Marla settled at the kitchen table, her gaze drawn to Luke kicking his legs, strapped into the stroller that likely cost a few hundred bucks. She didn't envy Tally all the gear she had to pack whenever she and Luke went out anywhere. That part would be a pain.

Tally, busy pouring them both mugs of coffee, didn't look her way. "Things are fine. You needn't worry about us."

Marla detected the raised pitch in her tone. "By the way, how is Ken's gemstone mine doing? Did you ever ask him about it after our last talk?"

"Yes, I did." Tally brought the cups over, plopped them down, then took a seat opposite Marla. She brushed a hand through her wavy blonde hair. "He sold his share. The mine was becoming less profitable, so it made sense. He's invested the money wisely this time, and his insurance firm is doing well."

So what's wrong? Marla wanted to ask. "Does he help you with Luke's care, or is he too busy at work?"

"Ken does what he can. Where are you going with this, Marla? Don't you have enough on your own mind?"

"I'm just concerned, that's all. I want the best for you. You know that."

"I do, and I appreciate it, but maybe this time you should stick to your own affairs."

Rebuffed, Marla fell silent. Tally had never snapped at her like that before. "So is Luke rolling over on his own?" she asked shortly, switching to a safer topic.

Tally's mouth, which had pinched during their conversation, eased into a smile. "He is, and I'm hoping he'll be able to sit soon. That will make going to the grocery store a lot easier."

"His head is still wobbly."

"I know. He's the dearest thing to me, Marla. And I know you love him, too. Promise me you'll take care of him if anything happens to us."

"Of course I will. But why are you even thinking like that?" *What the hell are you not telling me?*

"All parents worry about these things. How about you and Dalton? Any thoughts about having one of your own now that you are married again?"

Not you, too! "Heck, no. We have enough anxiety about Brianna driving."

"Tell me about the woman who died in your day spa. Any progress on the case?" Tally stuck a pacifier in Luke's mouth when he started fussing. He made loud sucking noises but seemed happy.

Marla marveled at his tiny hands and had an irresistible urge to kiss his fingers. What was it about babies that made you want to cuddle them?

Not all parents felt that same instinct. Some of them murdered their kids. She couldn't fathom the darkness in their souls.

"Val's friend Nadia was killed by a hit-and-run driver," she replied. "I wonder if it's because someone feared Val had confided in her. Or else it was because of the journal." She explained the latest findings to Tally.

"So Nadia belonged to the same gym as Lora Larue?"

"That's correct. She must have been meaning to tell me this when she wrote 'Pilates.' "

"For what reason? To point the finger at Lora in Val's death?"

"It's a possibility. But the gym instructor brought up a new angle. Val and Nadia were more than friends."

"Yes, I got that. Do you think this is why Val never remarried?"

Marla gave a firm nod. "It could be why she divorced her husband in the first place."

"And Lora knew about it but has said nothing to the police."

Marla sat forward as a thought occurred to her. "Lora belongs to that sports club, which might have other branches. I wonder if she visits their facilities when she travels to different cities, assuming they offer reciprocal membership."

Tally's gaze brightened. "Maybe Val knew what she did on those trips, if it wasn't all related to the organization's business. And since Lora knew Val's secret, Val had to keep quiet or risk exposure. Even with today's liberal views, people still care about such things."

"And Nadia had honored her bond of silence until now."

Marla sipped her coffee while mulling over the implications. "First Val is killed, then Jason, and now Nadia. I still can't see how it all ties together."

Tally got up, walked to the pantry, withdrew a box of cookies, and brought them to the table. "Here, I forgot to offer you something to eat."

Marla helped herself to a chocolate chip cookie while Tally peeked at Luke. He'd fallen asleep in the stroller. Perhaps he found their voices to be soothing.

"Let's start at the beginning," Tally said, retaking her seat. "Give me a rundown of what you've learned so far."

Grateful to have Tally's attention and mindful that it was a diversion from whatever bothered her friend, Marla put forth her theories. "Somebody hired our shampoo girl, Patty, to add liquid latex to the face cream Rosana used on Val. She'd accessed Rosana's records to see which jar to taint and also changed Val's appointment to first thing in the morning."

"How did Patty get hold of this substance?"

"Anyone can buy it on the Internet. Makeup artists use liquid latex in the entertainment industry for special effects. Patty could have been instructed on where to order it, or the killer could have provided it for her." Kat hadn't revealed to Marla how the girl had obtained the item. Hopefully, the detective had already thought to trace the source.

"What about that makeup lady at the fashion show?" Tally asked. "She'd be the most likely person to know about this stuff."

"Her name is Joyce Underwood. She was quite open about her resentment of Val, which dates back to their high school days when Val stole her boyfriend. But that was years ago, and Joyce would have nothing to gain by killing Val now." Or so Joyce had implied. But she was present at the scene of Jason's murder. Had Dalton or the other detectives determined when

Joyce had left the hotel in comparison to the time of death?

Tally frowned at a chipped fingernail. "What about the models at the show? Any of them moonlight in the acting biz?"

Marla felt a stab of sympathy for her friend. Gone were Tally's days of manicures and massages. For a birthday present, Marla should consider giving her a gift certificate to their spa services along with an offer to babysit.

"Joyce did point me in the direction of Ashley Hunt, the headliner model at the show. I spotted Ashley with Dr. Ian Needles, another board member. It appeared as if they were well acquainted. Ashley came to me later and confessed they'd been seeing each other. The doctor had dumped her, and she wanted to get even. She said I should tell Dalton that the doctor freely prescribed pain meds for his patients."

"How would she know?"

"She'd gone to him for a cosmetic procedure and mentioned a recent back injury. He offered to treat her with a prescription. If Ian was our killer, I think he'd have murdered her and not Jason. It doesn't make sense for either of them to be involved."

"Anybody else on your list have acting aspirations?"

"Not that I know, but it's a good point. We haven't looked into that angle."

"Okay, let's go back to Val. She had two passions: painting and historic buildings."

"Hence her support of FOFL, which she might have been about to withdraw. We've been down that path. Loss of her funding would affect several people. Lora's trips might be curtailed. The fashion show might not take place without another underwriter. And the group's finances would suffer."

"No problems there, I take it?"

"Howard Cohn is treasurer. I assume his bank is where Val has her accounts, as he's trustee of her estate. Howard is related to one of the men in her father's journal."

"That's a significant lead. But concerning Howard's role as the group's treasurer, has Dalton examined their ledgers?"

"He hasn't mentioned any irregularities, except the FOFL secretary might be inflating the catering bill from their annual ball and pocketing the difference from the actual expenses."

"That would give this woman a motive if Val noticed the discrepancy."

"Solomon Gold, the president, is another contender. He favors bids from companies for restoration work that help him in return with his personal remodeling projects."

Tally tapped her finger on the table. "Who else from this group has something to hide?"

"Andrew Fine, their publicist, has been slanting articles in favor of Rick Rodriguez, the developer. Rick wants to convert a strip of historic buildings on Hollywood Beach into condo towers. Val was fighting him on the group's behalf."

"So Rodriguez is another person of interest. What happens to his project with Val out of the way?"

Marla shrugged. "I haven't heard any more about it. I'll ask Dalton."

"Those are Val's business relations. What about her personal life? Is there anybody among her household staff, friends, or family who might have wanted her out of the way?"

"Sean, the brother-in-law, felt his wife should have inherited more of her parents' estate. I'm not sure why they left the house and the bulk of their fortune to Val. Either they didn't trust Cathy's husband, or Val had a more stable personality."

"Was Sean hoping Cathy would inherit everything from Val and regain her rightful inheritance that way?"

"Cathy was already dead when Val was killed. I believe the sister's portion will pass to her kids, not the husband, so I don't see Sean as a murderer. Anyway, he knew Val meant to leave a bequest to Friends of Old Florida."

"You said Val and Jason had a connection through the art gallery. Val's other passion was her painting. Could anything skanky be going on at that place?"

Restless, Marla stood and paced, careful not to disturb the sleeping baby. "But then, how would Nadia be connected, unless the killer feared Val had told her what she knew?"

"Maybe Val put her paintings in that particular store so she could keep an eye on Yolanda's shop next door." Tally reached for a cookie, but Marla also noticed her furtive glance at the clock.

"I showed Yolanda the photo of Henutt and the other guy Jason had sent me. She said he was a funeral director."

"Has Dalton interviewed him?"

"I'm not sure if he's gotten there yet. But how could this guy be involved?"

"Jason sent you their picture for a reason."

"I know. Maybe he was only guessing who might be involved in Val's murder, if that had been his purpose in sending me the photos. For whatever reason, Jason got himself killed." Marla paused. "I should go talk to the funeral director on my own."

"Don't forget to investigate Lora Larue," Tally advised her. "Lora knew both Val and Nadia, and perhaps Jason as well. Who hired him? Was he there for Yolanda's benefit or the organization's publicity?"

"He told me Yolanda had hired him. But that's enough for now. Thanks so much for letting me vent. This has helped immensely."

Tally stood and brushed off her pants. "If you don't mind, I'd like to lie down while Luke is snoozing. His nap won't last long."

"Of course, I'm sorry to keep you." Marla grabbed her purse and gave her a hug. "Are you sure there isn't anything I can do for you while I'm here?"

"You've already cheered me up. We'll talk again soon. Bye, Marla." Tally walked her to the door, where Marla took her leave.

Her body felt lighter as she strolled to her car, her burdens somehow relieved. It had helped to discuss things with Tally as always. She only wished she knew what was going on in their household.

Meanwhile, she absorbed her surroundings. The December air smelled of wood smoke. Somebody must have a fire going in a fireplace nearby. Christmas lights decorated many of the houses in Tally's development. And flowers bloomed, a winter sight she never failed to appreciate. She buttoned her sweater, feeling she'd need a jacket by the evening.

So what conclusions did she come away with? On the drive to work, Marla reviewed the points in her mind. Did any of these people moonlight as actors? What was the relationship of the funeral director to Henutt? Was anything crooked going on at the art gallery? What did Lora do on her business trips? Could she be trading favors with other hotel managers for free hotel stays?

One item they hadn't discussed was Warren's journal. Val and then Nadia had possessed the book. Now both of them were dead. How could Jason be involved?

Maybe he'd been digging into Val's past and came across an article relating to her father's trip. A news piece about Warren might mention Howard's father as well, if the two men were connected as Marla surmised.

Excited by this possibility, she added another item to her mental list. They needed to track down newspapers from that time period. Jason's demise could be the key to unlocking the puzzle.

CHAPTER FOURTEEN

Marla's mother called before she reached the salon. "Have you eaten lunch yet?" Anita said, her voice filling the space via wireless connection.

"I'm driving to work, Ma."

"So? You don't have to be there until one. Do you have time to stop for a bite to eat?"

"Only if it's fast." Marla glanced at the clock. It wasn't quite noon yet. She'd planned to grab a sandwich at Arnie's place but could make a detour. "I'll meet you at the diner."

"Good, I'm ten minutes away. See you soon."

Wondering what Ma had on her mind when they'd just seen each other two days ago, Marla headed east on Broward Boulevard. The parking lot by the restaurant was crammed, so she got a space nearer to Publix. By the time she'd walked the few paces toward the corner eatery, Anita was waiting for her by the front door.

"So what's up, Ma?" Marla said after the hostess had seated them and the waitress took their orders. She examined the interior, crowded with patrons. With its varied menu and reasonable prices, the place was always busy.

"We didn't have much chance for a private chat at Christmas. It's so odd to see a tree in your house, but that's the way of things these days."

"We're an interfaith family now. Get used to it." Her skilled eye took in Anita's short white hair, red painted fingernails, and

201

stylish pants set. Ma looked well, so surely she didn't have some dire ailment to report. What else could be on her mind?

"The dinner conversation devolved to crime solving again," her mother remarked. "When are you going to stop chasing criminals and do your duty to the family?"

Marla took a sip of water. "What do you mean?"

"Are you and Dalton planning to have a baby?"

Marla coughed, spewing water droplets. She grabbed a napkin. When she'd recovered, she regarded her mother with a disgusted glance. "Is that what you wanted to talk to me about? You know how I feel about having children."

"Yes, but you've been married a year now and you're not getting any younger. If you change your mind later, you'll run into complications."

"It's my choice, Ma. Besides, you already have grand-children." Thank goodness her brother had fulfilled that obligation.

"That's not the point. You're dissatisfied with the salon business as your sole focus. So be a mensch and have a kid. If you're worried about your mothering abilities, you'll do fine. You've proven it with Brianna. She's turning into a lovely young lady."

Marla smiled at the compliment. "Yes, she is. It helps that we're past her hormonal surge, although her driving lessons are riling Dalton something fierce."

"I've no doubt." Anita reached forward to cover her hand. "I know your soul craves something more. Push aside your fears and move on with your life."

She snatched her hand away. "It's not fear holding me back. I don't want kids to tie me down. I've never traveled anywhere, except for our honeymoon. There are places I want to go and things I want to see. Once you have children, you're stuck for twenty years, not to mention the cost." And yet a vision of what she'd be missing—an infant like little Luke smiling up at her—

intruded on her thoughts. Disconcerted by the notion, she shoved it aside.

Anita stiffened. "If you say so. I just hope you're happy with your choice when you are my age."

"We'll have Brianna, and I have my niece and nephew. We won't be alone." She bit her lower lip upon noting Ma's expression. *Well, that was tactless, Marla.* "Um, how are your mah jongg games going? Have any cruises coming up with the gang?"

"Not in the near future." They sat back while the waitress delivered their meals. "By the way, I've met someone."

Marla paused with a potato chip halfway to her mouth. "Oh, really?" *Maybe this is why Ma wanted to meet her today.* "Who is he? And why wait until now to tell me?"

"I didn't want to mention it in front of company. We met at my book club. He's the new group leader."

Marla had hoped her mother would be content without jumping into another relationship so soon after dumping Roger. When she considered it, though, Ma was only sixty-seven and could have many good years ahead of her. Why should she be alone if she could find companionship? It just seemed strange to think of her mother with boyfriends.

"Tell me about him," she said with a polite smile.

"Renfield is a retired literature professor. Conversation with him is so stimulating. He likes to go out and have fun, and he isn't stingy like Roger. We hit it off right away. There's one thing, bubeleh. Reed—that's his nickname—isn't Jewish."

Marla's jaw dropped. Hadn't her mother been the one to harp on her to marry a Jewish man? "I don't believe it. Here you were criticizing my Christmas tree. What a hypocrite."

Anita twirled her iced tea glass. "We enjoy each other's company, and that's what counts at our stage in life. But *you* have to worry about raising children."

"No, I don't. Soon Brianna will be going to college, and then

Dalton and I can travel to all the places I've dreamed about visiting."

"If you can afford it, between her college tuition and living expenses."

"I have money saved up in a vacation fund." They ate in silence until the waitress cleared their empty plates and left the bill on the table.

Anita tossed out a few dollars for a tip and picked up the tab. They'd pay at the cashier up front. "I'm glad we had this little chat. You don't call me very much these days."

"Come on, Ma. You know things are hectic during the holidays. I'll be glad when everything gets back to normal after New Year's."

"I don't know that I'd call crime solving getting back to normal."

Marla gritted her teeth in annoyance while Anita paid the check. They exited together.

"Let's do lunch again after the holidays are over," Marla suggested to mollify her mother. "Meanwhile, why don't you bring Reed to our New Year's Day party so we can meet him?"

"I'll see if he's free. Be safe, bubeleh."

They embraced, and then Anita turned in the opposite direction. As Marla neared the driver's side of her car, she frowned. Was something hanging beneath her vehicle? She bent over to get a closer look. It appeared as though a wire had come loose.

She froze, Dalton's warnings ringing in her head. Good God, what had he told her about car bombs? Look for dangling wires, aluminum foil, and she couldn't remember what else. Would it be foolish to call the cops?

Her nape prickling, she glanced up and down the asphalt, but no one appeared to be observing her. First Val had been killed, then Jason and Nadia. Was it her turn now?

Her eyes narrowed as she thought about Patty's actions. A

microphone placed at her salon station would pick up her conversations with Nicole. Did the bad guy hear her mention that she had Warren's journal? Presumably that's why he'd sent Patty to search her drawers and attempt to break into her car. He might be afraid of what she'd read in Warren's story.

She hurried back to the front of the restaurant. She'd call Dalton so she wouldn't seem like an idiot if this proved to be a false alarm.

Half an hour later, fire trucks with flashing lights convened in the parking lot. A bomb squad unit pulled in. Dalton spoke into his radio where he stood beside Marla, while she phoned the salon with yet another delay.

"I'll take you to work," Dalton said after he'd signed off. "You don't need to stay here."

"Is there really a bomb? I wasn't imagining things?"

"You were right to call me. I'm glad you were diligent." He gave her a quick embrace. "This could have gone wrong if you hadn't been alert."

"Will they be able to disarm the device without blowing up my car?" She'd finally given up the lease and purchased the Camry. She didn't want to lose it this way. That inane thought kept her sanity, otherwise she might cede into hysterics. Her body trembled, but she forced herself to remain outwardly calm.

"The guys are good at their job. They have to be. Come on." He guided her to his sedan. "The slimeball behind all this must believe you're a threat."

"I have to read the rest of Warren's journal. It has to be significant." Marla wrapped her arms around herself, wondering which of her recent moves had spooked the killer. If she hadn't noticed that wire . . . Her blood turned cold at what might have happened.

She cast aside her thoughts of the intended outcome even as her gaze darted to the side view mirror as they entered traffic.

Was the bad guy watching to see if his plan worked? And when it didn't, was he following them? She didn't note any vehicle behind, which reassured her for the moment.

"So what did you think about the Pilates instructor's statement?" she asked in a logical manner to get herself back on track. "Had you known Val was a closet lesbian?"

His gaze focused on the road, he crinkled his brow. "No, you're ahead of us on that one. It puts an interesting slant on things, that's for sure."

"Nadia and Lora were both in the same exercise class. Do you think they were involved in a love triangle?"

"All indications show Lora is fond of men, so I doubt that was the case."

"Oh? How so?"

"She oozes seduction when she's around the male sex. Or hadn't you noticed?"

Marla stared at him. The woman's oversized figure wasn't the rail-thin type most men preferred. But then again, Biggs Kahuna had a fondness for her. Marla wouldn't call him a hunk by her standards. Maybe Lora had a special appeal for men with a heftier build?

Her thoughts drifted back to the wires trailing underneath her car. What had she uncovered that threatened the killer? Could it truly be about the journal, or were there other factors she was overlooking because of her focus on that book?

"What did you learn in your background check of FOFL's board members?" she asked her husband. "Did you find out what Lora does on her excursions around the country?"

His hands gripped the steering wheel as they paused at a red light. "Her trips seem legit. She checks into a hotel at each location, visits the preservation society in the area, and tours their projects. We haven't turned up any red flags from her credit card charges or bank account. Well, then again, she does make a cash deposit after each trip."

"Is it a substantial amount?"

"I'll have to take another look. It could be meaningful, now that you mention it. We figured she was depositing a paycheck that she'd cashed in."

"If she's doing something else on those jaunts and Val discovered her purpose, Lora would have had reason to get rid of her."

"Perhaps, but that's a stretch." The light changed, and he pressed the accelerator.

They zoomed west in fairly light traffic. Westfield Mall passed by on their left. The Christmas tree market hadn't been dismantled yet. Crap, Marla hadn't even thought to go shopping for after-Christmas sales. She was missing out on all the bargains. At the very least, she should pick up some wrapping paper and greeting cards for next year.

"Do the group's board members get paid?" she asked, to divert herself from morose thoughts. There might not be a next year if they didn't catch this killer before he struck again.

"The four officers have paid positions."

"What about Lora's day job? If she's not on FOFL's payroll, what does she do for a living?"

"Lora is a commercial real estate agent."

"Really?" Marla straightened her shoulders. "She couldn't be working in cahoots with Rick Rodriguez, could she? I mean, he's a big-time developer. Maybe they do deals together."

"From what I've seen, Lora seems dedicated to her preservationist ideals. I don't believe she could be compromised that way."

"Andrew Fine seems to have compromised his ideals. His latest articles are slanted in favor of Rodriguez's acquisition of those properties on Hollywood Beach."

"I know. He's operating in opposition to the group's goals.

It's a puzzle to me why they're keeping him on."

"It's only that one project. Maybe he truly believes those buildings would be better off torn down. Solomon Gold can't be the only owner. Perhaps the other homeowners would rather be rid of the headache and move on."

"Marla, why don't you relax? You've had a stressful day. Let me worry about these things."

"When somebody just tried to blow me up? I don't think so. Tell me, does Lora work for a firm that has franchises in these other cities she visits? Maybe she's a regional supervisor of sorts who kills two birds with one stone during her trips."

"She doesn't seem to go anywhere except where I've said."

"Does she meet with anyone else at these projects? Someone who isn't part of the historic organization, I mean. She could be . . . oh, I don't know . . . a member of an anarchist group, for example. I'm just throwing that out there because you shouldn't discard her as a suspect."

"We aren't, but Kat and I need more to go on where she's concerned."

"Okay, does Lora have visitors in her hotel room?"

He glanced at her, his gaze darkening. "You think she's a high-class hooker?"

"It would account for the come-hither look you mentioned."

"That would be hard to pull off in different cities unless she belonged to a network."

"Is there such a thing nationwide?"

Dalton shrugged. "Could be. I'll ask the guys in that department."

"So the FOFL officers are paid positions. Do any of them work elsewhere? I believe Howard Cohn is a bank manager. How about Solomon Gold, the president?"

"Gold administers the day-to-day business at the group's office. He's responsible for writing the monthly newsletter and for supervising restorations on their projects. But on a personal basis, he gets a substantial income from his rental properties. I imagine managing those places keeps him busy."

"I've only met the veep once. What does he do?"

"Joseph Mancini handles fundraising and development activities, submitting grant applications, and nominating sites for Historic Place designation. He also coordinates educational webinars. He serves on the Florida Historical Commission and is a historical architect."

"Impressive. Did he have much contact with Val?"

"To a certain extent, but he seems clean. He was overseas on a family trip when Val kicked the bucket. The guy didn't get back until after the funeral and seemed genuinely upset about her death."

"That leaves Sue Ellen. Does the secretary even have time for another job?"

"She doesn't moonlight as far as I know. If she did, maybe she wouldn't have to dip her fingers into the annual fundraising pie. She has a snarky attitude, like she feels entitled to more. She'll face charges for embezzling once we solve the case."

"But you don't think she's guilty of plotting Val's murder? She could have been afraid of getting caught, especially if Val questioned the receipts."

Dalton compressed his lips. "I'm not writing her off yet."

Marla would still place her bet on Lora. "Who else is on the board of directors?"

"There's Dr. Needles. He's already under investigation for prescription abuse."

"Could he have offed Val because she posed a threat to his lucrative business?"

"Adding murder to his charges? Unlikely, but always possible."

"So who's left?"

"Three more board members. They consist of a nautical archaeologist, a prehistoric archaeologist, and a historian. I've written them off the list." Dalton turned into the parking lot for Marla's salon. He pulled up to the curb in front of her establishment. "Go to work and forget about this stuff. I'll pick you up tonight at eight."

She gathered her purse. "What about my car?"

"If it's been cleared, we can get it then or in the morning."

Marla leaned over to kiss him. "I love you."

"Love you, too. Stay safe."

She entered the salon, wishing she knew more about Lora's activities. That woman had to be involved somehow. First Val and then Nadia had died, and all three of them were connected through the same athletic club. That couldn't be a coincidence. Plus, Nadia had written herself a reminder to call Marla and mentioned Pilates.

Unfortunately, she didn't get a chance to process more from her conversation with Dalton. This was one of her busiest weeks of the year, and she found comfort in routine. She kept her lips sealed about why Dalton had dropped her off, saying her car needed repairs. It still concerned her that Patty had so readily entered the salon and riffled through her drawers. How would the shampoo girl have known when Robyn left to pick up their order at Arnie's deli unless she'd kept watch outside?

Marla's blood chilled. She paused with shears in hand, about to snip a customer's hair. What if someone kept track of her movements on a closer basis? She'd already suspected a microphone might be hidden nearby, but what about a video monitor? Going into automatic mode, she cut and combed while half her mind flitted elsewhere.

As soon as she was free, Marla shoved aside the irons in her bottom roundabout drawer searching for an item she had received as a holiday gift last year. She loved receiving presents from clients at the holidays, but she'd run out of counter space and had shoved this in here. There it was, buried at the bottom and still in its gift bag. A client had visited the Spy Museum in Washington, D.C., and gifted Marla with a bug detector. It was still in its wrapping.

After glancing at the front desk to see if her next client had arrived, Marla used her scissors to cut the plastic surrounding the device. It was a palm-sized rectangular scanner that could detect a wireless hidden camera or microphone. She read the directions. Pull out the antenna. Hold down the "A" button while panning the unit around the room. If it detects a signal, it will beep. Then hold down the "B" button and concentrate on that one area. When it beeps steadily, visually search for a hidden device. Interference could come from radio signals such as cell phones, televisions, or computers.

Oh, great. The instructions said a wireless camera could be smaller than a dime and needed merely a pinhole to view the entire room. It could be embedded anywhere and would broadcast up to seven hundred feet away.

She waited until everyone left at the end of the day before deploying the device. It beeped in a couple of places, once at her station and across the room where Jen worked. Was the day spa bugged, too? And who should she call about it? Dalton was due to pick her up any minute. Did she really want to add to his burdens, or should she notify her security company?

"I had a hunch," she told her husband during their drive home. "I was thinking about Patty and how she had known when to search my drawers. It was almost as though she had eyes on the place. And then I remembered this gift that a client gave me last year. It's a bug detector from the Spy Museum in D.C. I panned it around, and it beeped."

He shot her a glance from the driver's seat. "Meaning what?"

"It found a signal. I didn't locate a mic or hidden camera,

but I'm not experienced at this sort of thing. Should I call my security company in the morning?"

"Let me have my team inspect the premises. They know how to look for surveillance devices."

A camera would explain how someone knew she had the journal after watching her show it to Nicole. Marla's skin crawled. She didn't like the idea of being observed. "What's happening with my car?"

"A colleague dropped me off and I drove it home. Not to worry, it's as good as new."

"How about the explosive device? Did you get any clues from it?"

"The thing was homemade. Anybody could have gotten directions off the Internet on how to make one. There weren't any prints or other identifying factors."

"So the bad guy is cautious to cover his tracks. That doesn't help us."

That night, after they'd set their alarm and she huddled in bed, Marla brought out the journal again. She had to read more. Dalton, occupied in the bathroom, noted her movement in the mirror. "Hey, read it aloud, okay?"

They had a few nights to themselves. Brie had gone to Disney World with Dalton's parents. So Marla settled in with the journal on her lap and opened to where she'd left a bookmark.

"Remember the last part was where the men had uncovered the treasure chest," she reminded her husband, before reading aloud from that point onward.

" 'I had read the tales of shipwrecks along the Florida coast. Pirates were prevalent, too, and my mind recalled the story of the infamous brigand known as Red Ted. Born Thaddeus Montoya, he was a nobleman's son from Spain whose exploits with the ladies caused his hasty departure aboard a naval vessel. Because he could read and write, he rose to officer's status and got himself appointed as a liaison to the court. But his old habits died hard, and he once again found himself fleeing Spanish authorities. He commandeered a ship and set sail, forcing the crew to either join him or be hanged. His nickname came from his fondness for bloodshed.

" 'Wanting to get even with Spain, he set out for the next decade to raid helpless merchant ships. But his inflated ego eventually caused his demise just as he'd broken apart his lair in preparation for retirement. Unable to resist one last conquest, he'd aimed for a cargo vessel riding the waves. It turned out to be an American warship in disguise. Outgunned, he shot himself rather than be taken captive. When the sailors arrived at his lair, they discovered the treasure was gone along with any women or children.

" 'I figured this chest of gold might be part of the pirate's cache. George and I wanted to search the area for more loot. Ralph wanted to hand the chest over to the authorities and let them deal with the matter. The majority prevailed. We decided to dig up the chest, divide the coins, and mark the spot to return later for a broader search.

" 'But once we had the chest unburied, an argument broke forth. Ralph, whose moral compass exceeded ours, insisted on donating the goods to a museum to be enjoyed by all. What right did he have to cut George and me out of our share? After we buried the skunk in a separate hole dug for that purpose, we debated the issue. The three of us agreed to sleep on it and decide what to do in the morning. We fashioned a makeshift sled out of driftwood and dragged the chest back to our hut.

" 'In the morning, we went for a swim. Airing out the hut hadn't eliminated the animal stink from the night before, and we craved a cleansing. Now please don't think too badly of us from what happened next.' "

Marla paused, glancing at Dalton who listened in bed beside

her. She hadn't even been aware of him joining her. "I have a bad feeling about this."

"Go on. Why did you stop?" Lowering his brows, he thrust stiff fingers through his still-damp hair.

"Pirate treasure? Is that really what this is all about?"

"You won't know until you read further."

"Okay, let's see what happens." Marla found her place and cleared her throat. " 'We were swimming in the ocean when I heard a cry. Ralph had gone out farther than George and me, and he appeared to be in distress. Waves were rocking us. I'm a pretty good swimmer, but the undertow was strong. If I swam out that far, I might have trouble coming back.

" 'I shouted to Ralph to swim parallel to shore, knowing if you fought the current, it would be worse. Sometimes you could break free this way.

" 'George bobbed in the distance and waved. Wait, why was he heading toward the beach? He gestured for me to follow him. Was he afraid I'd get sucked out to sea, too?

" 'My heart pounding, I glanced between him and Ralph. Ralph's head became increasingly difficult to discern among the crests. I treaded water, hesitating between saving my friend and saving my own skin. Somehow I think Fate made the choice for me. Without Ralph's interference, George and I would be free to divide the treasure between ourselves. And while I was having these shameful thoughts, Ralph disappeared. I cried his name. I swam parallel, trying to catch a glimpse of him, but he was gone. With heavy hearts, George and I reported him missing and presumed drowned. They never found a trace of him. We split up our loot, hoarding it for years before we dared cash it in, claiming we'd inherited it from our granddads who were collectors. Luckily, the coin dealers didn't question us. We returned to the site but never found anything else from Red Ted's stash.' "

"So what does this prove?" Dalton said with a weary yawn.

Marla marked her place among the pages and set them on the nightstand. "It explains why three of them started on this trip and only two of them returned."

"So? It appears to be an accidental drowning."

"That they did nothing to prevent. Guilt must have weighed upon them."

"I don't see how it would affect events today."

"Both Val and Howard's fathers, assuming George is related to the banker, clearly were involved. They would have guarded their reputations. If their secret got out, they might have been viewed as greedy, or worse. For some men, that's enough motive to commit murder."

"But George and Warren are dead," Dalton pointed out.

"Their children aren't, at least not until Val died. Maybe Howard didn't know about his father's misdeeds until Val discovered the journal and told him."

"And he murdered her, so his dad's guilt wouldn't come out?" Dalton scoffed.

"Why else would Jason have sent me a photo of Howard? He had a point to prove. Jason also sent me a photo of Henutt and a funeral director. Maybe he wasn't sure which angle to pursue."

Dalton's gaze darkened. "I'd like to know which secret got Jason killed. What had he been investigating?"

"If it's about the journal, this could be why someone tried to silence me. They know I have the book now and would have read the contents." She felt her eyes widen. "Maybe this person believes the treasure still exists. There could be directions in here to the hut's location."

"Or a map to the loot, but that's a long shot."

"I wish we knew more about this pirate. It might tell us if we're on the right track." She tapped his arm. "Hold on. What if Nadia's message spelled Pirates, not Pilates? We might have

215

misinterpreted the middle letter."

"Hmm, that's true. But there's still that connection at the sports club between Nadia, Val, and Lora."

"And the connection at the art gallery between Jason and Val, plus possibly Henutt since his wife's boutique is next door. Oh, my God. What if Jason is the third son?" Marla's mind raced ahead. "Val was Warren's daughter. Howard was George's son, which you should be able to determine. It could be that Ralph had fathered a child, too, before he died. His friends might not have known about it. What if it's Jason who'd researched his father's history and turned up news articles that led him to question the truth of past events?"

Dalton grimaced. "You're making my head spin. Let's sleep on it and continue this discussion in the morning."

"All right, but we need to look up how Ralph's death was reported."

Marla turned out the light, but her dreams wouldn't let her go as she drifted into sleep. She woke up the following day gasping and choking as though she were drowning in the ocean like poor Ralph. They should try to access historical archives about the tragic accident.

But what if they were chasing down the wrong alley? What if the photo with Henutt and the other guy was the more significant one?

A visit to Gabriel Stone at his Parkland funeral home was in order. This took priority on her to-do list.

CHAPTER FIFTEEN

Dalton's space in bed beside her was empty when Marla grabbed a robe to wrap around herself. The morning air chilled her skin. Another cold front must have come through during the night.

From the tantalizing aroma of coffee in the air, she surmised Dalton had already gone into the kitchen and started the coffeemaker. She needed a boost of caffeine to awaken her senses and chase away the cobwebs of her dreams.

In the kitchen, Dalton sat at the table and watched the morning news. Marla poured herself a mug of java and added cream.

Once fully alert, she broached the subject on her mind. "Have you or Kat interviewed Gabriel Stone at his funeral home and shown him Jason's photo? I'm wondering how he explains his relationship to Hunutt Soe Dum." She smiled as she said the name. It sounded so ridiculous. However, the fellow himself was anything but a fool, especially if he had Asian mob connections.

Dalton glanced at her. With a lock of hair fallen across his forehead, his heavy-lidded gaze, and his stubbled jaw, he looked rakishly handsome. "We've talked to him. He claimed to be an acquaintance of Henutt. They'd spoken at the fundraiser ball where Jason snapped the picture. As we expected, he denied any further relationship between them. But the guys in our other department have traced an exchange of goods between Stone and Henutt that occurred via their intermediaries."

"What kind of goods?" Marla sank into a seat at the table across from him.

"We're not sure. Henutt sends shipments home to China. I'm thinking illegal organ harvesting, but nothing has been proven."

"From dead people? What would be the purpose?" She shuddered at the thought.

"Who knows? Medical experiments? Exotic food ingredients? Think of shark's-fin soup."

A hunch hit her that made sense. It would explain what Henutt was buying from the funeral director and exporting overseas. "Would you mind if I had a chat with him? My schedule is busy today, but I have a two-hour break at lunchtime that I left open after a client cancelled. I could run over to Parkland then."

"Not if you go alone. Take someone with you."

Despite her efforts, Marla couldn't get any friends to join her. Nicole and Robyn were busy at work. Tally couldn't accompany her with the baby. And her other friends were tied up with their own affairs. That left her relatives, and Marla wasn't about to involve her cousin or her mother. So Friday afternoon found her driving solo to the northwest quadrant of the county.

Her plan was to provoke Gabriel Stone to see how much he'd reveal. Dalton knew her destination as she'd texted him upon her departure. So if anything bad happened, he would know where to look for her.

The white-columned building was set back from the road by a long driveway amid a pleasant setting of pines. Beyond stretched the cemetery grounds. The property suited Parkland, an upscale community with gated neighborhoods and expensive housing. Marla had called ahead to make an appointment, saying she was a friend of Yolanda Whipp. The place appeared to be privately owned and not one of the chains. It did well, judging from the fresh paint and well-maintained trim.

The interior looked polished and clean down to the grout edging the tile floor. A sweet citrus scent pervaded the air as Marla entered a short hallway. She found the administrative office and announced herself.

Gabriel Stone hurried from an inner sanctum to greet her. He had white hair, a pleasant lined face, and a welcoming smile. As befitted the dignity of his establishment, he wore navy pants with a buttoned dress shirt and tie. In his office, she noticed a sport jacket draped over his desk chair, where he took a seat. She sat opposite in a comfy leather armchair.

"How may I help you?" he began. "Are you interested in a Pre-Need Plan?"

Marla crossed her legs. "Not really. As I mentioned on the phone, I'm a friend of Yolanda's. Her husband Henutt has an interesting background. Did you know he maintains his connection to China? Why, he sends packages home on a regular basis."

Stone picked up a ballpoint pen, clicking it on and off. "That's generous of him."

"Yes, isn't it? I can't help wondering what he ships there. It couldn't be money or electronics. You'd have to declare that to the government." She gave a low chuckle. "And if it were anything perishable, it would require refrigeration."

"I don't understand what this has to do with me."

"I own a hair salon and day spa. One of our clients was murdered. You might know the lady's name. Valerie Weston was a benefactress to Friends of Old Florida."

"Did we do her funeral? I don't remember the names of all the people that come through here."

"No, her memorial service was elsewhere. Val was an artist who displayed her paintings at a gallery next door to Yolanda's shop. A photographer also had his works for sale there. That same guy, Jason Faulks, snapped this picture of you and Henutt the night of FOFL's gala fundraiser." Marla showed him the photo on her cell phone.

He gave an audible gasp. "How did you get this picture?"

"Jason emailed it to me the night of the ball, just before he was murdered."

"What's your point?" Stone's eyes narrowed to twin slits.

She put the phone back in her purse. "I wonder if Val caught onto you and Henutt. I've done some research. Are you aware China is one of three major global buyers of human hair? The international marketplace calls it black gold. It's a trade worth nine hundred million dollars."

"I still don't understand why you've come here."

"I've read that hair from corpses could be a source of revenue. Perhaps Val or Jason figured out what was going on and threatened to expose your operation."

He shot to his feet. "Are you implying I had something to do with their deaths? How dare you make false accusations. I didn't harm either one of them. Besides, exporting hair isn't illegal."

Marla rose to stare him down. "No, but I'd bet the family members of the deceased might be interested to know what you're doing without their permission."

"What's your point?"

"Perhaps you weren't personally involved in Val's murder, but Henutt might not care to have his scheme exposed. He wouldn't even have to get his fingers dirty. He'd know who to call."

Stone's face darkened. "Why do you care about any of this?"

"Val died in my day spa, and a staff member is involved. I want to clear her name. My husband is the homicide detective on the case. It would be helpful if you cooperated with his investigation." She tightened the purse strap across her shoulder. "Consider this a warning. You might want to be more careful about the company you keep, or you could end up in one of your own coffins."

On the drive back to the salon, Marla's gaze kept darting to the rear view mirror in case she'd been followed. No one appeared to be tailing her, but she didn't let her guard down until she was safely at work. Then she gave Dalton a call to inform him of her results.

"I'd bet he's guilty of engaging in the human hair trade. That would be what Henutt is exporting. Stone wouldn't have permission from the families of the deceased to sell their hair cuttings."

"It wasn't smart of you to provoke Stone. I hope you don't have any repercussions from your visit."

She heard the dismay in his tone. At least Marla hadn't told him she'd gone there alone. "He knows you're a police detective. If he's wise, he'll start cooperating, unless he's too afraid of Henutt's reaction."

"Or else he'll tip Henutt off that you're aware of their enterprise."

"I'll be careful." Marla rang off and pocketed her cell phone. She'd spoken to him outside the salon, grateful his team had located and removed the hidden surveillance bugs inside.

So when Nicole asked her for the latest news on the case, Marla felt comfortable talking to her. They had a moment in between clients, and she wanted to share what she had learned.

"Ugh, that's awful," Nicole said, her nose scrunching. "He cuts hair from dead people and sells them for extensions?"

"I suspect Gabriel Stone sells the hair to Henutt who ships it to China. From what I've read online, the United States, Britain, and China are the three major world buyers. Forty percent of the hair sold is made into extensions."

Nicole stuck a comb into the Barbicide jar. "So what's done with the rest?"

Standing by her station, Marla looked up the notes she'd written on her smartphone. "Shorter hair from men is used by chemical companies. The amino acids in hair have multiple industrial uses, including food additives. It's cheaper than synthetic sources."

"Eww. How would I know I'm eating it?"

"Look for an ingredient labeled L-cysteine. It can be used to leaven bread, for example." Marla read from her notes. "Human hair is first dissolved in acid. The L-cysteine, isolated by a chemical process, is packaged and shipped to commercial bread makers. Other sources of this amino acid include chicken or duck feathers and petroleum by-products."

"That's disgusting."

"Listen to this. Most of the hair used to make the L-cysteine comes from the floors of barbershops and hair salons in China. There's also a temple in India where people donate their hair to their god as an act of humility. They shave your head, then women sweep it up and throw it into a giant steel vat. It gets sold at auction to the international market."

Nicole stared at the strands of hair littering their floor, the remnants of haircuts that the assistant had yet to sweep up. "So you're saying we're standing on a gold mine."

"So to speak. I've even read reports of Russian prisoners having their heads shaved against their will, and the harvesting of hair from corpses."

"Gross. I don't think I'll buy baked goods anymore."

"It's also a flavor enhancer and may have other uses in the food industry."

"So how can you tell where the L-cysteine ingredient comes from, whether it's animal in origin or synthetic?"

"There isn't any way to tell if it's not on the label. If you're concerned, I'd suggest trying kosher goods or vegan items. They'd be a safer bet. Hey, get this. Blonde is the most popular color for the human hair trade because it can be dyed more easily. Wavy hair has the best-selling texture."

"I think I've learned more than I wanted to know, thanks."

"Don't you agree this all fits? Henutt is buying hair from Stone and shipping it to China."

Nicole tilted her head. "So you think Valerie Weston somehow discovered their scheme and they killed her over it?"

"It's a distinct possibility, at least where Henutt is concerned."

They both got busy with clients, and Marla lost track of time. A notion struck her as she was preparing to leave for the day.

What if Lora Larue's trips to various cities coincided with visits to funeral homes in those areas? Could she be acting as a liaison in this shady black gold business?

Excited by the idea, Marla presented it to Dalton over a late dinner. "Did you ever get a list of the cities Lora has visited on FOFL's behalf?"

"Our focus has been more on the paper trail Lora Larue generates."

"You could just ask Sue Ellen at the group's main office. The secretary would file Lora's trip receipts for reimbursement. And you'd said Lora made cash deposits after these trips. That indicates she's getting paid, but for what? And how much of an amount is it?"

"Not enough to raise any red flags with the IRS. It's under five thousand dollars each time. She says it's a travel bonus but won't reveal the source."

"For all we know, Lora could be teaching real estate seminars in these locations. See if she's visited sports clubs during her trips, too. Her club might have branches nationwide." Marla grabbed his arm as another thought surfaced. "Does she go overseas? Maybe she visits hair salons instead of funeral homes on Henutt's behalf, soliciting new sources of hair for him to trade."

Dalton's mouth thinned. "We need a list of the cities she's visited and the dates. And I agree we should look more closely into her side activities on these trips."

"Are you going into work tomorrow?"

"Kat's on call this weekend, but I'd like to run with this while it's on my mind."

Saturday morning, Marla woke early and worked on salon book-keeping at home while doing laundry. Her mother called in the midst of her folding a load of dry clothes.

"Reed and I made plans to go on a cruise," she told Marla. "We're leaving in three weeks."

"What? You barely know the guy."

"I know him well enough. We're going on one of those Southern Caribbean ten-day trips. I'm so excited."

Marla grimaced. What could she say? Her mother was a grown woman who had her own mind. "Have you done a background check on this man? How do you know he's legit?" She'd heard of con men who preyed on widows.

"Oh, come on, cut me some slack. I'm not stupid. I thought you'd be happy for me."

"Of course I am. Did you invite him to join us for New Year's Day?" *I want to see who's snowed my mother and if he's right for her.*

"Yes, Reed is excited to come and meet the family. Tell me, how does Brianna like Disney World? Have you heard from her?"

"She's texted us. She is having a great time. They'll be home tomorrow."

"How does it feel to have an empty house? Soon she'll be heading off to college, as you pointed out. You're hoping to travel then, but Dalton will be tied to his job. You might think about feathering your nest now so you can have another focus."

"Yeah, Ma. I'll think about it. Now I've gotta go. I'm in the middle of doing laundry." She hung up, slamming the receiver harder than usual. How come she got annoyed every time she spoke to her mother?

Needing comfort, Marla dialed her friend, Tally. Having a baby meant Tally and Ken kept early hours.

Tally's sullen voice answered. "Hi, Marla."

"Hi, how is everything? I wanted to remind you that we're having a low-key party on New Year's Day, if you can make it. We'd love to have you, and you could bring Luke."

"Thanks, I'll talk to Ken about it."

"Is the baby okay? Is he sitting up yet?" She didn't expect that a few days would make a difference, but who knew? Kids developed rapidly during their first year.

Tally chuckled. "Not quite, but he's getting there. I adore him so much, Marla. You'd be a good mother too, if you gave it a chance. I'm glad you'll be there for Luke if he needs you."

Marla's heart skipped a beat. What was up with this?

"Of course I will, Tally. Why, is something going on that you're not telling me?"

"No, I'm just a nervous new mom who needs reassurance. How is Dalton's case coming along, by the way? I hope he won't have to spend the holidays at work."

"He's narrowing the suspects. It won't be long now before he pinpoints the culprit."

"You're probably one step ahead of everyone, like always. Don't neglect the things in life that really matter, Marla. You'll regret it one day. Now I have to go. Luke needs me. Bye."

Marla stared at the mobile phone in her hand. Did Tally just dismiss her without saying anything of substance? Worry lines creased her brow. Something was wrong over there, and she'd bet it involved Tally's husband.

Dalton's call distracted her. "Hey, pack an overnight bag. We're going to Key West."

"What? Why?" Marla halted in the kitchen after bringing the

dogs in from the backyard. What had Dalton learned that led to this trail?

"According to Kat's research, Lora Larue has been there recently. And Kat found a news article in the archives that mentioned Ralph, the missing person in that journal."

"In Key West? I thought their log cabin was east of here somewhere."

"It was, but this article is more recent. It's by a former salvage expert speculating about a Spanish galleon that had floundered in a storm. We should talk to him, and we can check out the hotel where Lora stayed while we're there. What time can you get off work?"

Marla groaned. Saturday was her busiest day, and she was fully booked. But time was running out. They had to wrap this case quickly before anybody else got hurt. And this weekend was convenient with Brianna away from home.

"Pick me up at the salon at ten. Hopefully Robyn can switch my later appointments to next week. I'll call the kennel to see if they can take the dogs."

Key Largo was the first big island in the Keys after a long and boring stretch through swamp territory south of the mainland. They made their first stop at the inviting Chamber of Commerce Visitor Center to stretch their legs, use the bathroom, and inquire about recommended restaurants for lunch. Marla liked the sound of Fish House, Sundowners, or Snapper's Waterfront Restaurant.

After a pleasant meal amid tropical breezes and a sunny ocean view, they moved on toward their goal. Marla made note of various restroom stops along the way. She'd been down to the Keys once before but it had been years ago, and she'd forgotten what facilities were available. Supermarkets, gas stations, and fast-food chains were good bets.

"Don't tell me we have two more hours to go," she said as they entered Islamorada. Numerous eateries advertised as they drove south on Route One toward the end of the line. It would be nice to stay at one of these resort hotels for a long weekend. Too bad they were in a rush.

"Look, there's Crane Point Museum and Nature Center," Dalton mentioned when they'd reached Marathon. "Many of these islands have marine attractions or research facilities for dolphins and turtles. We should bring Brie with us next time."

"Did you notify your parents we were going to Key West in case we get back late for some reason?"

"Yes, I told them to keep Brie with them until we come by. We'll pick her up on our way home tomorrow."

Spectacular views captured her attention. The Atlantic Ocean sparkled to their left and the Gulf to their right as they sped down the Overseas Highway. She sank into the seat cushion as tension ebbed from her bones. They really should get away more often.

After checking into their hotel in Key West, they left their bags in the room and went outside. "What should we do first, trace Lora's movements or talk to the salvage expert?" Marla asked, donning her sunglasses.

Dalton checked his watch. "It's already after three, and this is Saturday. The salvager is on the staff for a community newspaper. He writes a weekly column featuring the area's history. I called ahead to make sure he'd be there today, but it's getting late."

"Let's start there, then. Here's a map I picked up in the lobby. What's the street address for the newspaper?"

They stood out front on the sidewalk. Their hotel had a prime downtown location near the Historic Seaport District. They were a few blocks from Duval Street, the main strip of shops, bars, and restaurants. The historic attractions were within walking distance, too. Marla would have liked to take the Conch Tour Train for its descriptive overview of the island, but she'd reserve that activity for their next visit.

They passed the train depot and gift shop as they headed up Front Street. Marla watched her footing, the sidewalk being strewn with plant debris. Palms and other tropical foliage shaded the area, providing needed respite from the blazing sun. It was hot at this southernmost tip of the United States, and she was glad she'd worn white capris with a turquoise top.

"Which way?" Dalton asked as they hit the intersection at Duval. It looked as though the pub crawlers had already started, judging by the number of people sitting outdoors at the saloons and cafés lining the street.

"Let's keep going until we reach Whitehead Street. Then we need to turn left toward the post office."

"I wish we had time to see Truman's Little White House," Dalton said in a wistful tone. He propped a pair of sunglasses on his nose as they walked along.

"I know. And I wish we had more time to go shopping." They would have to make another trip to see the historic sites, parks, beaches, and other attractions.

Glad Dalton had the foresight to make a dinner reservation in advance, she strolled along, peering longingly at the shops displaying souvenirs, tee-shirts, island spices, aloe products, sandals, and more. Several shops selling homemade Key lime pies made her mouth water. She'd have to get that for dessert tonight.

The newspaper headquarters was nestled between a tattoo parlor and a ghost tour ticket office. Fortunately, the guy Dalton contacted earlier was waiting for them. Sam Flint looked like a sea captain with his peppery hair and beard, nautical cap, and gold-rimmed spectacles. His skin, tanned from years in the sun, had those dark spots people get in tropical climates.

"Have a seat." Sam gestured to a couple of battered wood chairs facing his desk. "So what can I do for you folks? You'd mentioned an article of mine that interested you?"

Dalton nodded. "That's right. You'd written about an unsolved mystery involving a man who disappeared off the coast of Broward County in 1934 and was presumed drowned. His name was Ralph Flint. Wait a minute. I just made the connection. You have the same last name."

Sam sank into a desk chair. "Ralph was my father. He drove to Florida from up north searching for adventure that year and wound up dead. At least, that's what I figured happened to him."

Marla sat forward. "We'd wondered if he had a child." So Sam, and not Jason, was Ralph's son.

"Ralph was engaged to my mother. She was pregnant when he left on vacation, but my dad didn't know it at the time. I was born after he died."

CHAPTER SIXTEEN

Marla needed a moment to assimilate this information, which opened a new chapter in the story started by Val's dad. All three men in the journal had descendants. How many of them had known about each other?

"Did your mother tell you anything about Ralph while you were growing up?" she asked.

Sam straightened his eyeglasses. "Mom ended up marrying another man who raised me as his own. It was only in my later years that Mom revealed I'd been adopted by my stepfather. She never really knew what had happened to Ralph. The authorities told her he'd drowned."

"So you started looking for him?"

"I traced his movements to Miami, where he was last seen. A newspaper there had a small article about an incident involving Warren Brookstone and two friends. Warren had reported that he had last seen my father swimming too far out to sea. Ralph didn't heed his warning to come in and vanished beneath the waves. The other guy, George Cohen, verified his story. A body was never found."

"George Cohen? How do you spell his last name?"

"C-o-h-e-n. You're thinking of his son, Howard?"

"Yes, he must have changed the spelling to C-o-h-n. So they *are* father and son." That confirmed her theory. "And both George and Warren claimed your father was the victim of an accidental drowning?"

Dalton jabbed a finger in the air. "It's not unusual in Florida. Drownings off our coast are a common occurrence, especially for tourists who don't respect the undertow. We also have sharks that pose a hazard. They swim closer to the beach than people realize."

Sam nodded. "That might be true, but I suspected more was going on once those coins surfaced."

"Let me guess," Dalton said, crossing one knee over the other. "They were Spanish in origin."

"They showed up on a collector's circuit. I didn't recognize them from any of the known shipwrecks. It got me to thinking. Both George and Warren didn't lack for financial means after their trip. What if those boys had made a discovery and disagreed on how to divide the loot? And what if my father was the odd man out?"

Marla and Dalton exchanged a glance. "So you think they found some buried treasure," she said, "and sold one or two pieces when they needed money? Until they deemed it safe to sell more?"

Sam's gaze fixed on them. "I'd read an interview with Warren where he claimed to be descended from pirates. I called his daughter and confessed my identity. All she knew were the stories her father had told her. So I looked up George's son, Howard. He'd changed the spelling of his last name, as you surmised. But I still found him. He was reluctant to talk to me. And he said something strange. 'If only he'd known,' Howard said about his dad. If only George had known what? That Ralph had fathered a son? Would that have made a difference?"

"You guessed right about the treasure." Dalton told him about the journal and his current investigations. "I assume Val hadn't discovered her father's book yet when you called her."

Sam's face paled. "Oh, my God. Do you think Howard is going around killing anyone who discovered his father's crime?"

"The friends didn't actually kill Ralph. Their crime, if any, was one of neglect."

"But their lack of action killed my father nonetheless. Howard might be afraid the truth would affect his reputation."

"Or maybe the boys' find is more significant than a single chest of gold coins," Marla suggested. "Tell us about shipwrecks in the area."

Sam moistened his lips. "Well now, that's a favorite topic of mine. Are you ready for a history lesson?"

"Go ahead," Dalton said. "It might be important to this case."

"The waters around Florida have seen ships flounder for decades, starting with Native Americans who used dugout canoes to travel up and down the coast. As civilization increased, ships and boats became vital to our development. Waterways were the most efficient means to transport people and cargo. Florida became a hub for maritime trade routes, but our waters can be treacherous. Hence we have a large number of shipwrecks offshore."

"What about treasure ships from Spanish fleets?" Marla asked, shifting in her seat. The hard wood bottom hurt her derriere.

An avaricious gleam entered Sam's eyes. "My estimate is that maybe thirty to forty Spanish ships, dating from the 1500s to the late 1600s, lay at the sea bottom. The Spaniards would pick up gold, silver, jewels, and rare spices from the Caribbean islands and the South and Central Americas. Sometimes, they'd stop at a mint in Mexico before grouping together to return home. Or they'd gather in Havana and leave from there under convoy."

"But not all of them made it."

"That's right. They'd get grounded on our reefs or floundered during hurricanes. For example, the Tierra Firme fleet set sail in 1622 from South America. Twenty-eight ships headed home to Spain. They ran into a fierce storm off the Florida Keys. Both the Nuestra Señora de Atocha and the Santa Margarita were lost. In 1985, Mel Fisher discovered the Atocha's resting place and its treasure."

"I'm hoping we have time to visit his museum," Marla said.

"Was the other ship ever found?" Dalton's rapt expression showed his fascination.

Sam's face folded into a frown. "The problem with that wreck site, unlike the deeper water where the Atocha sank, is that undercurrents cause shifting sand dunes. The Santa Margarita broke apart in a wide debris field. Through the years, people have discovered many of its relics, including a lead box filled with sixteen thousand pearls."

"That's amazing," Marla said. "Those ships must have been heavy with all the gold coins, silver bars, and jewels aboard. No wonder they sank. How many more ships like those two remain undiscovered?"

"Quite a few." Sam got up to pace the room. "Most of the known wreck sites are charted on maps. They're part of the state's historical preserves."

"Who owns the salvage rights to a sunken ship?" Marla asked, wondering about laws regarding lost treasure.

"According to the Abandoned Shipwreck Act of 1988, any historic find becomes the property of its respective state."

"Is that what happened when Mel Fisher discovered the Atocha?"

"He won a case in the U.S. Supreme Court to recover the treasure, but he had to donate a percentage to the state. Anyone who wants to explore a historic shipwreck today has to get a permit. The state won't always grant it, preferring for history to remain undisturbed."

Dalton stood to face the other man. "What about pirates? Did they capture any of these treasure ships?"

"Oh, yes. Unarmed merchant vessels were a prime target."

"I presume the pirates took their loot ashore. What happened to it?"

Sam pointed a finger at him. "You're thinking that the chest uncovered by those boys might have been part of a pirate's stash? There's one story that some folks take for legend, but it's based on a real person. A pirate nicknamed Red Ted, because of his lust for bloodshed, plied the waters off the Florida coast. He died in battle with an American naval warship. But when the troops arrived at his camp near St. Augustine, it was empty. No captives, no loot."

"Yes, I read about him." Even to Marla's own ears, her voice reflected her excitement. "Warren mentioned this guy in his journal. He thought they might have uncovered part of his hoard."

"Before his last voyage, Red Ted was getting set to retire. He'd loaded his goods onto a mule train and told his second in command to take it to Key West, where he planned to hole up in his later years. Then a sighting came for one more merchant ship that appeared to be unarmed. He couldn't resist this last kill and set sail. The vessel turned out to be a warship hiding under a merchant flag, and Red Ted shot himself rather than be captured."

"What happened to his mule train?" Marla asked.

"They were attacked by Indians on the route south. The natives made off with horses and mules and left them with fewer pack animals. They had to lighten their load and so buried some of the chests. They didn't have much better luck as they headed into swampland and were beset by storms as well as bandits. With dwindling resources, they buried more loads along the way."

"Hopefully someone kept track of those locations," Dalton said in a wry tone.

"Only one survivor staggered into Key West. He waited for Red Ted until word came that the pirate king was dead. Ravaged by disease, he tried to sell his map but nobody believed him. He headed north, afraid he'd be identified as a pirate and hanged. That was the last anyone heard about Red Ted's treasure. But the man had a pouch of uncut emeralds on him that provided him with a cushy lifestyle in the end. In my mind, that indicates the tales of Red Ted were true."

"And no one found any trace of this loot until Warren and his buddies dug up that buried chest?" Dalton asked.

"That's correct." Sam stroked his jaw. "Warren didn't have a map in his journal, did he? Because by rights, part of that treasure should belong to me."

"Unfortunately, no. To our knowledge, Warren and George never found more gold."

"It's all water under the bridge now, as far as I'm concerned," Sam said with a shrug.

"But not for us." Dalton gestured for Marla to rise. "We have our murder cases to solve. At any rate, it's been nice meeting you, Mr. Flint."

Outside, they strolled toward Duval Street. "Do you want to see if Mel Fisher's museum is still open?" Dalton suggested.

"Okay. So do you believe Sam? Do you think he had any further contact with Val or Howard?"

"I don't see what he'd accomplish. He couldn't blame the kids for what their fathers did."

"No, but you heard him," Marla persisted. "He'd want a cut if either of their fortunes were based on the discovery of that chest."

"But he hadn't read the journal. So how would he know what they'd found? He was only guessing."

"You have a point." She studied her map. "We're going the wrong way. The museum is located on Greene Street. We have to head back toward Mallory Square."

Dalton paid their entry fee inside the main entrance. They wandered through the historical exhibits that took up two floors. Awed by the artifacts, Marla lost track of time.

The staff chased them out at five o'clock, all too soon in her opinion. This place warranted another visit. She hadn't seen nearly enough in one hour.

"Now what?" Marla glanced at her watch. "We still have time before our dinner reservation. I don't relish walking to Louie's Backyard. It's at the opposite end of the island."

"Let's head back to the hotel. We can get changed, and then we'll take the car."

"I'll meet you," Marla said, spying a store she wanted to visit. "You go ahead. I have a few stops to make along the way."

He regarded her with a bemused smile. "We still have tomorrow morning."

"It's Sunday. These places don't open early. And we have to head home to be there for Brianna."

By the time she returned to the hotel, her arms were laden with packages. She rushed to get dressed for dinner in time for their seven o'clock reservation. She hoped Louie's Backyard lived up to its reputation.

She wasn't disappointed. Palms shaded the sign out front identifying the Victorian house originally built in the 1900s by a wealthy sea captain. Converted into a restaurant in 1971, it was further renovated by new owners and now was listed on the National Register of Historic Places.

They stepped up to a covered veranda with white columns where a series of rocking chairs invited guests to linger. As they entered through the front door, a hostess greeted them. High ceilings, crown molding, and polished wood floors gave the place a homey ambience. A staircase rose to a second level, where the restaurant's Upper Deck served small plates and a selection of wines.

They'd requested a table in the outside dining area at the rear of the house. Their white-clothed table held wine glasses, bread plates, and a glass-enclosed oil candle. They faced east and the Atlantic Ocean. The view to the side enchanted Marla with its sandy beach and graceful coconut palms, but she couldn't see the water stretching out to sea. The sky had darkened, and the moon didn't provide enough illumination.

After they had sampled their first glass of Chardonnay, they placed their orders. Dalton chose the miso-glazed grilled yellowfin tuna, and Marla ordered potato and olive crusted salmon. Dalton, sitting next to a potted red croton plant, reached for a slice of crusty bread.

"We forgot to ask at the hotel about Lora," Marla said, not allowing the ocean breeze to distract her. "What was the credit card charge that led you here?"

"It was a bar bill. Oddly enough, we didn't see any room charge."

"Hmm, just like the night of the ball. We should speak to the manager who was on duty that night."

"Tomorrow is Sunday. Let's hope he'll be there. If not, somebody else might be able to clue us in."

Marla took a sip of the wine. "Speaking of clues, what did we learn this afternoon?"

Dalton fingered his water glass. "I don't think Sam had anything to do with the murders. He's more interested in learning the truth about his father than leading a wild goose chase for a legendary pirate treasure."

"But what else do you think Nadia meant with her message? If not pirates, then that brings us back to Pilates."

"I know, and I'm not sure." His brow furrowed. "It's possible Howard believed there might be more gold coins hidden out there, but why kill Val? Because she'd learned about what his dad did so long ago? Or because she might want a cut of the treasure?"

"We should have shown Sam the photos Jason sent me." Her breath hitched. "Omigosh. Sam looks like the other guy in the picture with Howard."

"Let me see that one again." Dalton took her cell phone when she handed it over. He squinted as he brought up the photo images. "You're right. It's Sam without his beard."

"Does this mean he lied to us? He must have been there the night of the fundraiser."

"So he spoke to Howard at the event. Just because Sam was present doesn't prove anything. He could have come to gain news about his father."

"Then why not tell us he'd met Howard in person that night?" Marla bit her lower lip. "You know what I'm thinking? Jason sent us this photo. What if his research led him to Sam, and he realized Sam and Howard knew each other?"

"And then one of them killed Jason? For what reason?"

"Maybe they're both on the trail of buried treasure, and Jason discovered their plans."

"It bears further investigation, but not tonight. Let's focus on us." His hand snaked across the table and grasped hers. "We're having a romantic dinner. I want to enjoy my time alone with you."

"Tell me about it. We rarely get to have private time together anymore."

His brows waggled suggestively. "I suggest we take advantage of it. But there's one topic that concerns me. Don't you think it's time you went off the Pill?"

"What?" She withdrew her hand.

"You've been on it for a long time. We don't know the long-term effects. And if one day you decided to, you know, expand the family, it could be difficult. Your body would need time to adjust."

Oh no, we are not having this conversation now. "I'll think about it," she said in a chilly tone. Any romantic notions she might have had fled into the night.

He studied her face. "I'm only saying you might change your mind in the future, and then you could have difficulty getting pregnant. And it's a healthy choice to stop taking hormones. We'll use other means for birth control."

You're hoping we'll slip up, and I'll carry another little Vail inside.

"I'll give it serious consideration, but you know how I feel about having more kids in our household." A vision of tiny Luke came to mind. She mentally sniffed his baby scent and kissed his adorable toes.

No, Marla, don't go there. If you do, you'll lose twenty years of your life.

But what would she gain? The joy of watching your children grow to adulthood, their friendship as you got older, and their offspring to remember her after she passed on. Was she willing to risk the pain along with the pleasure? *It's not in my cards, thanks.*

"So did I tell you my mother is dating someone new?" she said in a bright tone to change the subject. "I'm relieved she's gotten rid of Roger, but don't you think it's too soon for her to be jumping into another relationship?"

Dalton took a moment to answer, sipping his conch chowder while Marla munched on a leaf from her Boston lettuce salad. "I don't think you're in a position to judge your mother's actions. If this guy makes her happy, that's what counts."

Marla bristled at his attitude. "She has to watch out for scam artists who prey on widows. I merely have her best interests at heart."

"Do you?" His sharp gaze pinned hers. "Or is it still difficult to accept that Anita might like another man besides your father?"

"Of course I want her to be happy. This man, his name is Reed, is a retired literature professor. He isn't Jewish."

Dalton pretended to be shocked. "Oh, my, what is the world coming to these days?"

She gave his hand a mock slap. "Like we should talk. You're right, I should be glad for her. But I'll feel better about it after we meet the guy."

"I know. It's your strong protective instinct speaking."

Marla's fingers crawled up his arm. She didn't want his thoughts to slide to her motherly instincts next. And so she flirted with him for the rest of the meal.

When they got back to the hotel, playing in the room was the sole thing on their minds. And so it wasn't until Sunday morning that Marla regained her senses and remembered their purpose in coming to Key West.

"We should see which hotel manager was on duty that evening," she told her husband, after reminding him of the bar bill engendered by Lora Larue.

They stood by the front desk where Dalton had gone to check out. Marla guarded their luggage while he settled the bill. The airy lobby had ceiling fans, potted palms, and furniture cushioned in tropical prints.

They'd had breakfast in the restaurant overlooking the water. Key West easily seduced its visitors into languor. The island ambience made you want to don flip-flops, sit on a bar stool, or lie in a lounge chair all day.

A yearning for travel gripped her. She'd always dreamed of going to Tahiti. Marla still kept a list of places to visit when her schedule lightened. How could Dalton even harbor the thought of having more kids when the world awaited them?

He made their inquiry at the registration desk, and the clerk scrolled through his computer records. "The manager was Paul

Otero on that date. He's just coming off night duty and might still be on the premises. Would you like me to ring him for you?"

"Please, I'd appreciate it." Dalton tapped his foot while waiting for a response.

A few minutes later, a middle-aged guy in a rumpled suit headed their way. He had tired eyes and a sagging jowl. Dalton introduced Marla and identified himself as a detective from Broward County.

"Do you know a woman named Lora Larue?" he began, spelling out her name.

Mr. Otero's face paled, and he glanced toward the front desk. "Um, I've met a few ladies by the name of Laura. What do you want to know?"

"This person stayed here as a guest and recommended the resort, but when I asked her the room cost, Lora said she didn't pay for her accommodations because her visit had been comped."

"Is that right?" Otero drew a finger around his collar. "Do you have the date when she checked in? Maybe she was a conference speaker or here on other business, and her company paid the tab." He had the desk clerk check their files. "I'm sorry, there isn't any such woman registered on that date."

"If Lora was here on business for Friends of Old Florida," Marla said, "they would have paid for Lora's room. But wouldn't it still be registered under her name, even if she didn't get a bill? Hotels always ask for your credit card for incidental charges."

"Regardless, we have no one by that name listed on our records. Why are you interested in her, anyway?"

"I'm investigating a murder. Three murders, actually, if we count a hit-and-run incident."

The manager swallowed, his Adam's apple moving visibly.

"You don't think this lady is some sort of merry widow killer, do you?"

Dalton's eyes narrowed. "I hadn't thought of her that way."

"I'm sorry I can't be of more help, but obviously if she stayed here, she didn't register under her own name."

"Dalton, may I have a word?" Marla drew her husband aside. "That guy isn't going to admit anything. We should talk to the bartender."

He glanced at her askance. "At this hour of the morning? The lounge is closed."

"Yes, but we can find out where he lives and track him down. He might have more information."

"Okay, we'll try that angle." Dalton approached the manager. "Thanks for talking to us, Mr. Otero. We won't keep you any longer."

As soon as the man had scurried away, Dalton slipped the desk clerk a twenty-dollar bill. "We need the name of the bartender who was in the lounge that night and where we can find him."

Shortly thereafter, they shoved their luggage into the trunk of Dalton's sedan before piling into his car. The bartender lived on the other side of the island. As they drove around, the magnificent view of the ocean stole her breath. A wide sidewalk bordered by a low concrete wall on the water side allowed bikers as well as walkers to enjoy the vista as they got their morning exercise. Fluffy clouds dotted the sky, its deep blue reflected in the sea.

Marla rested her elbow on the median between their seats. "I've been thinking. Lora might not pay for her room because FOFL covers it. If she travels on business for them, it makes sense."

"She'd still have a room assigned to her name. I believe there's more involved. You saw how Otero acted. He was

z

242

nervous. And that remark about a merry widow? Larue is up to something on these trips."

He turned down a lane edged with royal palms that led to a residential development. The homes were weathered one-story structures that had withstood the ravages of storms. Yards, overgrown with tropical foliage, led to houses that weren't nearly as grand as the ones in town. Nonetheless, these residences must still be pricy due to their location.

A television blared from within the yellow painted house they approached from a front walkway. Marla adjusted her purse strap as Dalton rang the bell. The noise dimmed and footsteps sounded.

"Who is it?" a man's gruff voice called.

"My husband and I are visitors to the island. We want to have a word with you about a customer at the lounge where you work," Marla said, since she sounded less threatening than Dalton. "Her name is Lora Larue."

The door swung wide. A thirtyish guy with lanky hair and an unshaven jaw stared at them. He wore a tee-shirt and shorts. "The name isn't familiar. What's she look like?" When Dalton gave the woman's description, his mouth fell open. "Well, what do you know? That sounds just like Lingerie Lora."

CHAPTER SEVENTEEN

Now it was Marla's turn to gape. "Lingerie Lora? What do you mean?"

"That's her stage name, or so I assume."

Marla gulped. This wasn't at all what she'd expected to hear. What kind of side business was Lora running? "I don't understand. Can you explain?"

"Why do you care?"

"I'm a detective from Broward County," Dalton replied. "She's involved in a case I'm investigating." When the guy remained mute, he handed over a couple of twenty-dollar bills.

Pocketing the money, the bartender averted his gaze. "She, you know, has customers to her room. The night manager is one of them. But I don't believe her claim that there's no funky business going on. I mean, come on, have you seen her website?"

A dog barked from another yard, and Marla shifted her feet. "Um, no. What's the URL?"

Dalton scribbled notes into a notepad while the man spoke. "Thanks, we'll look it up. How often does she come down here?"

The fellow's nose wrinkled. "Not that often. From things she's said, I've gathered she has clients all over the country. People talk to me at the bar. It's like they need someone to listen."

"I'm sure they do," Marla said in a soothing tone. "So how does she obtain her clients?"

"Guys contact her. It's all explained on her website."

"Have you heard of a woman named Valerie Weston? Did Lora ever mention her?"

"Sorry, the name doesn't ring a bell. I don't know much else about the lady except she's a generous tipper. I hope she visits us again soon."

Dalton gave him a business card. "If she does, will you send me a text message?"

"I suppose. I hope she isn't involved in anything bad. Her business might be kinky, but it isn't illegal, or so she says."

"Don't they all," Marla murmured. "Thanks so much for your cooperation," she told the guy, managing to withhold the sarcasm from her tongue. "Lingerie Lora? Would you believe it?" she said to Dalton once they were out of earshot.

"I wasn't expecting that, I'll tell you, but it might explain her extracurricular activities."

At the curb, Marla slid into their car, wincing at the broiling hot interior.

"Look it up on your phone while I drive." Dalton angled his broad shoulders through the driver's door. He buckled up and started the engine. A welcome blast of cool air poured from the vents.

Once they were headed north, Marla put "Lingerie Lora" into her browser search window. A number of sites popped up.

"Wow, would you believe there are videos, news articles, and more?"

"Go to the official website." Dalton repeated the Web address they'd been told.

Marla waited while the phone connected. "Lord save me. It's Lora." She stared at the screen, mesmerized by the image of Lora Larue's ample body in black lacey underwear.

"What's it say?" Dalton's brows shot up as he caught a glimpse.

"She gets paid to 'squash' men, but her site claims there's no sex involved. Yeah, right." Marla accessed the photo gallery. "Ugh, she sits on top of men's faces and does other poses."

A sordid image came to mind. What view would those guys have from beneath her bulk? *You can't tell me this isn't a turn-on for her customers.* Marla's nose wrinkled at the mental visions.

"I can't wait to see the YouTube videos," Dalton said with a teasing grin.

"I'll bet. We'll have to wait until we can access the desktop computer. I don't want to look at them now. This view is too amazing." She shut her phone down to peer out the window at the vista of sea and sky. This had to be one of the most beautiful drives on Earth.

With a stop for lunch, they didn't get home until nearly two. Since Dalton had called ahead, Brianna was there waiting for them along with Kate and John, who'd picked up the dogs from the kennel.

"We couldn't leave Brie here alone," Kate said, following Marla into the kitchen where she went to wash her hands.

Dalton deposited their luggage in the bedroom and then returned to properly greet his parents. "Hey, pumpkin," he said to Brianna, giving her a hug.

"Dad, can I go over Heather's house until New Year's? It's only for two nights."

"What? You just got home."

"Is that what you really want, honey?" Marla asked, willing to comply if it meant more private time for her and Dalton.

Brianna nodded, her long braid swinging at her back. "You're probably tired from your trip, and it's boring here. Heather's parents are having a New Year's Eve party."

John slapped Dalton on the shoulder. "Let her go, son. She'd rather be with her friends than with you old fogies." He winked at them. "Once Brie has her driver's license, you won't be seeing much of her."

"How was Disney World? We want to hear all about it." Marla hoped her husband wouldn't start his rant about teenage drivers. She spooned some coffee into the coffeemaker filter, needing a jolt of caffeine to face the remainder of the afternoon.

"It was great." Brianna proceeded to tell them about the rides she'd been on and what was new at the theme park.

"Sounds like you had a wonderful time." Marla beamed at her after turning on the device. Soon the aroma of brewing coffee filled the air. "Did you have lunch? Kate and John, can I get you anything to eat?"

Kate gave her an indulgent smile. "No, thanks, we're fine. We need to go home and unpack." Her mother-in-law's hair was nicely arranged, Marla noted idly. Kate wore a pleasing red and white skirt ensemble that looked suitable for a ladies' luncheon. Maybe she and John had plans for later on.

"I'm sorry we kept you."

"No problem. So did you learn what you set out to do?"

Dalton leaned against a counter. "We gained some valuable information. The hotel was great. We should take you there sometime," he told his daughter.

Brianna rolled her eyes. "I can't wait. I'm going to tell Heather that I'm coming over."

Dalton, realizing he was defeated, spread his hands.

"Hey, we should go visit Lora if she's home and tell her we've learned her secret," Marla suggested.

"That's not a bad idea. And I should check in with my partner to exchange news. Mom and Dad, are you going so soon?" he asked as his parents headed for the door.

"Yes, we really have to leave." Kate turned to face him and Marla, who'd trailed along. "Happy New Year in advance. Don't drink and drive. I'll see you on January first."

Brianna skipped after them to embrace her grandparents and say goodbye. Then she rushed to her room to phone her friend.

An hour later, Marla and Dalton sped east on Sunrise Boulevard toward the address he had for Lora Larue. The buxom lady lived on the twentieth floor of a high-rise condo. Its prime beach location would offer a view of the ocean on one side and the Intracoastal on the other. As a real estate agent, Lora might have gotten a good deal on this expensive piece of property.

Gripping her purse and comfortable in a pair of jeans and a knit top, Marla stepped out into the warm air at the parking garage. The humidity made it feel like summer. They needed another cold front to give the semblance of a Florida winter. At the front desk, she and Dalton each provided a picture I.D. The receptionist phoned Lora's apartment while Marla held her breath. Would she be home? And more importantly, would she see them?

An elevator ride later, they emerged onto her floor and found her door number. Lora wore a caftan-type ensemble with a turban on her head as she bade them enter. Her place smelled like chicken soup. Coming down the hall, Marla had sniffed various aromas as they walked along. Why did interior corridors like this always transmit cooking odors? It was merely one among many reasons why she'd never live in a high-rise unit.

"We're sorry to bother you on a Sunday," she said with a friendly smile. "Thank you for letting us in."

"We weren't sure if you'd be home or not." Dalton roamed the living room, peering at various knickknacks lying around. "You travel so frequently on behalf of FOFL."

"I don't do much traveling over the holidays. It's too expensive and not a lot of work gets done. My trips will resume in mid-January," Lora explained.

"You're lucky the group pays your expenses." Marla settled onto an armchair and crossed her legs. Lora had expensive tchotchkes but no family photos. Whoa, was that one of Val's paintings on the wall?

"So what is it you want?" Lora asked with a wary expression.

"We know what else you've been doing on your trips. How come you didn't mention it when I first interviewed you?" Dalton stood facing her, his taller height imposing.

Lora thrust her chin forward, no easy feat since she had a couple of them.

Bad Marla. Don't be so critical. This woman has hordes of customers for her alter ego.

"You didn't ask about my extracurricular activities, Detective. Nor are they relevant to the organization. What I do in my private time is my business."

"Did Val find out and threaten to curtail your trips?"

"Hell, no. She might have curtailed them by dying, unless she left our group a bequest like she promised."

Marla leaned forward. "We've seen your Internet site, Lingerie Lora."

Lora's complexion reddened. "So what? I'm careful to be discreet."

"Yet how would the Friends of Old Florida board members feel if they knew how you moonlighted on these travels? Maybe they wouldn't want you representing their organization."

"If so, I'd just raise my fees so my clients paid the travel fare."

"Is that why you don't register for your hotel rooms? You seduce the managers into becoming your customers to get your incidentals comped?"

"I don't seduce anyone. I get hired to do what I do. It doesn't interfere with my business for FOFL. I'm very dedicated in that regard."

Dalton paced across the carpet and back again. "I understand you belong to the same health club as Nadia Welsh. Did you ever overhear her talking to Val about the journal that had belonged to her dad?"

"Huh? I have no idea what you're talking about."

"Don't you find it more than coincidental that both Val and Nadia were killed?"

Lora stared at her. "Omigod, you don't think I'm next, do you? Is there some sort of serial killer going around picking out victims at sports clubs?"

Marla had to chuckle at that one. "Don't worry on that score, Lora. We doubt that's the case. But their deaths are related and so is Jason Faulks, the photographer from the fashion show. Do these photos mean anything to you?" She showed Lora the pictures on her cell phone.

Lora examined them and shook her head. "I recognize Howard in that one but I have no idea who this other guy is with him. And that's Yolanda's husband with a stranger. What does this mean?"

"They're clues Jason sent me," Marla said in a patient tone. "Nadia had a note on her person when she died that mentioned either Pilates or Pirates, depending on the middle letter. That's how we got onto the health club."

Lora sank into a seat and covered her face with her hands. "I'm truly sorry Val is gone. Despite what you think, she was a friend. I don't have many women friends, so that's saying a lot."

"How did you get started in this other business?" Marla asked, genuinely curious. "And how do potential clients contact you? I didn't see any email listed on your website."

"Believe it or not, I get booked through an agent. Once I'm with a client, I'll give them my personal contact info. I get a lot of repeat customers." Her ample chest puffed with pride. "If you think it would bother me to be let go by FOFL, you're mistaken. I make a six-figure income from my private business, not to mention my real estate clients."

"And you sit on people?" Marla scrunched her nose at the thought.

"Men like it. I fulfill their sexual fantasies. But I'm never naked and we don't have sex."

Marla could just imagine. She shut out the distasteful images and changed the subject. "So how did Val learn about your secret identity?"

Lora snorted. "She made a pass at me." The large woman noted their expressions. "You discovered she was gay, didn't you? It shocked the hell out of me. I would never have suspected it of her. When I turned her down, it put a strain on our friendship."

"Did she seem upset about anything in recent times that you noticed?" Dalton asked, settling onto a coastal-style sofa with beige upholstery, rolled arms, and a cherry wood frame.

Marla glanced around, taking in the tasteful furnishings and the accent pillows with their palm leaf motif. Lora had a keen eye for design. The woman continued to surprise her, but she found herself liking Lora despite their differences. Her gaze fell upon a paperback tossed on a side table titled *The Duke's Revenge*. Good heavens, Lora was a fan of romance novels. Who knew? Then again, maybe Lingerie Lora was still looking for love.

Lora twisted her hands together. "Val mentioned that she had misgivings about Howard handling her money. Have you spoken to him?"

"Howard is the trustee on Val's estate," Dalton replied. "We understand his father and Val's dad had been friends. That's likely how he obtained management of their accounts."

"Val preferred for other people to handle the mundane details of her life. She probably didn't question his role for years."

"Did Val ever talk about her dad in his youth?"

"He claimed that he might have been descended from pirates.

251

Val doubted his history was so colorful."

"What do you think happened to make her distrust Howard Cohn?"

Lora shrugged. "Maybe she took a look at her investments for a change and asked Howard about them."

"How well do you know the group's treasurer?"

"We're just acquaintances through the organization, although I've run into him a couple of times at those Renaissance festivals."

Marla interceded. "What do you mean?"

"We both belong to a creative anachronism society. You know, we dress up once a year in medieval costume and have a fair. I like to play a tavern wench. But Howard, he's a real actor. He'll usually go for the role of a highwayman or bandit, but I've seen him play a pirate, too."

"You're kidding." Marla couldn't picture the staid banker in costume, let alone hamming it up as an outlaw. How far from the truth was the part he played?

"You talk about my secret life." Lora's blue eyes sparkled. "Ask Howard about his moonlighting activities. I haven't seen him in the playhouse myself, but I hear he's pretty good."

"In the playhouse? Are you saying he actually works as an actor?"

"Oh, yes." Lora gave a low chuckle. "It's amazing how we all hide a secret side of ourselves. What's yours, Marla?"

"I'm too busy at work to have time for anything else."

"That's a shame. We all need a creative outlet." She pointed to Dalton. "And you, Detective? Are you a workaholic, too?"

He allowed a small smile to play about his lips. "I grow tomatoes, do crossword puzzles, take walks in the park. But I don't paint or do photography or act in the theater, if that's what you mean. Did you know Val displayed her artwork in the same gallery as Jason Faulks? He was a photographic artist. The gallery is next door to Yolanda's shop. Is that a coincidence?"

Lora got up to pace the carpet. "Val was devoted to her art. It gave her great pleasure to spend time in her studio."

"Do you think the fashion show will continue without Val's patronage?" Dalton asked in a mild tone.

Marla recognized his interrogation technique. This might appear to be a friendly conversation, but he was digging for information.

"I hope so," Lora replied. "It's a critical fundraiser for FOFL."

"Are you really interested in old buildings? How did you get involved in the group?"

She stopped to glare at him. "I care about our history. It's important to preserve our past. My day job is in commercial real estate. So often we see old structures torn down to make place for the new. We lose our heritage. If I come across a piece of property that has historical value, I'll notify Friends of Old Florida so they can get involved."

Marla uncrossed her legs and leaned forward. "What you do think of Yolanda? Her event generates press and attracts a crowd to your fundraiser. I found her missing headpiece, by the way, and returned it to her."

Lora's face brightened. "I'm glad to hear it. Where was the thing?"

"A person stole it who later had second thoughts. I doubt she's anyone you know."

"I like Yolanda. She's extremely talented."

Marla swallowed, her throat dry. Lora hadn't so much as offered them a glass of water, but then, they were invading her privacy on a Sunday. Her legs restless, she squirmed on the chair. They'd sat all morning in the car driving up from the Keys, and now this. They should take a walk to get some exercise. But she remained silent, letting Dalton lead the conversation and providing him with her support. Besides, she might pick up on something he missed. What had Lora said about Howard Cohn's hobbies?

Dalton rose to stretch his limbs. "In your real estate work, how much contact do you have with Rick Rodriguez?"

"I've dealt with him on several occasions. He's usually successful in his bids to acquire land for his various projects."

"Tell me about Val's fight with him over that strip on Hollywood Beach. I understand Solomon Gold owns some of those structures, and Val was opposing Rodriguez at FOFL's request. Or did Gold have more personal interests in mind for prompting her intervention?"

"Val loved that architecture from the thirties. She didn't get involved because of Gold's concerns. It was her genuine belief that those buildings belonged on the historic register."

"How far would Rodriguez go to obtain a property he deemed valuable?" Dalton asked.

Marla gave him a sharp glance. Where was he going with this line of questioning? Did he know something she didn't? A wisp of suspicion crept into her head. What had Dalton learned from his partner when he'd called Kat earlier? Now that she thought about it, he hadn't mentioned their conversation.

"Rick can be pretty obstinate," Lora said. "He's always juggling several projects. But I assume you've spoken to him. Do you consider him a suspect in any of these cases? Or me, for that matter?" Her eyes rounded as though she'd just had the thought.

"We're looking into all the possibilities, Miss Larue. Is there anything else you'd like to tell us? Or anyone whom you think might have wanted to cause harm to Val or Nadia?"

He didn't mention Jason, Marla noticed. Was that because his murder hadn't been premeditated? It had appeared to be a crime of opportunity, whereas Val's demise had been meticulously planned.

Lora's brow folded. "No, but I hope you catch the person. It's horrible how Val died. And Nadia, too. I still can't believe it." She shivered and wound her arms across her chest.

Marla hoped Lora wasn't next on the list. The killer might believe Lora knew something, putting her in danger.

"You've looked into Dr. Needles, I presume," Lora blurted suddenly to Dalton.

He gave her a startled glance. "We have. Why do you mention his name?"

"Ashley, the model, says he's the go-to person for prescription pain meds. But I want to consult him on a different issue. I'd like to know what you've learned about his surgical skills. Are there any malpractice suits against him? Are his patients satisfied?"

"I don't understand." Dalton frowned at her.

"I've asked him about weight-loss surgery. It's an option I've considered, especially since I'm at risk for developing diabetes."

"It's a risky procedure, isn't it?" Marla said, not too familiar with the options.

"In more ways than one." Lora mashed her lips, her expression tormented. "I should lose weight for health reasons, but then would men still want me? They like my size the way it is. I'd stand to lose everything."

"Not everything, Lora. You'd have your important work for FOFL, your real estate business, and your other hobbies. You could still play a sexy tavern wench at the medieval fair." Marla regretted her last words when Lora looked about to cry. This choice must have been weighing on her mind.

A wave of compassion hit her. She felt sorry for Lora, who seemed lonely in this tower apartment all by herself. Lora had admitted to not having many female friends. Maybe her secret identity was her way to gain affection.

"My sister makes fun of me, you know," Lora said, her head

255

down. "She says I don't do anything to help myself, and I've let myself get this way. But my sister was always Mom's favorite. She doesn't understand."

So you began eating to comfort yourself, Marla surmised. Maybe Lora feared she'd slip back into her old habits even if she had the weight-loss surgery. It was a dilemma, all right. But the woman would never succeed unless she liked herself first.

"Have you considered counseling?" Marla suggested in a soft tone. "You might want to look into why this role as Lingerie Lora is important to you. You're a valuable asset to Friends of Old Florida, and you sell commercial real estate. Do you really need this other side business that you have to hide?"

"I like the money aspect, but I suppose I could get by without it. What would I tell my fans?"

"Exactly what you've told us. You had to lose weight for health reasons. You might be surprised. They might still want your, er, services."

"You're right." Lora swiped at her eyes. "Maybe I should talk to someone first. I'm glad you stopped by, but I don't think I've helped you much with your case, Detective."

"We appreciate everything you've told us," Dalton said in a formal tone.

Marla sprang from her seat, unable to sit any longer. Inwardly, she smiled at Dalton's reaction. He was great at interrogating suspects but less so when it came to expressing empathy.

"So what now?" she asked him once they were back inside their car and cruising south. It was getting late. The ocean glistened to their left, a murky green until it deepened further out to sea. Strollers crowded the sidewalk bordered by a low concrete wall in a wave design, while cafés on the other side of the street bustled with patrons seated outdoors.

Once again, Marla vowed to lessen her load so she could

enjoy life at her leisure. But would she be happy that way? Or would she only be satisfied with tasks to accomplish each day?

"Now we pay a visit to Howard Cohn and see what he has to say."

She glanced at Dalton's stern profile and thrilled to his strong presence. It didn't fail to astound her how he valued her input. A surge of affection made her pat his arm and smile. "I'd much rather park and walk along the beach. My legs need the exercise. Promise me we'll come back here when we have some free time."

"Sure, Brie would love it, too. But first, we have to wrap this case before anyone else gets hurt."

"I know. What did Kat tell you when you called her earlier? Did it have something to do with FOFL's treasurer that you want to visit him next?"

"Kat found something fishy going on with Val's investment accounts. She believes the trustee might have been siphoning money for years by putting it into phony funds that supposedly fizzled. Val only got wind of it recently when she wrote a check on her account that bounced due to lack of available cash."

"Do you think Val questioned Howard about it?"

"I'll bet she did and threatened to get an audit."

"So Howard could risk losing millions and going to jail. That's motive for murder."

He gave a grim nod. "Let's see if he's home. An unexpected visit might throw him off guard."

CHAPTER EIGHTEEN

"I should be visiting Cohn with my partner instead of you, but we're close by and I'd rather not waste time," Dalton told Marla. "If things go south, promise me you'll leave to get help."

"Don't worry; I'll clear out if there's any threat." *It should be okay if they keep this a friendly chat. Dalton can come back later with the handcuffs if necessary.*

Howard Cohn lived in Mangrove Isles, a community of pricey homes bordered by canals in east Fort Lauderdale. His Mediterranean-style villa had iron grillwork on a second-story balcony, ceiling fans on a covered porch, and hurricane-impact windows facing the front lawn. Tropical greenery bordered a paved walkway to the door.

"Does Howard have a family?" Marla asked, unable to recall his marital status.

"He got divorced eight years ago. His kids live with the ex-wife."

Unfortunately, no one answered the bell or their loud knock at the front door.

"Could he be out back?" Marla suggested. "Maybe he doesn't hear us."

"I'll go check. Wait for me, and don't make any moves on your own."

"I have an idea," she said when her husband returned and shook his head in defeat. "Lora mentioned that Howard works as an actor at a playhouse. This is Sunday evening. He might have a performance."

"You could be right, but I need something to eat and then I'm taking you home."

"Heck no, I want this to end as much as you do. We're getting close. I can feel it in my bones."

"It's *my* duty to solve this case, not yours. Your safety is paramount. I shouldn't have brought you here."

An hour later, while they sat in a restaurant and waited for their check, Marla accessed the Internet and cross-referenced Howard's name with community theaters in Fort Lauderdale.

"Give it up, Marla. I'm driving you home." Dalton peered anxiously for their waiter.

"But we're close by. I just found a place with his name listed. It's a theater east on Sunrise. We could possibly reach him before the curtain rises."

"Damn, you're stubborn. All right, but you'll stay in the car."

However, when they arrived, only ten minutes remained before curtain time. Dalton bought tickets for them both at an old-fashioned glass-enclosed booth under an overhang with bright signage. Marla had never known a theater existed here. This structure looked to be quite old.

They were lucky to get seats, having decided to confront Howard after the show. He was playing in the latest musical rendition of *Peter Pan*. A number of families with children sat in the audience. Marla leafed through the playbill before the lights dimmed, noting Howard's role as the infamous Captain Hook. So he liked pirates, did he?

"Hey, look at this." Dalton nudged her. "In the credits, the theater company thanks Howard Cohn for his patronage. He must be a big donor."

She couldn't envision the prim banker belting out a tune, but he surprised her on stage. Under his makeup and cosmetic enhancements, she could hardly recognize him.

Hold that thought. Cosmetic enhancements? Did he use liquid latex to create those scars on his face? "Look at his makeup," she whispered to Dalton. "He might have a supply of the stuff that killed Val Weston."

"Quiet," someone hissed from behind.

Dalton raised his eyebrows but remained silent. They'd head backstage as soon as the lights came up. There wasn't any intermission, as the performance only ran for an hour and a half. Marla zoned out as various puzzle pieces fell into place.

Howard, son of George from the journal, had a fondness for history and shipwrecks in particular. Hadn't he told her so himself? Dr. Ian Needles was a certified diver. Did they work together searching for Red Ted's downed vessel? Did Howard believe the pirate had treasure aboard? Or was his search confined to land in the vicinity where his father had camped? Was he stealing from Val's investments to fund these expeditions?

Eager to determine the truth, she headed backstage with Dalton after the last curtain call. It took a good fifteen minutes to get past the crowd and locate the entrance to the rear area. But a hefty security guard blocked their way.

"Sorry, folks, you'll have to wait out front with the others. The cast should be there momentarily to greet guests."

"We need to have a word in private with one of the actors," Dalton said, flashing his badge.

They argued for another five minutes until the dressing room doors opened and actors—dressed in street clothes—spilled past toward the front lobby. Howard wasn't among them.

"Where can we find Howard Cohn?" Dalton demanded, his patience gone.

"Dressing room number three. But he should have come out with the others."

He didn't. His space was empty when they'd pushed through

the unlocked door. A quick search of the other rooms left them with one conclusion. Howard had fled. Maybe he'd spotted them in the audience, or maybe he'd just had to leave early for some reason.

While Dalton sped for the street exit at the end of the corridor, Marla gnashed her teeth in frustration. She scanned the room's contents, looking for a hint of where Howard might have gone. An array of colorful costumes hung on a rack. Shelving held wigs and beards, pirate hats and leather belts. She walked closer to the dressing table that faced a mirror. It held a selection of cosmetics, including a bottle labeled Liquid Latex.

Ah, the proverbial smoking gun. With the finger of guilt pointing at Howard, Marla wondered at his motive. Was it really about buried treasure? Or was it about removing the threat to his reputation from his father's misdeeds? Or maybe the past wasn't the reason at all. Maybe Val had latched onto Howard's theft of her money after all these years. He had means and motive, and via Patty the shampoo assistant, also opportunity.

She scoured the room, halting at a diagram and photos tacked up on the wall. What was this? It looked to be a construction project with various standing structures earmarked for renovation. Puzzled, Marla traced each one with her forefinger. In the bottom left corner of the blueprint was a note that said "Pirate's Playground."

She'd never heard of a place by that name. Where was it located? Accessing the Internet on her cell phone, she did a search. What came up made her gasp in astonishment.

"Listen to this," she said to Dalton when he'd returned empty-handed. "Pirate's Playground used to be a theme park in Hollywood. Built in 1966, it stood on one hundred acres of land off Sheridan, east of Federal Highway. Rock concerts were held there, and the site was also featured in film and television shows."

"No way. What happened to it?"

"Disney World opened and drew the crowds away. It went into bankruptcy and closed in 1976. A bid to open a biblical theme park there fell through when Orlando was chosen for the site. The property has gone through various owners since then but has never made it past the planning stage."

"So what is it to Howard Cohn?"

Marla clicked on another link, frowning at the small screen. She hadn't planned to upgrade her smartphone but maybe it was time. "Here's an article that says a new owner has purchased the property and plans to erect condominiums, but the redevelopment is being opposed. Another party wants to get the site declared a historic property and restore it instead as a monument to the past."

"In this case, I'd probably support the redevelopment. Who needs another theme park? And even restored, would it merely serve as a museum on an expensive piece of land, or would it actually be operational?"

"That's not the point. How is FOFL's treasurer involved?"

Dalton shrugged his broad shoulders. "If I had to guess, I'd say he's the one interested in the preservation angle. Look at this diagram. It lists all the attractions as they must have been in the park's heyday. He wants to see it restored."

"Of course. Howard loves pirates. It would suit his nature." Having learned enough, Marla turned off her browser and stuck the phone in her jeans pocket.

"Cohn could be supporting this effort with funds he stole from Val."

"Among his other interests, like this theater." She examined some papers lying about on an armchair. "Looks as though he wants to renovate this place, too."

"It needs fixing," Dalton agreed, pointing to the marred baseboards and worn carpet.

He looks tired, Marla realized. They should go home and pick up where they left off tomorrow. She was about to make this suggestion when her glance fell upon a note card in the trash can. *Meet me at PP after the show.* Bending over, she plucked it from the receptacle.

"Look, do you suppose this is where Howard went? It could mean Pirate's Playground."

"Why would he meet someone there after dark?" Dalton took the message to examine it. Then he rummaged in the trash can but soon gave up. "There's nothing else, not even an envelope. Somebody might have delivered this note to Cohn. I can ask around."

"Or not. How far are we from the theme park site? If it's off Route One, we'd just have to drive south for a bit."

"I suppose we could check it out. I need to nail this guy." Dalton yanked out his cell phone. "I'll notify Kat for backup."

With all the traffic lights and fumbling around the territory trying to find the place without any signage, it was nearly eleven by the time they reached the place. Dalton pulled into a deserted parking lot filled with potholes and weeds. A lone street light provided dim illumination. After shutting the ignition, he withdrew a couple of sturdy flashlights from one of the interior compartments. But he hesitated before handing one to her.

"You'd better stay in the car until I check things out."

"Why don't you wait for Kat?"

"I want to see if Cohn is here before I waste her time."

"Fine, then I'm coming with you." Should she take her purse or leave it here locked up? Better to keep it, she thought, considering the mini can of hair spray and metal nail file she kept inside. They might come in handy. Nonetheless, she slung the strap diagonally across her chest so she'd be hands free.

"If Cohn is here, we'll wait for reinforcements." Outside on the asphalt, Dalton moved forward. "I wish we had a map. This place is spooky at night."

"I snapped a picture of Howard's diagram on my cell phone." Her shoes crunching on gravel, Marla shivered at the sight of ghostly rides rising in the gloom.

"That won't help us. We don't know which way he went."

"Look, two cars are parked at that end, in the shadows. One of them should belong to Howard. Maybe he left footprints we can follow."

They spoke in low tones so their voices wouldn't carry. Over by the corner, Dalton shone his flashlight at the ground, revealing shoe imprints in the soft grass. But the trail ended when they reached a concrete path.

"Here's the old ticketing stand." Dalton pointed to a toll-booth type structure beside a rotted wood fence. A gate swung in the breeze, making creaking noises.

"It's sad how these old places fall apart and are forgotten," Marla said, kicking at a pebble.

"This land would be worth something, though. Let's go inside. Who could Cohn be meeting and why?"

"Maybe the builder means to offer him a bribe if he halts his opposition to the redevelopment project."

"You could be right."

Inside the gate, they paused to survey the territory. A full moon came out from behind a cloud, providing enough illumination to discern shadowy forms looming in the dark. A huge replica of a pirate ship rose on their left, its ropes clanging in the wind. Cannons were aimed at the walkway. Marla guessed they had been loaded with water to shoot passersby.

"There's another ship somewhere on a fake waterway," she said. "Pirates fired at the vessel while it sailed on the so-called river. The crew shot back to protect their passengers. I imagine it was like a variation of the jungle cruise at Disney World."

"This must have been a fun place when it was open."

Marla's scalp prickled. Where could Howard have gone? As an actor who liked playing pirate, what would have been his favorite attraction?

An observation tower drew her attention. It had cages suspended in the air. From what she'd read, people considered this a thrill ride back in the day.

Up ahead to their left rose a twisting rollercoaster. A cool breeze lifted the hairs on her arms and brought with it the aroma of dry dirt. She shut off her flashlight to conserve power, letting Dalton lead with his turned on when the moon slipped behind a cloud.

They passed the remains of a log flume and a water slide, skirted a funhouse called Pirate's Den, and ended up beside an arcade. Marla studied the ring toss game. She'd never been good at that sort of thing.

"It's too quiet here," Dalton said in a hushed tone. "I don't like it."

"Of course it's quiet. What did you expect?" Marla paused in front of a shooting gallery. She figured that was one game where Dalton would excel.

Hey, was that man-sized target moving? The hanging figure was dressed as a pirate. He looked hauntingly similar to the character played by Howard Cohn onstage.

She poked her husband. "Be subtle about it, but take a look at the target for that shooting game. Am I imagining things, or does he resemble Howard more than he should?"

The moon emerged, allowing them to see more clearly.

"Stay here," Dalton told Marla before he strode around the corner.

She saw him emerge and prod the target, but she couldn't see much else beyond. "Well? Is it real or a dummy?"

"It *is* Howard Cohn. He's dead. And his body is still warm."

A loud crack sounded, and a whoosh of air zinged past Marla's ear. "Somebody's shooting at me!" She crouched down, wondering which way to run. She couldn't tell the direction of their assailant.

"Get over here," Dalton called before disappearing out the exit.

She scurried around to meet him. He hovered at the rear of the structure, waiting for her with his weapon drawn.

"We'll head toward the park entrance," he said, his face grim. "Could you tell where the shooter was located?"

"No idea, sorry. What's he still doing here?"

"Your guess is as good as mine, unless this was a setup for all of us."

"I'd hoped you might be tailing Howard," said a deep voice from behind.

They whirled around. Rick Rodriguez aimed a gun at them. Or rather, he aimed it directly at Marla's head.

"Lower your weapon to the ground, Detective. If you fire, I can get off a shot before I drop. It'll kill your wife."

Marla sensed Dalton's hesitation. Then he bent slowly, placing his gun on the ground.

"Kick it away out of reach."

Dalton complied but kicked it in her direction. He'd taken her to the firing range. If they could distract Rodriguez, she might be able to scoop the weapon up and use it.

"Why would you want Howard dead?" she asked to get the developer talking. Dalton had called for backup. How long before Kat arrived?

"The idiot played his pirate role too well. He'd been stealing money from Val Weston's accounts, and she caught on to him. She interfered with my projects, too. So I got rid of her as a favor to us both. This site, when redeveloped, will be worth millions. I'd hoped to gain Howard's support, but he had his own dreams to restore the theme park. The guy was nuts about pirates and the past. We couldn't come to an agreement, so I shot him."

His matter-of-fact tone sent chills up Marla's spine. "So this has nothing to do with the journal written by Val's father, Warren?"

Rodriguez gave a snort of laughter. "Not for me. Their parents did a bad thing together. Howard told me all about it and how Ralph's son had entered the picture."

"Jason Faulks caught them on camera together at the ball. Did one of them kill Jason?" Marla asked, keeping her voice even.

"Faulks had the notion he'd make a good journalist. He'd been researching articles about the region's past and its history of shipwrecks. He might have exposed Howard's secret expeditions, and that publicity would lead to closer scrutiny. Howard had been funding his treasure hunts with money from Val Weston's accounts. So Howard took matters into his own hands. He killed Faulks and stole his camera."

Marla gasped. "Howard confessed to you?"

"Yes, and he killed that other woman, too. Val's friend. Once he heard about the journal, he tried to get his hands on it. All he cared about was finding that pirate stash. But looking for buried loot was never my goal. I want the gold in this ground, meaning the land development. I'm not about to let anyone get in my way, including you."

"Is that why you bribed Andrew Fine into slanting his articles in favor of your latest projects?" Marla said hastily, seeing his gun arm raise a notch.

"That's so." He spared a glance around them. "Now let's see. Where can I stage your death so it looks like a horrible accident?" His gaze halted on the observation tower. "I can use the manual lever to hoist you to the top. And when that cage comes crashing down, people will wonder why you were so fool-ish as to explore this site at night."

"You won't get away with it," Dalton said in a calm tone. "I've called for backup. They know we're here."

"But your pals think you're tracking Howard, right? No one will be looking for me."

No, but they'll see your car in the parking lot if we can stall you long enough. Marla's heart raced as she fixated on the gun pointed at her.

"Head over to the tower," Rodriguez said, his silver hair glint-ing in the moonlight. His hooked nose, determined eyes, and fighter's physique would make him a worthy opponent in a fist-fight. Marla hoped they could subdue him another way.

"Tell me one thing," she replied, not moving. "How did you learn about Val's allergy? That method of killing her was diaboli-cal. I'd think you would have gone for a more direct approach, like a hit and run."

He grinned in pride. "That worked for Howard in getting rid of Nadia. I figured with the allergic reaction, either the beauti-cian would be blamed for Val's death or that stupid shampoo girl would take the fall. I paid her to sabotage the face cream and change Val's appointment."

"So Howard didn't supply you with the liquid latex? It wasn't his idea?"

"Hell, no. I bought the stuff on the Internet. It's easy enough to obtain. As for who told me about Val's allergy, that was Lora Larue. She's the commercial real estate agent handling the sale of this property."

Marla sucked in a breath. "So she's in on this with you?"

"She agrees this site is ripe for redevelopment. Is she involved in anything else? Nope. The broad is too dumb to see beyond her nose. But I'm not, and I know you're stalling. So move."

They hadn't walked a few feet at gunpoint when a flight of

geese took off with wild squawking in front of them. Dalton pushed Marla to the side.

"Run! We'll split up and meet at the lair."

Marla dashed away, her shoes kicking up dirt as Rodriguez cursed and fired wildly into the night. Her chest heaving, she ran until she had to pause to take a breath. And then she realized she had no idea where she was or what Dalton had meant by a lair.

CHAPTER NINETEEN

Marla stood still to regard her surroundings and get her bearings. A large ship rose at a dock to her left, but it wasn't the same one as the ship at the park entrance. This vessel rode on water, unlike the other replica. And it actually appeared sailworthy. It must be the water ride she'd read about, where the crew fought pirates to protect their passengers and Indians pretended to shoot arrows from the shore.

The rippling current sparkled in the moonlight. For a moment, she wondered if the waterways led to an outlet, or if they'd been constructed here for this purpose. It was tempting to look for a boat or raft and find out. But if it did have an outlet, the water might also harbor alligators. No, thanks. She'd better locate another escape route.

But Dalton hadn't asked her to leave. He'd wanted to lure Rodriguez somewhere. And the crooked developer might have the main exit blocked from access anyway, depending on where he was located.

She patted her purse, still strapped to her shoulder, but didn't dare retrieve her flashlight inside. She'd have to stumble around in the night. The wind had picked up, whistling through the park's derelict rides and causing the ship's wood to creak and its lines to clank against each other. The eerie sounds in the deserted park gave her the shivers. Is that where the pirate phrase, "Shiver me timbers" came from?

Wait, could Nadia have meant this place when she scribbled

that note? Perhaps she'd been attempting to write Pirate's Playground, and not Pilates or Pirate? And how did she figure things out, anyway? She must have put the pieces together from what Val had told her.

It didn't matter now. Marla listened acutely for footsteps or heavy breathing but heard nothing indicating another human within range. Maybe she should text Dalton and ask him where he meant they should meet. But his phone might jangle and give away his position, so she discarded that option.

He said to go to the lair. Where could he mean?

One possibility took precedence. The Pirate's Den attraction would fit that description.

She'd lost all sense of direction. She stood immobile, afraid to move and yet desperate to make a run for it. If only she knew what her husband had in mind. It was unlike him to abandon her like this. Yet in doing so, it showed his trust that she would figure it out. She couldn't let him down.

Leaving the walkway, she trod on soft grass, attempting to use the moon for guidance. She could take out her cell phone but the glare might be too revealing. At the front entrance, the moon had been overhead at two o'clock. She pictured her map. The den was at a far left corner of the park. So the moon should be behind her, right?

She got confused at the angles and moved forward. It wouldn't accomplish anything to stand there. Maybe she'd make her way back to the car through an opening in the fence further along. It had to be in disrepair same as the attractions.

Her glance fell upon the rollercoaster stretching toward the sky. Hey, she could use that structure plus the observation tower for landmarks. Those should help guide her toward the rear corner she sought.

A loud honk made her jump with fright and her heart pound so fast she felt dizzy. A couple of geese picked at the grass ahead.

Damn, they were noisy things. This must be a feeding ground for them.

She sidestepped past and kept moving, her sixth sense alert for any unusual sounds. Her breath huffed in the cool air and cold chills racked her. She wriggled her fingertips, icy from fear. Momentarily distracted, she didn't watch where she was walking and crunched on a big twig. Tree debris covered the grounds where the landscaping had overgrown.

A cough sounded from behind. Her pulse throbbed in her throat, and she hastened forward. Judging from the tower, she must be headed in the right direction. She prayed Dalton would be there, otherwise she'd be lost.

Think, girl. You've used your own wits before to defeat a killer.

Why would Dalton choose this particular attraction? Pirate's Den must be some sort of tunnel ride. Were there scenes depicting the brigands' treasure and their captured slaves? Tableaux of debauchery after a raid in town? Skeleton figures popping out of nowhere to scare visitors? Images of similar rides at other theme parks came to mind.

Those attractions had models of pirates wearing gun belts, knives, and axes.

Yes, of course. Dalton could pick up a weapon there, assuming they weren't all made of rubber.

She stumbled upon the place by accident, roaming past the log flume that snaked through the park. Canals crisscrossed the property and served as fictional rivers for the play land.

Light flickered from within the gaping maw of the den entrance. Constructed of fake boulders, it resembled a cave. Aware she'd be presenting herself as a target, she stepped across the threshold. Lit torches in wall sconces emitted smoke and provided enough illumination for her to see where the space narrowed ahead so guests would have to form a line. Faux calcite columns and stalactites contributed to the illusion of a cavern.

She peered around but the edges remained shadowed. She couldn't see what was beyond the torch light. Dalton must have gotten here first to light them.

"Move inside," he commanded in a low tone. "Stand in the center."

Unable to identify his position, she obeyed, her teeth chattering. One wrong move and Rodriguez would shoot her. Where was Dalton hiding? She turned in a circle, but her narrowed gaze couldn't discern his tall figure anywhere.

"Stop right there," Rodriguez called from behind.

She spun to face him, putting on a brave front. He stood silhouetted in the ride entrance. Could she sling her purse far enough to strike him? Her breath came in short, labored bursts as she noticed his gun pointed her way. Could he hit her at that range?

He stepped closer, allowing her to see the triumph on his face. His mouth widened in a sneer as he neared. "Where's your husband?"

"I don't know. I lost him."

"Liar. He must be around somewhere. Who else lit these torches?"

"Rick, please don't do this. You might as well give up. The authorities will be searching for you. Dalton can make you a deal."

"I'm not going to rot in prison. Besides, you've been a pain. I'll enjoy this." He raised his gun arm.

"Marla, duck!" Dalton yelled.

She dove to her right, which was to Rodriguez's left as he fired from his right hand. Then he cried out and fell to his knees as another shot cracked the air from behind him.

Dalton sprinted forward, holding an axe backward, and

brained him with the handle.

Rodriguez crumpled to the ground.

As Marla shakily rose to her feet, Dalton holstered his ankle gun and whipped out a pair of handcuffs that he kept in his pocket when off-duty. He proceeded to secure the suspect.

His cell phone rang. "You take it and tell Kat where we are," he ordered. When she'd hung up, his solemn gaze met hers. "Marla, I would never put you in danger. I had him the minute he stepped inside."

She looked in the direction where he was pointing. He'd been standing on a ledge to the side of the entrance. It was part of a narrow path for guests to follow toward the exit in case the power failed.

A smile played about her mouth. "I know. I love you."

"I love you, too. You're the best."

"I am, aren't I? But we're better as a team."

CHAPTER TWENTY

"Ma is late. She should have called by now," Marla told Dalton in the kitchen on New Year's Day. Brianna was back home, and all of their other guests had arrived. Her mother was always on time, which is why Marla worried. "Maybe I should text her. She might have run into car trouble."

"Don't worry, there could be any number of reasons why she's delayed. The new boyfriend might have been late to pick her up. They're probably on their way."

She checked the steamer trays in the oven. Tonight had called for Italian food, and she'd shamelessly ordered it from her favorite restaurant. Dinner would be buffet style with casual seating. Everyone was still tired from last night.

It had been a fun evening, even though Marla missed spending it with Tally and Ken. This had been the first year in forever that they hadn't clinked champagne glasses together at midnight. A pang of hurt gnawed at her that her best friend wouldn't even stop by today with the baby to say hello.

She plastered a smile on her face, picked up a tray of hot mini-quiches, and took them into the adjacent room where people stood chatting. Besides family members, they'd invited friends and neighbors. Dalton's mom dogged her heels as she headed toward the refrigerator to replenish the ice bucket. Marla's mother-in-law wore a sweater with fashion jewelry and belted pants. Comfort was the dress code for this informal gathering.

"Are you sure you don't need any help?" Kate asked.

"No, but thanks for offering. Go sit and relax. Can I get you a cup of coffee?"

"I'm good, thank you. Will you be coming to the art fair next month? John has a booth to display his stained glass designs."

"I know. We've reserved the date. I'm excited for him."

Kate glanced toward the front window. "Where's your mother?"

The doorbell rang. "Maybe that's her." Marla put down the ice scoop in her hand and hastened to the foyer. From somewhere out back, the dogs barked. They were secured in the fenced yard, out of harm's way. She didn't want them inside with food lying around, and they'd bother the company with their demand for attention.

Anita stood on the stoop along with a handsome fellow with graying reddish hair and a trim beard. "Marla, this is Renfield Westmore. Reed, this is my daughter, Marla Vail."

They shook hands. Marla appreciated his firm handshake and friendly smile. Lines crinkled beside his eyes as though he smiled often, and he had a pleasant quirk to his lips. She couldn't help her quick glance at his lean torso as she stood aside for them to enter. He dressed well, wearing a tweed sport coat and pressed pants.

She introduced him around and was grateful when Dalton led the man to a quiet corner and engaged him in conversation.

The two mothers greeted each other and proceeded with their usual annoying behavior of one-upmanship.

"We've nearly finished decorating our condo," Kate said to Anita, while Marla checked the food in the oven again. "Our designer did a superb job of finding the exact couch I wanted."

"How lovely. It must feel good to be settled in. Me, I could never live in an apartment with other people all around. I like my house."

"You've never considered downsizing?"

"What for?" Anita spread her hands. "I need the room when my grandkids come to stay." She sniffed the air. "Yum, garlic and basil. My mouth is watering."

"The food will be done soon, Ma. Have some appetizers," Marla suggested to get them out of her way.

Kate cast a glance at Marla. "A three-bedroom unit is spacious enough for us. Brie has her own room when she comes to stay. Now, if there were two or three more grandchildren, that would be a different story."

Marla felt her face redden. "Don't look at me. I'm busy enough with my salon."

"You'd have more time if you gave up your crime-solving escapades." Anita wagged a finger at her. "It's time for you to settle down. Kate and I aren't getting any younger."

Marla enjoyed the look of affront on her mother-in-law's face at that pronouncement. She finished scooping ice cubes into the bucket and turned away from the fridge. The other two trailed her into the family room, where she put her load down on the drinks table.

"Did I hear you mention crime-solving?" Dalton said, looking glad for the distraction. He turned away from Reed, whose face held a supercilious expression.

What, did the former literature professor consider a cop beneath his class? Usually Dalton could give as good as he got. Maybe he'd appeared to be more dimwitted than usual, in order to coax confidences. Marla didn't care for the idea of her mother going on a cruise with a man she'd barely met, so she had asked Dalton to subtly interrogate him. Doubtless the guy would be impressed once Dalton gave him the full force of his sharp mind.

"Marla needs to give up chasing crooks and focus on family," Anita told Dalton in an admonishing tone.

Robyn shouldered her way through the crowd. "I'm glad she discovered who killed Val. Now we can put that sadness behind us at the salon."

Brianna approached, holding a glass of ginger ale. "Tell them who did it, Daddy. You know they want to hear the sordid details."

"Let's go into the living room," Marla said. This wasn't for the children's ears. She double-checked to make sure the patio door was secured with its childproof lock. With small kids visiting, she'd taken extra precautions. She smiled at the dogs' antics as they dashed after a squirrel across the backyard.

"Did Marla tell you how she and Dalton nailed the building developer at an abandoned theme park in Hollywood?" Nicole prompted.

"It was called Pirate's Playground." Marla related the tourist attraction's history. "Rick Rodriguez meant to buy the land and erect condos there. It's a prime piece of property on the east side of town."

"So how did Val figure into his schemes?" Brianna asked, her face eager.

"She fought the redevelopment. Val had powerful friends, and he figured with her out of the way, his path would be clear. Rick bribed Andrew Fine, the publicist for FOFL, to write articles in his favor. They weren't all about that strip of historic structures on Hollywood Beach. Fine lobbied to local politicians on his behalf."

Nicole spoke up. "So it was never about the journal?"

"Well, partially." Marla glanced at Dalton in case he wanted to explain. He gave her a nod, so she carried on. "Howard was the one interested in hunting for any remaining pirate loot. Rick knew Howard wouldn't condone razing Pirate's Playground to the ground to make way for condos, so he tricked him. He led Howard on with promises of funding his hobby."

"Howard had been stealing from Val's accounts for years," Dalton cut in. "Not only did the group's treasurer need the money to remodel the theater that was his other passion besides pirate loot, but he'd been secretly funding expeditions to locate Red Ted's hoard. Unfortunately, when Rick tried to persuade Howard this last time to support his project, Howard vowed to oppose him. So Rick killed him."

"But what about Jason and Nadia? Are you saying Rick was the culprit there, too?" Nicole persisted.

Marla gazed at her with fondness. The other stylist loved reading mystery novels. She'd follow this trail until all loose ends were tied off.

"Jason wasn't only a talented photographer. He had ambitions to become a true journalist. In researching the region's history, he discovered an article about a mysterious drowning. He tracked the boys' descendants and realized Howard and Sam knew each other. Howard, along with Dr. Needles who's a diver and Sam who is a salvage expert, worked together to search for the rest of Red Ted's treasure. They planned to keep it for themselves if they ever found it and not turn it over to the government. From his work at the bank, Howard knew collectors who would pay handsomely for any find."

"I still don't get it," Nicole said, shaking her head. "Jason took those two pictures at the ball. You're saying Yolanda's husband wasn't involved in any of these murders?"

"Correct." Dalton directed his intense gaze at her. "Henutt Soe Dum may be involved in the so-called black gold trade of human hair, deriving some of it from corpses along with the help of a local funeral director, but he didn't kill Val."

"Even though her paintings and Jason's were exhibited next store to Yolanda's boutique?"

"That's right. I suspect that was just coincidence. Or maybe Yolanda recommended the gallery to Val. I spoke to the proprietor of the place. Val wasn't happy with the pricing on her paintings. She thought her sales might be better with a lower price tag. The owner disagreed, feeling she'd be devaluing her work that way. But it doesn't matter now. Neither Henutt nor the art gallery director were at fault in this case."

"So who killed Jason? It must be the other photo that ticked someone off?" Nicole took a handful of honey-roasted peanuts from a bowl on the cocktail table and popped some into her mouth.

"It was Howard," Marla pointed out. She explained again how Howard Cohn had been embezzling money from Val's accounts to fund his search for more treasure and lately, to renovate the theater that supported his passion as an actor. "The man was obsessed with pirates, and I suspect he half-fancied himself a modern-day version. He stabbed Jason because of the photo Jason took of him and Sam together. And he killed Nadia because he feared she'd read the journal and might expose his soiled family history, causing too much scrutiny to fall on him."

"And then Rodriguez killed him when Cohn wouldn't support his plans to redevelop Pirate's Playground," Dalton added, with a scowl at the memory of their recent encounter with the fellow, now in custody.

"Everyone had secrets," Marla said, thinking about Val's relationship to Nadia that went beyond friendship, Lora's erotic secret identity, and Sue Ellen's inflation of the catering bill.

"How sad." Kate hung her head. "It only goes to show that many families, even the wealthiest ones, hide skeletons in their closets."

Marla raised an eyebrow at her. Was Kate speaking about herself?

Staring at a flickering candle on the cocktail table, she thought about the Hanukkah menorah she'd just put away. The discovery of that travel journal could be viewed as the true miracle of the season. It had brought to light a past injustice and pointed the way to the truth. Val and her father could now rest in peace, and so could Ralph's spirit from so long ago.

The phone rang, and Dalton excused himself to go into the den to answer. He must have picked up the mobile phone and walked down the hallway because she couldn't hear him under the sudden silence that fell. She hoped it wasn't another case, not so soon after this last one.

"Marla, is that burnt food I smell?" Anita said, rising.

She gave her mother a startled glance. "Omigosh, I forgot all about the lasagna."

Fortunately, the dish was crisp around the edges but still okay. She reheated the garlic rolls in the microwave and mixed the Caesar salad. Dalton needed to uncork another bottle of wine. She shot an annoyed gaze at the doorway into the kitchen. What was keeping him so long?

Heck, she shouldn't complain. Their lives might always be disrupted by his job, but at least they had each other. No matter what came around the next corner, they'd be together.

She smiled fondly at Brianna, who helped her place the food on the kitchen table for the buffet. She'd already laid out the utensils, plates, and napkins.

What more could she want? She had a loving husband and stepdaughter, and they were surrounded by friends and family. Life couldn't be more complete.

"*Kinehora*," she said aloud, remembering to say the superstitious phrase to avert the evil eye. Otherwise, just when you thought all was perfect, calamity would fall.

The universe sought balance and would find ways to achieve it. She'd learned not to tempt fate. Just in case, she knocked on wood as well.

"Come on, everybody. Let's eat," she called to her company.

As guests filed in to get their dinner plates, Marla smiled with satisfaction. Some people might complain about hosting so many holidays, but she considered it a privilege. You never knew when things might change. Better to enjoy being with your loved ones while you had the chance.

AUTHOR'S NOTE

The journal in this story, *Florida Escapade,* is based on a 1935 travel memoir written by my father, Harry I. Heller. In *Florida Escape,* you can read the real exploits of three intrepid explorers during their adventurous trip to the Sunshine State. Some of these passages are excerpted in *Facials Can Be Fatal.* For more details, please visit my website at *http://nancyjcohen.com.*

The theme park, Pirate's Playground, is modeled after a defunct attraction in Dania, Florida called Pirates World. It was built in 1967 and lasted until its doors closed in the 1970s. The land was rezoned for residential use, and today condominiums inhabit the site.

If you enjoyed *Facials Can Be Fatal,* please spread the word. Here are some ways you can help:

Write an online customer review at Amazon,
Goodreads, or BN.
Post about this book on your social media sites
and online forums.
Recommend the Bad Hair Day Mysteries to
reader groups and book clubs.
Gift a copy of this book to a friend.
Consider giving a Bad Hair Day mystery as a gift to
your hairstylist.

ABOUT THE AUTHOR

Nancy J. Cohen writes the humorous Bad Hair Day Mysteries featuring hairstylist Marla Vail, who solves crimes with wit and style under the sultry Florida sun. Titles in this series have made the IMBA bestseller list and been selected by *Suspense Magazine* as best cozy mystery. The author of over twenty published works, Nancy has also written the instructional guide, *Writing the Cozy Mystery*, an easy-to-follow reference on how to write a winning whodunit. Nancy's imaginative romances, including the Drift Lords series, have proven popular with fans as well. These books have won the HOLT Medallion and Best Book in Romantic SciFi/Fantasy at *The Romance Reviews*.

A featured speaker at libraries, conferences, and community events, Nancy is listed in *Contemporary Authors, Poets & Writers*, and *Who's Who in U.S. Writers, Editors, & Poets*. When not busy writing, she enjoys fine dining, cruising, visiting Disney World, and outlet shopping, plus frequent trips to the salon for research.

Nancy loves to hear from readers. Contact her at *nancy@ nancyjcohen.com* or sign up for her newsletter at *http://nancyjcohen .com/newsletter/*.